"I prefer horses to people," Devlin said. "They might bite or kick if frightened or provoked. But they don't lie."

Thea weathered the blow—it was justified. "I didn't think a harmless fabrication would hurt anyone…" Her voice trailed into silence.

"And when nothing worked, you got desperate."

"Desperate," she repeated. "Have you ever been desperate, Mr. Stone? About anything?"

"Yes. But never enough to cheat, or beg or deceive."

"Then you've never been desperate."

"I don't know what to think of you, Miss Pickford. Is that your real name, by the way?"

"It's actually my mother's maiden name." He slid the question in so neatly Thea answered before she realized it. "Please don't ask for my real name. I don't want to lie to you anymore."

"Ah." Another one of those flicks of blue light came and went in his eyes. "We're in accord, then. I don't want to be lied to."

**Books by Sara Mitchell**

Love Inspired Historical     Love Inspired

*Legacy of Secrets*             *Night Music*
*The Widow's Secret*       *Shelter of His Arms*
*Mistletoe Courtship*
  "The Christmas Secret"
*A Most Unusual Match*

## SARA MITCHELL

A popular and highly acclaimed author in the Christian market, Sara's aim is to depict the struggle between the challenges of everyday life and the values to which our faith would have us aspire. The author of contemporary, historical suspense and historical novels, her work has been published by many inspirational book publishers.

Having lived in diverse locations from Georgia to California to Great Britain, her extensive travel experience helps her create authentic settings for her books. A lifelong music lover, Sara has also written several musical dramas and has long been active in the music miniseries of the churches wherever she has lived. The mother of two daughters, Sara now lives in Virginia.

# SARA MITCHELL

## A Most Unusual Match

Steeple
Hill®

Published by Steeple Hill Books™

**STEEPLE HILL BOOKS**

Steeple
Hill®

Recycling programs
for this product may
not exist in your area.

ISBN-13: 978-0-373-82854-8

A MOST UNUSUAL MATCH

Copyright © 2011 by Sara Mitchell

www.SteepleHill.com

**Printed in U.S.A.**

Do not say, "I'll pay you back for this wrong!"
Wait for the Lord, and He will deliver you.
—*Proverbs* 20:22, NIV

He hath...sent me to heal the brokenhearted,
to preach deliverance to the captives,
and recovering of sight to the blind,
to set at liberty them that are bruised.
—*Luke* 4:18, KJV

To Melissa Endlich, my dear editor, for her consummate
editorial skill, and her faith in me.
Thanks for everything.

## Acknowledgments

Profound thanks to the following, all of whom were
gracious with their time and generous with their
information. Any historical errors are *entirely* the author's
doing.

Once again to the staff members in the U.S. Secret
Service Office of Government and Public Affairs, and
the staff of the U.S. Secret Service Archives, for their
courtesy and invaluable assistance.

### <u>Saratoga Springs, New York</u>

Mary Ann Fitzgerald, City Historian, Saratoga Springs

Allan Carter, Historian, Saratoga Racing Museum

...and all the other wonderful individuals up in
Saratoga Springs I spoke to a time or two,
or exchanged emails with.

### <u>Jekyl Island</u>

Gretchen Greminger, Curator, Jekyl Island—
spelled "Jekyll" from the 20th century onward!
(so nobody will be confused....)

Clint and the rest of the staff at the Jekyll Island Museum.

Gretchen, many, many thanks for helping me perfect the
plot and make it work! You're a perfect example of a
peach of a Georgia gal!

God's blessings to one and all.

# Chapter One

*Saratoga Springs, New York*
*June, 1897*

Theodora Langston watched Edgar Fane stroll across the lobby of the Grand Union Hotel. A half smile lurked at the corners of his mouth, while a swelling crowd—mostly ladies—clustered about him. His gray fedora tipped forward jauntily and one pale hand lightly swung a brass-handled walking stick, tapping the marble foyer with each step. Mr. Fane epitomized a gentleman out to enjoy his season at Saratoga Springs. He had the right, seeing he was a son of one of the richest men in the country.

Thea watched him, and her heart burned with hatred.

As he passed the marbled pillar where she stood, the indifferent gaze passed over her as though Thea were part of the pillar. Edgar Fane, she had discovered over the past ten days, preferred his female admirers long and willowy and adoring, or dainty and luscious and adoring. She could feign adoration, but since her unextraordinary face and physique failed to capture the scoundrel's interest, Thea would have to try a different strategy. She had spent the last of her deceased grandmother's trust fund on this crusade, and would not abandon her quest until Edgar Fane was behind bars, where he belonged.

Her troubled glance fell upon Grandmother's ruby ring, snug on Thea's engagement finger. She was accustomed to ink from a printing press, not fancy rings. Still, the facade of wealth was necessary to gain access to the higher echelons of Saratoga Springs society. Justice did not come cheaply. The ring might be real, all the lavish gowns she'd purchased from Bloomingdale's with the rest of the trust money might be the latest fashion, but she was living a lie.

She could hear her grandfather's voice as though she were standing in their library on that rainy afternoon a month earlier. *Thea, you mustn't think such things about him.* He had sounded so gentle. Gentle, and defeated. *Mr. Fane proclaimed his innocence with equal vehemence. No proof of malfeasance on his part has surfaced.*

*You are innocent, but you're the one they arrested, you're the one those awful Secret Service operatives treated like a common criminal!*

*I was the one who tried to deposit counterfeit funds.*

But it was Edgar Fane who had paid Charles Langston with those bogus funds.

The burning hatred inside Thea seethed, cauterizing her heart. No use to pray for forgiveness, or ask for divine help. Her grandfather could pray all he wanted to, but Thea doubted God would oblige Charles Langston with an answer. Because of Edgar Fane, her grandfather's faith had dimmed to the stub of a barely flickering candle. As for Thea, life had finally forced her to swallow an unpalatable truth: She could not trust anyone—God or man—to see justice served. If she wanted Edgar Fane to be punished for his crimes, she'd have to do it herself.

For all her life she'd played a part—the good child, the

grateful girl, the admirable woman—while inside, insecurity and anxiety clawed with razor-stropped spikes. Now she was about to embark on her most ambitious role. She did not enjoy the risk and the public nature of the charade, but she was confident of her success.

The crowded hotel parlor seemed to lurch, and Thea braced herself against the grooved pillar until the sensation dissipated. She never should have used her mother's maiden name, a constant reminder that no matter whether her present life be truth or lie, she remained the abandoned daughter of a wayward youngest son and a vaudeville singer from the Bowery. No surprise that for most of her childhood she struggled with dizzy spells.

As for faith, life had finally forced Thea to swallow an unpalatable truth: something was lacking in her, something missing from birth that made her unlovable to everyone but her grandfather.

Despite Charles Langston's attempts to give her the life of a privileged young lady, perhaps she was Hetty Pickford's daughter after all.

The high-pitched whinny of an alarmed horse cut through the noisy road traffic on the Saratoga Springs Broadway. Moments earlier Devlin Stone had emerged from the Indian encampment arcade, where he'd spent the past two hours shadowing a suspect. Scarborough disappeared into one of the sidewalk eateries, and Devlin let him go, instead searching the street until he spotted a foam-flecked bay hitched to a surrey in front of the Columbian Hotel. Hooves clattered on the cobblestones by the curb and the horse's head strained against the checkrein. The driver, stupid man, yanked on the reins while shouting an unending barrage of abuse.

Anger flaring, Dev approached just as the terrified horse

reared in the traces and plunged forward straight toward a pair of young boys on bicycles. Dev leaped in front of them. "Move!" he ordered, whipping off his jacket.

The two boys scrambled for safety but the horse swung his head around, ears flat and teeth bared. Devlin grabbed the driving reins just behind the bit, then flung his jacket over the blinkers to completely blind the horse.

"Easy, boy...calm down, you're all right. Nobody's going to hurt you now."

"Hey! Whadaya think you're doing?" the driver yelled, sawing on the reins in a vain attempt to regain control.

With his free hand Dev reached for his pocketknife. "Probably saving this animal's life, and unfortunately yours," he responded in the same soothing tone as he lifted the knife, slicing both reins twelve inches from the bit. "There you are, fella. No more pressure on your mouth. That's it...just relax."

He dropped the knife back in his trouser pocket, unlatched the checkrein. The driver's complexion had gone from the boiling flush of rage to dirty-sheet gray. Good. Devlin held his palm in front of the horse's nostrils, waiting until a hot fluttering breath gently blew over his fingers before he slowly removed his jacket. A single quiver rolled through the flanks, but the horse stood still, watching Devlin.

"Good boy. You're all right." He applied light forward pressure and the horse docilely allowed Dev to lead him across Broadway onto a calm side street.

Devlin turned to the driver. "Get out of the buggy."

"I'm not paying for the harness you ruined," the man complained, climbing stiffly down from the surrey.

"How about you shut up and hand me the rest of the reins?" Before Devlin pummeled the bounder himself.

The lash of temper did the trick, for without further

argument the man complied. In seconds Dev formed a makeshift hackamore, and secured the end to a hitching post.

"You know horses well enough," the driver observed grudgingly. "Guess I owe you. Don't know what spooked the stupid animal."

"Try having a piece of metal crammed in your mouth, then have someone yank on it until it bleeds." Devlin eyed the other man with disfavor.

"Yeah…well, I don't usually do my own driving." He glanced at the now-quiet horse, a flicker of admiration warring with the sneer. "Anytime you want a job as coachman, look me up." He reached into his vest pocket and tugged out an ivory calling card.

"No, thanks. I'd have to be around you." Devlin rummaged for a fifty-cent piece, flicked it so the coin fell with a soft thud onto the packed dirt inches from the man's shiny shoes. "Enjoy a cup of coffee at the Congress Spring Pavilion. I'll return this animal. Where'd you rent him? The livery on Henry Street? By the way, you are right about one thing." He waited a moment before continuing, "I strongly suggest you do hire a driver. Because if I catch you mistreating a horse again, rest assured you'll feel a lot worse than the animal."

The driver bristled anew. Then, jaw muscles working, with his heel he ground the coin into the dirt, swiveled and stalked off down the street.

An hour later, mostly recovered, Devlin stood on the piazza of the Grand Union Hotel, surrounded by a herd of chattering humanity instead of a spooked horse in a herd of Broadway traffic. He wished, not for the first time, that he was back in Virginia, surrounded by his own horses, none of which had ever known the cruelty that poor livery hack endured. The pasture would be lush and green, and if he looked up he would see the ancient Blue Ridge Mountains against a summer sky instead of rows of massive white marble columns supporting a structure billed as the largest hotel in the world.

Over the aroma of ladies' French perfume and men's sweat he caught a whiff of popcorn. Maneuvering his way between a cluster of ladies debating on whether to visit Tiffany's before or after a promenade along Broadway, Devlin shouldered his way over to the vendor to buy a bag of popcorn.

Bright summer sunshine poured over Saratoga, onto the twenty-plus thousand tourists enjoying a season at the place touted as "America's Resort." An ironic smile hovered at the corners of Devlin's mouth. How many of the guests would scramble for the first train leaving the depot if they knew an operative for the U.S. Secret Service prowled among them?

Perhaps he should have flashed his badge at that lout earlier—except Dev was here undercover, the badge and credentials safely hidden in his own hotel room.

Of course few operatives—if any—could spend an entire season playing the part of a wealthy gentleman of leisure. In the first place, Congress would never approve the funds. To Devlin's way of thinking, such shortsightedness plagued a lot of government officials. He'd only been with the Service for two years, and at the moment did not feel adequate to match wits with the Hotel Hustler.

In only three years, the invisible thief had cost unsuspecting dupes somewhere in the neighborhood of fifty million dollars—and nobody could figure out how he managed it.

The previous autumn, Service hopes had soared when a call came in from the chief of the New York City office; they'd arrested a man at the bank where he tried to pass bills matching the Hustler's work. Infuriatingly, the man denied all knowledge of counterfeiting, claiming the false bills had come from Edgar Fane. Corroborating evidence could not be found either to support his claims or prove his guilt, and they'd been forced to release Charles Langston. Edgar Fane hadn't even been arrested, much less charged. Another dead end in this impenetrable maze.

Counterfeiters were a despicable bunch. Pervasive as flies, they swarmed the country, mostly in cities, undermining the national currency. A few of them had committed murder. Over the last decade, for the most part the Service had done a crackerjack job closing down the worst of the gangs.

But the Hotel Hustler had them stumped.

Devlin accepted that pride as well as a dose of cussedness had concocted this present undercover infiltration scheme. Chief Hazen reluctantly sanctioned it, telling Devlin he certainly wouldn't look a gift horse in the mouth.

He'd laughed when he said it.

Dev shook his head and resumed watching the front of the Grand Union Hotel. Six weeks earlier, a reliable snitch had informed another operative that the Hustler would be at Saratoga, but as always no other information, such as a description, had surfaced. Three guests, one of them Edgar Fane, warranted surveillance, based upon these scraps of evidence tirelessly gleaned over the past twenty months.

Some ten minutes later patience was rewarded. Dev watched the impeccably clad Edgar Fane emerge onto the piazza, surrounded by his throng of hangers-on. Dev had been shadowing the cultured, congenial fellow for three days, and the man did not fit the usual profile of a criminal. Privileged son of the owner of exclusive emporiums all over the country, Fane scattered money and bonhomie wherever he traveled. The money thus far was genuine. Dev wasn't convinced about the rest. Edgar Fane reminded him of a Thoroughbred he and his uncle once reluctantly agreed to train for the owner. Flashy specimen of horse-flesh, conformation of champions—but not an animal to turn your back on.

Edgar Fane paused, lifted his hand. Several women approached, and Devlin watched in some amusement as they jockeyed for position—the buxom redhead boldly thrust her arm through Fane's, while a regal blonde offered a narrow white hand adorned with several rings, which Fane adroitly kissed even as his other hand patted the red-head's arm. The trio merged into the crowd, easy enough to follow since the redhead sported a gigantic hat the size of a saddle.

Devlin shouldered away from the column, then paused, his gaze returning to the third woman, the one Fane had barely seemed to notice as the other two women led him away. She stood very still, and in this chattering, gesticu-lating, endlessly restless crowd that stillness piqued Dev's interest. Without fuss, he tucked his hands in the waistband of his trousers and sauntered down the steps, pretending to scan the crowd while he memorized the young woman.

Unremarkable height and build in comparison to the luscious redhead and slender blonde. Like most society women, she styled her mass of honey-colored hair in the current Gibson girl fashion. Creamy magnolia complexion and a soft mouth, large dark brown eyes gazing after Edgar Fane with an expression of—Devlin's eyebrows shot up. Was that anger, or fear?

He wasn't to know, because the woman abruptly turned in a graceful swirl of skirts and hurried off in the opposite direction.

## Chapter Two

Thinking fast was one of the Service's unwritten requirements: intrigued, Dev followed the spurned woman instead of shadowing Fane, keeping at least a dozen people between them. When a potential masher approached her, his manner a trifle too familiar, Devlin's fingers twitched with the need to intervene.

Wasn't necessary. The young woman laughed, said something; the vanquished masher tipped his hat and moved away. So. The lady knew how to dismiss louts without causing offense.

Perhaps she'd had a lot of practice.

For several more moments Devlin followed her, automatically memorizing traits, from the slight tilt of her head to the firm assurance in her steps, the swanlike neck and softly rounded shoulders. A fine figure of a woman, perhaps. But he needed to see that face again. Moving quickly, he wound his way along the teeming walkway until he was some twenty feet ahead of the woman. He bought a frankfurter from a sweating vendor, absently munching while he chewed over his response to this particular female.

With an internal jolt he realized his acute interest bordered on personal rather than professional. He needed to see her face not only to jot down an accurate description in his nightly notes, but to discover if that blaze of emotion in her eyes had been a trick of the sunlight, rather than a revelation of her character. In his experience, women didn't always feel like they acted, or acted like they felt.

Devlin might begrudge the instant attraction this particular female had tweaked to life, but he'd be foolish to discount its power. Last time he succumbed, his heart was kicked, stomped and tromped. The Blue Ridge Mountains would be flat as the Plains out west before he'd trust his heart to another woman. Yet without any effort on her part—she didn't know he existed, after all—this one touched a crusted-over piece of it. Annoyed with himself, Dev moved closer, assessing her like an operative instead of a calf-eyed rube.

She'd make a useful shover, flirting her way through the stores that fronted Grand Union Hotel, handing over bogus bills to cashiers too dazzled to notice they'd just been bamboozled. After stealing thousands of dollars in purchases, she and the cur who supplied the counterfeit goods would turn around and sell everything the deceitful little shover had bought. The game had been played with various permutations throughout the country.

*Not this time,* Devlin muttered beneath his breath, despising those who preyed upon the innocent, the weak, the gullible. He bit off a tasty chunk of hot frankfurter.

Less than three paces away, a matronly woman draped in deep pink lace lifted her arm and waved to someone. "Miss Pickford?" she called out. "Theodora? Is that you?"

Amazingly, the woman Dev was following started, then offered a smile only someone watching her closely—such as himself—would recognize as strained. For a moment she wavered. Then she blinked and the smile warmed into cordiality. "Mrs. Van Eyck. I'm sorry, I didn't see you. The crowds…"

Dev took another bite, and eavesdropped without a qualm.

"How lovely you look today, dear," Mrs. Van Eyck gushed. "Have you heard from your darling fiancé this week? Do tell me, you know how much I adore those dashing British aristocrats. You must join me—I was just on my way to the springs for a healthful dose of the waters. I must say, the practice of charging for a drink these days is depressingly crass.… Where is your chaperone, Theodora? Mrs.…oh, dear, I can't seem to recall her name."

"Mrs. Chudd. She doesn't care for crowds, or heat, so I've left her reading a book in one of the hotel's parlors."

So Miss Theodora Pickford conveniently ditched her chaperone, and had already snagged herself a man. One who doubtless loved her in blissful ignorance of her interest in the son of one of the richest men in the country. Like a cloud passing across the sun, disillusionment shadowed Devlin's mind. His successes with the Service might satisfy an inchoate longing to serve his country, but the scope of human greed continued to catch him off guard.

"Where is Mr. Van Eyck today?" the two-timing flirt inquired.

Well-modulated voice, Devlin noted grudgingly. Warm, with a dash of humor. She smiled with her eyes as well as her mouth, and nobody would believe her to be anything other than genuine. Nobody except an undercover Secret Service operative whose belief in humanity had just endured another drubbing.

"Oh, you know Mr. Van Eyck. Playing cards at the Casino," Mrs. Van Eyck babbled along. "Annoying, when the weather is fine, isn't it? My dear friend Esmeralda—I introduced you the other day, did I not? Her husband's second cousin is distantly related to Queen Victoria, you know. I was quite mystified to learn your fiancé was unacquainted with him. You did tell me your intended is an earl?"

"I did, but you may have forgotten that dear Neville feels tremendous responsibility for all his family properties. They're scattered all over the British Isles, not to mention a villa in Italy, so he's rarely in London."

Why, the minx was lying! The slightly elevated voice, restless movement of her hands, dilated pupils—subtle signs but clear indications all the same.

More likely her absent fiancé was a butcher from Cleveland, or some gout-riddled banker twice her age. She might even be lying about having an intended at all. The particulars could be supplied with time. All that mattered for the moment was that Miss Pickford had an association with one of the suspects on Devlin's list, that she felt no qualms in wandering about without escort or chaperone and that she was a liar.

*Too bad for you, darling,* Dev thought. He detested liars, personally as well as professionally.

Unless the liar happened to be himself.

His conscience grumbled as it always did when he thought of the deceptions necessary in his undercover work; Dev reminded it that he had sworn an oath to defend the United States against all persons engaged in practices designed to undermine the country's economic sovereignty. This girl might be another bored society belle, but she was also clearly hiding something. And if that something was of a criminal nature, she might be in league with the Hotel Hustler himself, given the winsomeness of her charm.

Casually he stepped around Mrs. Van Eyck, placing himself within touching distance of Miss Pickford.

"Miss Pickford! Good afternoon." He doffed his straw

boater and bowed, his smile deepening at her look of consternation. "What a stroke of good fortune to find you in this crush. I just arrived from London last night. Neville was overjoyed to learn my visit to Saratoga would coincide with yours. He planned to send you a telegram—did you receive it? Well, never mind, what matters is the special message for you, that he asked me to pass along in person." He leaned forward, adding in a dramatic whisper, "We should probably retire to somewhere more private. Since Mrs. Chudd is happily reading in the parlor, so much the better."

"How thrilling," Mrs. Van Eyck cooed, "to have something more…physical…than a telegram or letter bringing word from your beloved." Her eyes twinkled. "Do join me later, Miss Pickford, and share everything this handsome messenger imparts. Young couples in love liven things up. Brings back happy memories of myself and Mr. Van Eyck, three decades ago."

"I don't think…" Miss Pickford began as she fumbled to open a brightly colored Chinese fan. "I didn't receive a telegram."

"Well, it's doubtless waiting at the desk. We'll fetch it later." Devlin clasped her elbow in a display of seeming gallantry which also effectively edged Mrs. Van Eyck farther away. "Is this heat too much for you? Let me escort you over to that patch of shade under the elms."

"Yes, of course."

Beneath the flimsy lawn overblouse he could feel the tensile strength of her slender forearm. A twitch of puzzlement feathered the base of Devlin's neck. For an accomplished flirt and a liar to boot, at close quarters Miss Pickford struck him as…fresh, unspoiled, even. Untainted by the slight aura of dissipation that hovered around Saratoga. He could lose himself in those expressive dark brown eyes. Her bones were those of a finely bred Arabian instead of the massive draft horses he bred and trained at StoneHill.

*Something didn't fit here.*

Grimly he focused his attention back on the plump, perspiring Mrs. Van Eyck. "Forgive me for absconding with your friend. I wouldn't intrude except I'm planning to attend the races—the first is at one forty-five, I believe. Before that I'm to meet someone at Hathorn Spring, so have little time to spare. Miss Pickford? Shall we?"

Two spots of red now burned in the young lady's magnolia cheeks, but the tangled emotions swimming through her eyes jarred Devlin. He'd expected anger and possibly a show of outrage....

"I'll try to see you later, Mrs. Van Eyck," Miss Pickford promised, twisting her neck to address the older woman and in the process managing to discreetly free her arm. "Dear Neville is a dreadful tease. This past spring he sent a young fellow dressed like a medieval troubadour to my house. I was treated to a ballad—poorly sung, I'm afraid— about all of Neville's goings-on that week."

Her eyelashes fluttered and her lips curled in a smile as she moved the fan back and forth in front of her face, possibly to disguise a significant "tell": the corners of her eyes didn't crinkle, which told Devlin her smile, like Miss Pickford, was artificial.

"How droll," Mrs. Van Eyck offered after a pause.

"Yes, isn't it? Um…I'll speak with this gentleman, then how about if I meet you at the Congress Spring Pavilion? Say, in a quarter of an hour?"

Between the two of them, Mrs. Van Eyck didn't stand a chance. After a final sideways perusal of Devlin, she retreated.

"You're quite good," he began, "though might have been safer promising to meet her at—"

"I much prefer to converse with a gentleman if I know his name, especially when he claims to be acquainted with my fiancé." She stood still, fan now dangling forgotten from her wrist. One hand was planted on her hip, but the other had curled into a fist at her side.

So she wanted to prolong the game, did she? "Ah. How remiss of me. Devlin Stone, of StoneHill Farm, Virginia, at your service, Miss Pickford."

"I thought I detected a Southern drawl." For a moment she seemed to hesitate before tossing her head. A fine pair of amethyst earrings dangled in the sunlight. "Well? What is the message dear Neville requested you to deliver? You have a meeting with someone and races to attend, after all. You'd best get on with the delivery before you're late for your appointment."

"You've got me, ma'am." Devlin swept an astute appraisal over her person, noting how the pulse in her throat now fluttered faster than the second hand on his pocket watch. He wished he didn't admire her nerve as much as he did her creamy skin. "I've actually never met your dear Neville. I overheard your conversation with Mrs. Van Eyck, and couldn't resist the opportunity to meet a lovely lady."

"I doubt that very much, Mr. Stone." Humor flitted across her face—the second honest emotion she'd revealed. "Mrs. Van Eyck is devoted to her husband. She might be diverted by the dimples in your cheeks, but she would never dream of establishing a liaison with a strange man, no matter how attractive. Now if you'll excuse me, I did promise to meet her. I'll pass along your regrets."

She stepped back into a bar of sunlight while Devlin struggled to untangle the mess her wit, and her poise, had made of his mind. For the first time he noticed the scattering of faint pockmarks that marred the creamy complexion in several places. For some reason, after her magnificent charade the slight imperfections tilted his opinion in favor of charity instead of contempt.

Ruthlessly Dev squashed the emotion. "Before you leave, do you think you'll be running into Mr. Fane again soon? He's an attractive, personable fellow, isn't he? And one of the country's richest men. I wonder how your fiancé would feel, knowing of your interest in someone whose reputation with the ladies is ofttimes…less than gentlemanly?"

She gawked at him. "You know Edgar Fane?"

"I know of him. He scatters largesse wherever he goes. Perhaps that explains why he's always surrounded by a particular sort of woman."

"And what sort of man makes vile speculations about a woman he's only just met?" she whipped back. "Are you insulting, or threatening me, Mr. Stone?"

"Perhaps you should tell me, Miss Pickford?"

For a suspended moment he wondered if she planned to dig in her heels, or flee. The back of his neck itched like sunburn; he was ashamed of how he was baiting her. Yet he couldn't allow what might be the only lead in eleven months of fruitless investigation to vanish because the lead was a lovely liar struggling to hide her vulnerability.

Slowly a hint of color crept back over her cheeks. The dark eyes searched his, and Dev's own pulse quickened when her tongue darted out to moisten her lips. "Both," she whispered, and before he recovered from her unexpected honesty she vanished into the crowd.

This time, Devlin let her go.

# Chapter Three

Theodora pushed her way through the crush of people strolling the Broadway. The energy that had fueled her encounter with Mr. Stone leaked away with each step until her feet barely lifted from the ground. A dozen yards from the Grand Union Hotel she stopped underneath the base of one of the elm trees shading the Broadway, needing a moment to collect herself. After several calming breaths, the spinning sensation receded; she fixed her gaze upon a fancy-goods storefront full of ladies' gloves while she thought about her reaction to the stranger.

How had this Mr. Stone known she was acting? His eyes, a mesmerizing blend of gray, slate blue and…and ice, had pierced every one of her painstakingly formulated masks. At the moment she should be prostrate with vertigo, her reaction to a bone-searing insecurity spawned early in her childhood. She kept this weakness relentlessly hidden from everyone but Mrs. Chudd, the widowed neighbor she'd hired at Grandfather's insistence to be her companion "while you work this mad scheme out of your system." Until the previous year, most of the attacks had disappeared altogether. Then Grandfather was arrested and spent a week in jail—for passing counterfeit money. The money Edgar Fane had paid him. The police and several Secret Service operatives had treated an innocent Charles Langston like a common criminal, but they hadn't even charged Edgar Fane, the lying, cheating snake.

Thea wasn't sure who she despised more, Edgar Fane or the sanctimonious Secret Service operatives with their closed minds and weak spines.

Edgar Fane was a villain. Thea had dedicated her life to proving his guilt, regardless of debilitating spells of vertigo. She owed that life to Grandfather, but would never enjoy it until she found a way to restore the twinkle in his eye and his wilted faith in God. For Thea, waiting for the Almighty to pursue vengeance was no longer an option.

Dizzy spells, however, might prove to be something of a conundrum. Certainly her first few brushes with Mr. Fane triggered the symptoms, probably because he'd ignored her. It was also turning out to be far more difficult than she imagined, projecting an attraction for a man she planned to skewer with the pitchfork of justice.

Devlin Stone claimed to know Edgar Fane. Perhaps...?

Perhaps she could jump off a cliff, as well. It might be less hazardous than pursuing Devlin Stone, who made her pulse flutter and caused a most unusual sensation in the region of her heart. Apparently Mr. Stone triggered a multitude of strange feelings, but not a single swirl of vertigo.

And he might be the only person able to help her.

Thea's hands clenched the Chinese fan. Mr. Stone's threat to expose her to her imaginary fiancé Neville could be discounted, but the threat itself would have to be dealt with. She'd learned Edgar Fane planned to leave Saratoga in three weeks. Less than a month...

Another swirl of dizziness batted her, a warning she would do well to heed.

So don't think about him, or Devlin Stone's unsubtle threats, Theodora. Think about how to persuade him to share everything he knows about Edgar Fane. Think about Charles Langston, and retribution. Think about flinging evidence at the Secret Service and humiliating them as they had humiliated her Grandfather and ruined his life.

But instead her mind reached back to the instant Mr. Stone had touched her. Strength, vitality and authority wrapped around Thea as securely as his fingers enclosed her arm. The impulse to confess everything had overwhelmed her senses, a terrifying prospect. Worse than the dreaded vertigo, she had been tempted to cling to a *stranger,* because…because unlike her reaction to Edgar Fane and despite all common sense, she had been drawn to Mr. Stone like penny nails to a powerful magnet.

There. She'd admitted the truth, to her conscience at least.

The whirling inside her head abruptly diminished.

She supposed she ought to be grateful. Regardless of Devlin Stone's too-perceptive gaze, apparently he only muddled her senses. If thoughts of him *lessened* the vertigo, she'd recite his name a hundred times a day.

Cautiously Thea straightened and headed for the hotel.

An hour later, dressed for her afternoon at the races, she left Mrs. Chudd reading a book and sipping fresh lime-ade. A spare woman with iron-gray hair, Mrs. Chudd was exactly the sort of chaperone Thea required: indifferent, and incurious. After confiding to her about the spells of vertigo, the woman had nodded once, then remarked that she wasn't a wet nurse but if called upon would do her duty. Today, her "Mind you use your parasol else you'll turn red as one of those Indians," constituted Mrs. Chudd's only gesture at chaperonage. At least this was Saratoga Springs, where guests discarded societal strictures like a too-tight corset.

After leaving a note of apology for the desk clerk to have delivered to Mrs. Van Eyck, Thea joined a dozen other guests in queue for one of the hotel wagons headed for the track. She felt awkward; there were those who disapproved of the entire horse-racing culture, denouncing the sport for its corruption and greed. Until she arrived at Saratoga, Thea had never paid attention one way or the other, though she remarked to someone at her dinner table how thrilling it would be to watch the powerful creatures thunder down the track at amazing speeds.

Today, however, was a hunting expedition, not a pleasure excursion. The tenor of her thoughts stirred up fresh guilt. After three weeks Thea could mostly block the insistent tug by remembering how her grandfather looked behind bars the only time she visited him in that foul hole of a cell. Voice cracking, fine tremors racking his stooped form, Charles begged her not to return. Because she saw that her presence hurt him beyond measure, Thea gave her promise.

Promises made to loved ones must be kept.

No matter how despicable her actions now, she would never break her word like her father with all his picture-postcard promises to come home, or abandon anyone at birth like her mother did Thea. Richard Langston and Hetty Pickford—what a legacy. Yet never once had her grandfather condemned their only child for the behavior of her parents.

Impatient with herself, Theodora glanced down at her blue-and-white costume, self-consciously running a finger over the perky red braid trimming the skirt and basque while she turned her mind to the afternoon ahead. A tingle of anticipation shot through her at the prospect of matching wits with Devlin Stone again.

She'd thought long and hard while she changed into her present costume. For some reason Mr. Stone had singled her out of a crowd of thousands of available, far more beautiful females. Based upon Thea's admittedly scant personal knowledge of romantic liaisons, all that was necessary to assure a gentleman's continued pursuit would be to indicate her willingness to be pursued. Very well, then. With a bit of pluck and a whole bucketful of luck, through encouraging Mr. Stone's interest in her, in turn she hoped to procure enough insight into Edgar Fane's habits to at last secure an entrée into the scoundrel's inner circle of friends. She refused to crawl home in shame and defeat.

Her tactics troubled Thea. If she ever blew the dust off her Bible and strove to establish a better communication with the Lord, she would doubtless spend many years on her knees, begging forgiveness for the sordidness of her present behavior. Even though he did not approve of her decision to pursue justice, Grandfather had understood her motives. Hopefully God would understand, as well, and help her achieve her goal. He was, after all, a God of justice. *If You help me now, perhaps I'll believe You're also a God of love.* If God helped her in this quest, perhaps she could also forgive Him for allowing her parents to abandon her, and an innocent man to be flung in jail.

But if she couldn't procure justice, and restore Charles Langston's faith, she saw no reason to waste time on her own.

As for Devlin Stone, she would ignore the prickle of attraction, maintain her distance with the laughing quips and smiling rebuffs that had thus far served her well with other flirtatious men. By the time Theodora Langst— The mental lapse stabbed her like a hatpin. For the rest of the way to the track she mentally repeated her assumed name—Theodora *Pickford*, Thea *Pickford*...Miss *Pickford*—and envisaged herself the privileged heiress whose beauty, grace and supreme self-confidence had won the love of a dashing Englishman. *Is Neville a baron, or an earl?* Inside her frilly lace gloves Thea's palms turned clammy; she gripped her lace parasol more tightly.

Her cause was just, her purpose noble, she reminded herself staunchly in a mantra repeated often these past weeks. The only person who would be hurt by her actions was the man who deserved it. Sometimes the end did justify the means.

It was ten minutes until post time when the load of passengers descended onto the velvet green lawns surrounding the racetrack. The crowd streaming into the grandstands looked to number in the thousands, not the hundred or so Thea had naively anticipated. Spotting Mr. Stone would be more difficult than she'd anticipated. Stalling, she opened her parasol and hoped she looked as though she expected her escort to appear any second. Beneath broad-trunked shade trees, jockeys fidgeted while trainers saddled the horses for the next race. Striped tents fluttered in a stray breeze, shading hundreds of race goers. Dust filmed the air. At one end of the sweeping slate-roofed grandstands she noticed a separate, open-sided structure full of odd-looking little stalls on stilts.

"What's going on over there?" she asked a passing gentleman studying a copy of the *Daily Saratogian*.

"Betting ring, ma'am. But that one's only for the gents. Ladies' betting is up on the top landing, rear of the grandstand. You a maiden filly, right? Well, you're in luck. Track was closed last year. But you can see for yourself the people have spoken, and the sport of kings is back at Saratoga. You go on up there, purchase yourself a ticket.

Rensselaer looks good in the Travers. Good luck to you, miss."

"Thank you," Thea said faintly, staring after the man.

Older, shadowy emotions stirred inside, greasy splotches of childhood memories. One of the cards her father had sent to her years ago had been postmarked "Saratoga Springs." Now, though surrounded by faces full of excitement and nervous anticipation, for some reason she had to fight the urge to weep. In the distance a bell clanged several times, and the surge of humanity pressed upon her, sweeping her up in their rush to reach the stands.

*Theodora, you dinglebrain, what were you thinking?* She would never reach the stands, much less succeed in locating Devlin Stone in this sea of faces.

Abruptly she turned, elbowing her way through all the bodies rushing in the opposite direction. Breathing hard, she at last reached a broad dirt avenue, and her gaze fixed upon the less-peopled stables to the southeast of the track. Perhaps over there she could snatch a moment or two of privacy, just enough to stiffen her spine again and set her to rights. She wasn't deserting the field of battle, nor abandoning her quest. She just needed to hush a few unpleasant voices from her childhood, and to come up with a more workable plan to locate Devlin Stone.

# Chapter Four

Upon reaching the stable area Thea was disconcerted to find herself confronted by a stern-faced man, standing with folded arms under the boughs of a massive pine. At her approach he shoved back the rim of his bowler hat and looked her over.

"You an owner, miss? Not supposed to let race goers wander hereabouts unescorted."

"I'm…I'm looking for my escort, a Mr. Stone?"

She was taken aback when the suspicion on the man's face relaxed into friendliness. "Ah, he's been here for a bit. Nice feller, told me about his horse farm in Virginia. Sure has that Southern drawl, though." He tugged out a brightly patterned handkerchief and dabbed his sweaty forehead, then gestured toward the stables. "Go ahead, miss, but mind your step and your skirt. It's not as busy, now the racing's commenced. But you stay clear o' that aisle." He pointed. "Trainers are bringing out the horses for the next race, owners are jawing at the jockeys, the horses can be fractious. So don't go bothering them none, else you'll get us both in Dutch."

"Thank you. You're very kind. And I'll be very care-ful." Flummoxed by her extraordinary luck, Thea smiled at the guard, closed her parasol and strolled with thudding heart toward the cool shadowed aisles in stables devoid of activity. Several grooms glanced over at her distractedly but nobody challenged her presence. By the time she reached a row of stalls near the back, the only person she had encountered was another groom, dozing on a fruit crate, his cap pulled over his eyes. All the stalls in this row were empty.

Earthy scents surrounded her, of hay and oats and leather and manure, all overlaid by the lazy heat of sunshine on old wood.

Gradually the knots in Thea's stomach unsnarled; she slipped down the cool, deserted aisle, then with more confidence approached the next row of stalls. A couple of stable boys touched their caps to her as she passed; some curious equine heads poked over stall doors, ears perked, nostrils whiffing. One horse, a chestnut with a white stripe down his forehead, nickered softly. Thea had never been around horses much, but after the tumultuous activity elsewhere, the tranquility here tugged her heart. Soon she found herself edging close enough to gingerly pat the chestnut's muzzle, which was softer than a fur muff. Warm air gusted from flared nostrils as the animal nudged her hand. Delighted, for a moment she savored the interaction, the unfamiliar scents swirling pleasantly around her. Then the horse retreated back into his stall, and with a lighter step Thea continued down the aisle. For the first time in her life she began to understand the compulsion to participate, even with only binoculars and betting tickets, in a sport where a rider harnessed himself to the horse and flew like the wind.

When she turned the next corner her gaze froze on the figure of a man standing a dozen paces away, his back to Thea. One of his arms draped companionably around a horse's neck, and Thea could hear the soft Southern cadences of his voice speaking to the animal. The pose struck her as almost intimate, and she found herself unable to shatter the peacefulness of the moment. Instead, drawn by a yearning that caught her even more off guard, Thea crept closer until she could hear Mr. Stone's words.

"…treating you like they should? You're a handsome fella, aren't you? For a Thoroughbred, that is. I'm used to something more substantial, say a Suffolk punch, or a Percheron? Magnificent horses, they are, and easily twice your size. But you'd put 'em to shame on a racetrack. Ah… easy, son. Touchy spot? Sorry. How about here, on the poll… Yeah, you like that, do you? That sweet spot between your ears, where the cranium meets the vertebrae."

Mesmerized, Thea watched the calm authority of his hands, deftly moving over every part of the racehorse he could reach from forehead to neck, moving only his arms. Never had she known a man could build such a connection with a beast that most likely weighed over a thousand pounds. Unlike the friendly but aloof horse that had allowed her brief pat before turning away, the horse with Mr. Stone had lowered his head over the stall door. The two of them looked as though they were, well, *talking* to each other.

Without warning, Thea's eyes stung, with a longing more forceful than the thirst for revenge that had dominated her life for nine agonizing months. What would it feel like to have a man lavish affection upon her, not merely a brief handclasp over her elbow? A man who communicated care and tenderness, like Mr. Stone with that horse? Plainly he loved the animals, and perhaps owned one or two himself. If so, he might be a man of some wealth.

Which meant, if she cozied up to Mr. Stone, he'd be justified in considering her as one more Saratoga sycophant, like all the women trailing along in Edgar Fane's wake.

Uncertainty glued Thea's feet to the ground.

One of the horses in a nearby stall snorted, then kicked the boards with his hoof. An involuntary gasp escaped before Thea could stifle it. Mr. Stone glanced casually around. Slowly he removed his arm from the horse's neck and turned to face her, the gentleness on his face hardening to—to stone.

"Miss Pickford. What a…surprise." Without looking away he gave the horse a final pat, then ambled down the aisle toward her. "I admit to chagrin. I…ah…wasn't prepared to see you again so soon, certainly not in this setting."

Thea squared her shoulders. "I didn't expect to find you in this setting either." He was taller than she remembered, his shoulders broader. Without the straw boater to soften his appearance, an aura of danger hovered around him now more than ever. Not the danger of a snake like Edgar Fane, but that of a thunderstorm—and she stood unprotected in an open field while lightning stabbed the sky. Thea focused on his hands—a stupid mistake because all she could remember was how they looked gently stroking a horse. "I have an important matter to discuss with you."

"Ah. Hmm." He seemed to hesitate. "Very well, I'm not one to gainsay a lady determined to ignore her fiancé's existence—Miss Pickford? Are you all right?"

Unstrung by the bald reminder of the nonexistent Neville, Thea almost backed into several stacked bales of straw. "I'm perfectly all right," she said.

In the dim stable his light eyes bored into hers; he lifted a hand to shove a lock of hair the rich color of polished mahogany off his forehead. Despite herself, Thea stiffened. Something flickered in his expression, then without fuss he stepped back a pace or two and folded his arms. "Are you a horse lover, Miss Pickford?"

"I've never been around them enough to know. But I admire them, very much. A chestnut with a white strip down his nose let me pat him for a second. I...you love them, don't you?"

"Yes. More than just about anything else on this earth. Most of the time, I prefer them to people." He hesitated, then added matter-of-factly, "Don't be afraid, Miss Pickford. I don't abuse horses, or women. Those who do best keep out of my way, however. May I offer an apology, for frightening you this morning?"

"I wasn't frightened, but an apology is definitely called for," she agreed.

The lock of hair fell back over his forehead. He brushed at it, and Thea stared, transfixed anew at the long supple fingers, the tanned wrist almost twice the size of hers. Why, that hand looked strong enough to break a brick, yet a moment earlier his touch had transformed a high-strung Thoroughbred to a purring kitten.

Blinking, she reminded herself of her purpose in hunting this man down. "You voiced several ungentlemanly accusations, which I'm willing to overlook because I—" The words faltered into awkward silence until she added breathlessly, "Mr. Stone...you're staring at me."

"Merely returning the favor, Miss Pickford. I'm flattered. You're a lovely young woman, but I'm thinking your fiancé should conduct his courtship from a much shorter distance than the other side of an ocean."

Thea's parasol slid free and fell with a soft plop onto the packed dirt stable floor. Mortified, she bent to retrieve it, but Mr. Stone stepped forward and swooped it up instead, his fingers brushing hers as he returned the parasol. The jolt of sensation fried the air between them. "I would never dishonor my fiancé…" she began feebly, the once-facile lie now stumbling from her lips. "I merely need to ask you something, about someone else."

"Oh?"

As if in a dream Thea watched him idly stroke the side of his nose. The vivid image of that finger brushing *her* nose burned a fiery trail all the way to her toes. Hot color scorched her cheeks. Her grandfather was right: despite her sophisticated education and her acquaintance with numerous intellectual gentlemen, until today she had remained unblemished emotionally. A perfectly rolled and floured biscuit which had never seen the inside of an oven.

The friendly courtship she had enjoyed the previous summer with a neighbor's grandson by comparison now seemed a tepid thing, ending without fanfare when the young man returned to Boston. In Thea's opinion, romance between a man and a woman was vastly overrated.

*This is not a romance, you limp-noodled ninnyhammer.*

"Miss Pickford? You wanted to ask me about something, or someone?" Mr. Stone prompted.

"Oh. Yes, yes I did." Thoroughly rattled, Thea snatched a piece of straw from the bale of hay and distractedly wove it between her fingers. "I wanted to ask you about… about—you told Mrs. Van Eyck and me you planned to attend the races. It's, ah, past two o'clock.…"

"So I did, and so it is." Mr. Stone's eyes narrowed, and for a moment he stared down at her without speaking. "I don't know what to do about you," he eventually murmured, his voice deep, the drawl warm and lazy. "You need to be more careful when you lie, and how you look at a man when your heart is promised elsewhere."

"Well, I'm not doing it on purpose," she blurted, stupidly. "As for telling lies, *you're* the one who pretended an acquaintance with my fiancé. How would you feel if I reported you to the local constable, or alerted—"

The words backed up in her throat when Mr. Stone took a single long stride toward her. The scents of starch and sweat and horse filled her nostrils. Before she could react, he plucked the straw from her fingers and skimmed it along the line of her clenched jaw. "No, you won't. You have too much to lose, don't you, to risk that sort of attention."

Stepping back, he sketched a brief bow, then swiveled on his heel and sauntered down the aisle, turned a corner and disappeared.

Thea remained motionless, one hand braced against the rough stable wall while she waited for the churning in her stomach to settle. After several moments she lifted her hand to the cheek the straw had touched. A tingle still quivered along her veins.

This bizarre physical attraction could be contained and ultimately controlled. But the absence of any signs of vertigo from their confrontation alarmed her profoundly. Such a reaction indicated a moral weakness in her character far worse to Thea than the facade designed to procure justice on behalf of her grandfather. A godly young lady of impeccable virtue should be outraged, or even nauseous with that vertigo—the latter her reaction on the four occasions when she had spoken to Edgar Fane.

Despite her sheltered upbringing, perhaps she had truly become her mother, whose acting skill was superseded only by her affinity for men.

The possibility cast a murky film over the summer afternoon, but Thea refused to abandon her purpose. Life offered choices, her grandfather told her frequently. She wasn't doomed to follow her mother's path; she would simply choose to avoid any further encounters with Devlin Stone. Another opportunity would arise to ingratiate herself with Edgar Fane, a man for whom she would never feel anything but disgust.

*Stiffen your spine, Theodora, and get on with the task.*

## Chapter Five

With a theatrical flourish, Edgar Fane pulled the sheet covering his latest painting from the canvas. His appreciative audience—the fifty or so guests he had invited to join him aboard the *Alice* as the boat gently steamed across Saratoga Lake—applauded and lifted their champagne glasses to toast his artistic prowess.

The effort was not one of his better ones. He'd chosen a seascape—hence the unveiling on the steamer—but the colors were too bright, the people on the shore more reminiscent of paint smears. The frame, however, was a lovely antique gold.

He did like the frame, which he'd discovered in an antique store in Chicago. A satisfied tingle briefly tickled his insides.

"Who's the lucky recipient this time?" Richard Beekins gave his shoulder a congenial pat, wheezing noisily in Edgar's ear as he talked. "C'mon, be a good chap and tell your daddy's old friend."

Edgar gave the boozy fellow a smile, then used the excuse of setting aside the delicate champagne flute to turn away. "You know I never divulge privileged information. Everyone needs a secret or two in life. Besides,

I need a gimmick to heighten the interest. We all know I'm no Michelangelo." He winked at Dahlia, his chosen dinner partner for the afternoon boating party. "Even my charming companion here, lovely lady though she may be, couldn't inveigle the name of the new owner."

Dahlia obediently pouted and fluttered her eyelashes. Diamonds twinkled in her ears, at the base of her throat and on almost every finger on both hands. "Darling Edgar, I haven't yet tried."

Bored with feminine fawning, Edgar downed another flute of champagne as he smiled his way among the guests until he reached the prow of the slender steamer. Dahlia fortunately had been detained by Richard Beekins. Propping his elbows on the narrow rail, Edgar contemplated the undulation of the water, how the sunlight danced over the ripples and whether or not he could capture the effect on canvas. Not that it mattered. His forays into painting provided a useful outlet, but he'd never intended to pursue the craft seriously. On the other hand, perhaps a studied dedication would offer an antidote to the ennui plaguing him the past few years.

"You're looking far too solemn." Cynthia Gorman's scent filled the air before the woman herself joined Edgar, close enough for the wind to blow her lawn skirts against his trousers. "You've been brooding most of the afternoon. What is it, Edgar?"

"Can't a man enjoy the sun on his head and the wind in his face for a minute or two?"

"Not Edgar Fane, apparently." Her laugh drifted pleasantly over the water. "When I spied you off by yourself for once, I grabbed the opportunity. You're the only member of your family I can stand being around for longer than a half hour, you know."

"Because I don't try and seduce you out of your fortune, or because I don't talk about mine?"

"My dear man, yours is the only seduction I might contemplate, but we both know that's never going to happen, so why don't you try me as a confidante? I can keep a secret."

Edgar's impatience erupted in a burst of laughter, which naturally offended Cynthia. He laid his hand against her heliotrope-scented cheek. "Don't," he murmured. "You know I love you dearly—"

"As you love all the other women in your harem…"

"Precisely. All a delight to the eyes, but I have no intention of confining my delight or confiding secrets to any of them. Thanks to my brothers and sister making more money and producing heirs, I am free to live—precisely as I please, unencumbered by familial obligation."

"Never alone, but always lonely."

Annoyed, Edgar straightened and stepped away. "My dear Cynthia, if I want a philosophical lecture I'll hunt down a mesmerist. The boat will be docking soon. I think it's time I made the announcement." He lifted his hand and brushed his knuckles against her jutting jaw. "Since we're such old friends, I will share one small secret with you." He waited until her eyes kindled with hope, then leaned to whisper into her ear, "You *won't* be the recipient of my latest work of art."

A loud burst of masculine guffaws echoed through the cut glass doors of the Casino's barroom. Half-empty glass of springwater in one hand, Devlin paced outside the entrance while he chewed over what to do next. Two of his suspects were here. Upstairs in the game room, Randolph Lunt had suffered heavy losses at the roulette table, and when he left off gambling to drown his sorrows

Dev automatically followed; meanwhile, Joseph Scarborough was deep in a poker game with four other men. He looked to be on a winning streak and would likely stay in the game for a while. Back home, some of their wins, and many of the losses, would feed half the county for a year. Devlin sipped the now-lukewarm water while he fought the cynicism crusting, one barnacle at a time, over the idealism of his youth.

As for his remaining suspect, Edgar Fane—that slippery charmer had taken a party of guests out on the *Alice,* one of the steamers chugging around Saratoga Lake. They wouldn't return dockside until near sunset.

So Devlin paced, and pondered his options.

Moments later, across the room the narrow cut glass doors banged open, and Lunt shoved through. "Hey, you!" He headed toward Devlin. "Need change for a twenty. Help me out, won't you?"

"Let's see what I've got." Dev tugged out his wallet and made a show of leafing through the bills.

After handing him smaller bills Dev accepted the twenty in return, casually tucking it away with rock-steady hands, while inside his heart pounded like a kettledrum. When Lunt disappeared back through the doors, Dev exited the Casino and hurried down the street to his hotel room.

Thirty minutes after a thorough examination of what turned out to be a bona fide twenty-dollar bill, he headed back for the Park, his favorite sanctuary not only from the masses but his own foul mood.

Redesigned a quarter of a century earlier by Frederick Olmsted's firm, Congress Spring Park was a popular destination for guests and townsfolk alike. Meandering paths wove through neatly sculpted shrubbery and towering trees. Soft summer breezes carried the sound of the band playing hum-along tunes from a bandstand, built in the middle of a spring-fed pond at the center of the park.

Sunbeams turned the droplets of a fountain to twinkling crystal confetti. Steps slowing, Dev finally allowed the peace of the place to relax the knots in his muscles. The saw-toothed disappointment ebbed.

Most likely the soused Randolph Lunt was a dead end—a man who gambled away enough money to drive him to drink did not possess enough fortitude to be the Hotel Hustler.

That left Joseph Scarborough, Edgar Fane—and Miss Pickford, whose interest in Fane probably deserved closer examination, in light of her deceptions. By the time Devlin wound his way back through the pair of Corinthian columns flanking the entrance to the park he had settled upon a plan of sorts: shadow Miss Pickford for a few days, note who she saw and the circumstances, see if any pattern developed. He told himself this course of action was coldly professional, and had nothing to do with a pair of dark brown eyes or the longing expression he'd glimpsed when he first caught sight of her.

Nothing to do with the faint scent of lilacs or vivid blush when she looked at him and dropped her parasol.

Tranquil mood broken, Devlin headed for the lake to wait for Edgar Fane and his boating party to return. He could hunt down Miss Pickford tomorrow. After hiring a two-seater runabout, he drove the four miles at a leisurely clip, then left the horse contentedly munching a handful of oats beneath a shade tree. Dev wandered down toward the dock where several people were fishing, their poles stretched in ragged formation along the landing and the shore. Lake water lapped in lazy ripples, insects droned in the tall grasses and farther down the shoreline a pair of ducks took flight.

One of the anglers near the end of the landing was a woman, dressed in some sort of striped skirt, yellow overblouse and a floppy, wide-brimmed hat. Lake breezes stirred the blue-and-yellow ribbons tied around the crown and dangling provocatively down the woman's back. She was alone, the closest other fisherman a dozen yards away. When she half turned, Dev caught a glimpse of her face. The punch of disbelief—and elation—left him disoriented.

Theodora Pickford. Fishing alone, from the dock where Edgar Fane would shortly disembark?

Why should he be surprised? Dev shook his head. Though supposedly engaged to a supposedly beloved British aristocrat, the Jezebel had professed an interest in Devlin—and Edgar Fane—from the moment Dev met her.

On the other hand, he might be judging her too harshly. He wasn't in the best of humors, after all. And all right, he admitted to himself that the memory of their encounter in the barn burned in his brain like a brand.

His father, dead before Devlin's tenth birthday, would have thanked God for "arranging" this encounter, proclaiming it divine assistance. Dev however saw no reason to interpret Miss Pickford's presence here as anything other than deliberate design on *her* part, and luck on his. No divine intervention, no proof that God invested any interest in the species He'd created, and perhaps now regretted.

Absently Devlin kicked a pebble, his gaze on Theodora Pickford's distant silhouette. He was an independently wealthy man with an overdeveloped sense of responsibility and a restless soul. Two years earlier he'd gone to Washington looking for a half brother, and instead of returning home to StoneHill Farm, he'd become a Secret Service operative. On a good day, Devlin liked to think his path to the nation's capitol two years ago had been part of his destiny. That he had something to offer a world far beyond the boundaries of StoneHill, something grander, something…ordained. Something that kindled the internal jolt of satisfaction he felt when a herd of horses cantered over to greet him.

He'd never expected to experience that jolt just from looking at a woman who most likely he'd be arresting one day soon.

## Chapter Six

He retraced his steps to his livery horse. Late-afternoon sunlight sheened the lake in gold and tinted streamers of wispy clouds a deep rose-pink. Steadily chugging toward the landing, the narrow-nosed steamer skimmed across the water, returning Miss Pickford's unwitting human catch to shore.

Perhaps he should warn Edgar Fane.

Instead Dev settled back against the tree trunk and watched. Sweat trickled down his temple; absently he swiped the droplets away, lifting his face to the light breeze, and waited. The *Alice* arrived at the landing and passengers swarmed onto the dock, their voices loud in the peaceful late afternoon. With scarcely a glance they streamed past Miss Pickford and the other anglers. Miss Pickford suddenly began a wild struggle with her fishing pole. Several passengers paused to observe, and over the swell of a dozen conversations Dev heard her breathless voice.

"I've been here for hours, and was about to give up. Oh—" Her upper body jerked, then steadied as she wrestled against the taut line. "No, no, don't help me. It's very exciting, isn't it? I hope it's a largemouth bass. My grandfather is…" The rest of her words faded into the general babble.

A small crowd gathered, blocking Dev's view. He unhurriedly ducked beneath the gelding's neck to better monitor Fane's passage to shore, noting the instant the man's attention turned from the boat captain to Miss Pickford. *Poor fool,* Dev thought. Fane laughed and took a step toward the siren seducing him with her fishing antics, even as a shapely debutante decked out in a ridiculous mimicry of a sailor suit wrapped possessive fingers around his forearm.

Without warning, Miss Pickford emitted a cry of surprise, her arms stretching taut while she fought to haul in her catch, which suddenly soared out of the water in a graceful arc and landed wetly six inches from Edgar Fane's feet.

"I caught it!" she exclaimed, at last turning to face her spellbound audience. "Did you see? What kind of fish— oh." Even from twenty feet away Dev could read the emotions tumbling across her face—surprise, sheepishness, amusement…and guilt. "Why…it's a—a shoe! I've been fighting for ages, over a *shoe?*"

Laughter tittered through the group. Dev wandered closer.

"How embarrassing." Miss Pickford addressed Fane, a becoming shade of pink tinting her cheeks the same hue as the clouds. "I beg your pardon. Did my shoe ruin yours?"

The artful question, with its tint of good-natured humor, secured Edgar Fane's unswerving interest, Devlin noted. Miss Pickford had cast her lures with masterful expertise.

"Not at all." Fane leaned to pick up the "catch." "At least, not compared to this poor old thing."

"I suppose we could ask the cook at Briggs House if he's willing to try a fillet of sole?" Miss Pickford ventured, and the entire crowd burst into appreciative laughter.

"Ha! Not only a lovely angler, but a humorist, as well. I'm delighted to meet you, Miss—it is Miss, I hope?"

"Well…unofficially I do have a fiancé, but he's in Europe at the moment." After an appropriately timed pause she added, "My chaperone might not approve, but this is 1897, after all. Practically a new century, time to dispense with so many cumbersome formalities." And the chit had the audacity to offer her hand. "Miss Pickford. I'm very glad my catch didn't land in your face."

"Miss Pickford. Edgar Fane, at your service." He bowed, the gesture courteous but mocking. "Tell me, Miss Pickford, do you also bowl and don bloomers to ride a bicycle? Play tennis and golf? I'm intrigued by this new concept of femininity, unashamed to engage in all manner of outdoor sport. We must get together. Here's my card. Simpson? Where are you, man? Ah…this is Simpson, my personal secretary. Simpson, I'm hoping Miss Pickford will dine with me one evening this week. Can you check my schedule, and make arrangements? Miss Pickford? I look forward to sharing more of your exploits."

And with a final lingering perusal he left her with his secretary and joined the rest of his guests. They clattered down the landing and dispersed into various buggies and carriages, the secretary following a moment later. The pier was soon deserted save for Miss Pickford and a couple of other fishermen who steadfastly kept their backs to her. One of the trolleys that ran from the lake to the village clanged its pending arrival at the Briggs House hotel. Devlin's attention never diverted from the lone woman who stood at the end of the pier. She stared out over the lake, fishing pole drooping lifelessly in her hand. Nearby, the remaining anglers began gathering their equipment, likely intending to catch the last trolley.

Suddenly Miss Pickford leaned down, scooped up the shoe and heaved both it and the fishing pole into the lake. Then she whirled and marched down the landing, passing within a dozen paces of the tree where Devlin waited, a silent, cynical witness to her performance. Eschewing the trolley, she set out walking along the edge of the road back to town.

What kind of woman walked four miles when transportation was readily available? Certainly she'd hoped to secure a ride in Edgar Fane's private omnibus, but with that hope dashed she had nothing to gain now but blisters.

"Shortsighted a bit, weren't you?" Devlin commented aloud after she disappeared around a bend in the road. He climbed into the runabout. "Well, let's see what kind of line you'll try on me."

Ten minutes along the road, however, he still hadn't overtaken her. The sky was deepening to twilight, the trolley long gone and only three other horse-drawn conveyances and several bicyclists had passed; serve him right if Miss Pickford had accepted a ride in someone else's buggy. His report to headquarters would have to detail the account of how Operative Stone allowed both parties he'd been shadowing to slip through his fingers. Grimly he searched both sides of the road, slowing the horse to a plodding walk. Even so, in the gathering darkness he almost missed the flash of color behind a clump of bushes.

"Whoa…" he murmured, and set the brake, his gaze riveted to the bushes. There, another glimpse of creamy yellow, the same shade as the overblouse Miss Pickford had been wearing.

Then he heard a low moan.

\* \* \*

Panting, Thea propped herself on her hands, but the motion triggered another bout of nausea; she retched, sides heaving, perspiration mingling with the tears that leaked from the corners of her eyes. Not since the night she'd visited Grandfather in that dreadful jail had she suffered from an attack this vicious. Stupid, stupid, *stupid* not to have realized what might happen if her little scheme to attract Edgar Fane worked.

Or more precisely, didn't work. The blackguard might have noticed her, but she hadn't garnered sufficient interest for an invitation to return to the hotel with the rest of his more favored guests.

*Listen to yourself, Theodora.* Her entire life now reflected the moral virtue of a…a vaudeville singer.

Which punishment in Dante's *Inferno* did she deserve, for becoming that which she most despised? The dizziness intensified, sucking her down, down into the depths. God would never forgive her, because she would never forgive herself.

"What the—" a man's voice exclaimed, and strong hands closed around her shoulders.

"Don't…" Thea managed before her stomach heaved again and she gagged.

"Easy. Shh…don't fight me, you'll make it worse."

The deep, now-familiar voice soothed, but humiliation scorched rational thought. Better a party of drunken fishermen had stumbled upon her than this man. "Mr. Stone…" Thea managed in a hoarse whisper, "please leave me alone. I'll…in a moment I'll be fine. I just need…" The effort to converse overwhelmed her. She could only close her eyes and allow those competent hands to do whatever they pleased.

A musky yet pleasant aroma drifted through her nostrils

as he gently eased her back down on the warm earth. Instead of scratchy meadow grasses her cheek was cushioned by some sort of fabric. She tried to lift her hand, but flashing lights stabbed behind her closed eyelids. "Can't… please. Leave me alone."

"All right," Devlin Stone murmured. The air stirred vaguely, then stilled.

So. He'd listened, and obeyed. Life, Thea decided in utter misery, once again proved she was a worthless castaside, an inferior specimen of humanity nobody wanted. Both parents had abandoned her. Her chaperone ignored her. Edgar Fane gave her over to his *secretary*. And now Mr. Stone left her prostrate in the bushes, never mind that he'd only done what she requested.

*Lord? If You care anything about me at all, let me die so I'm no longer a burden to my grandfather.* Her quest for justice had failed. Her parody on the dock with Edgar Fane clung like a stench. No wonder Mr. Stone abandoned her, as well.

# Chapter Seven

"Miss Pickford? You haven't passed out on me, have you?"

The calm voice penetrated her miasma, but Thea still started when a damp cloth passed over the back of her neck, then down her cheek. Next she felt his palm—warm, the fingertips slightly abraded—press against her forehead. "No fever. Eat anything today to cause a sickness in your belly?"

"Not…sick."

"Nor up to talking, either, hmm?" There was a sound of splashing, then he laid the freshly dampened cloth over her eyes. "I'm unbuttoning your sleeves at the wrists so I can bathe them, and your hands. Don't be alarmed, and don't fight me, all right?"

As if she could. Sighing a little, Thea allowed his skillful ministrations to lull her into a semicatatonic state, akin to floating on her back in one of the lakes scattered over Staten Island, drifting in the lazy current while the sun and water bound her in a lovely cocoon.

Time floated by, until she was able to take a deep breath without choking on the nausea. Hesitantly she opened her eyes. The whirling had abated. "Thank you," she breathed, and scraped up half a smile. "I'm better now." And saying it, she could feel the truth soaking into her pores. Edgar Fane made her sick; Devlin Stone made her feel safe.

Of the two, Mr. Stone probably posed more of a threat.

"Want to tell me what happened?" he asked eventually with the tone that caused a high-strung racehorse to rest its head against him.

For some moments Thea didn't answer. The vertigo had subsided, but humiliation still burned deep enough to smudge his Good Samaritan kindness into something less benign. A glance upward through the screen of her lashes intensified the uncertainty: he sat at ease beside her, one arm draped loosely across an upraised knee. A light wind stirred the fine linen of his pin-striped shirt. He was hatless today, and the wind brushed the lock of hair over his forehead, lending him the relaxed air of a man with nothing on his mind but a day at the lake. Yet, veiled in shadow, his gaze rested unwavering upon Theodora. She had the impression he would sit there, calmly waiting until Thea offered an explanation even if it took until darkness enfolded them like a blanket.

Who *was* Devlin Stone?

She had nothing to gain by telling him the truth, and everything to lose if she didn't. She might not understand his interest, but over the past several weeks she'd witnessed all manner of masculine conduct toward women and this man was no Edgar Fane. He could still be a charlatan, preying upon vulnerable women at resort hotels; from the first she'd sensed his contempt for her. But his present compassion contradicted every definition of a genuine cad. No man she'd ever known willingly nursed a sick woman.

On a more pragmatic note, the severity of this spell had robbed her of the strength to safely hike back to town.

Whether the choice was wise or not, Mr. Stone remained her best hope. He might not be cruel, but something warned Thea he would leave her stranded if she wove another story about an English fiancé, or how much she loved to fish. "I…have dizzy spells." The words stuck in her throat. Clumsily she attempted to rise.

Without a word Mr. Stone wrapped a strong arm around her shoulders and eased her back against one of the outcropping of boulders beside the shrubs. "Here." He tucked his now-crumpled but still-damp handkerchief into her hand. "Wipe your face. It will help. Suck on this peppermint." He handed her the piece of candy. "Then you can tell me about these spells of yours."

"You've been very kind." The candy helped assuage the weakness. "If I told you I'd prefer not to talk about them?"

"I'd take you straight to a physician." He searched her face, then added without inflection, "Are you with child, Miss Pickford?"

*"What?"* She almost sputtered the peppermint into his face. "Did you say— Do you actually think— I told you I'm not married. Why would you ask such an insulting question?"

For the first time a glint of blue sparkled in his eyes, and that attractive dimple creased one of his cheeks. "Given your response, I withdraw the question. You may be a highly imaginative liar, but these days only an innocent would offer that answer to a man vulgar enough to broach the subject in the first place."

Well. Thea didn't know whether to be insulted or relieved. "You confuse me, Mr. Stone," she mumbled, ducking her head. "From the moment we first met, you've confused me. I know I'm a…a…I haven't been truthful. There's a reason. At the time it seemed the only way." She smoothed the crumpled handkerchief in her lap, folding it into a neat square, her fingers still clumsy with weakness. "I've been here at Saratoga Springs for almost a month. Until you, everybody believed everything I told them." It was difficult, but she made herself face him directly. "How did you know?"

"When I'm not indulging in the first pleasure holiday in a decade—" his smile deepened until dimples creased both cheeks "—I raise and train horses. Draft horses, to be specific, though we—my uncle and I—gentle the odd pleasure mount here and there. I've been around them all my life. Horses taught me a lot about observation, about sensing feelings, moods." He gave a short laugh. "When you're surrounded by creatures with hooves the size of a soup tureen, you'd better learn how to read them. Works the same with people. Although I prefer horses for the most part. They might bite or kick if frightened or provoked. But they don't lie."

Thea weathered the blow; it was justified. "I didn't think a harmless fabrication would hurt anyone, and it kept speculation about me to a minimum. It was the only way I could think of to attract..." Her voice trailed into silence.

"And when nothing worked, you got desperate."

Above them a burnt orange sky warned of encroaching night. Somewhere nearby, an insect commenced its ceaseless chirring. But between Thea and Devlin Stone silence thickened until each inhalation choked her lungs. "Desperate," she repeated, squeezing her hand until her fingers went numb. "Have you ever been desperate, Mr. Stone? About anything?"

"Yes. But never enough to cheat, or beg, or deceive."

"Then you've never been desperate, and faced with

impossible choices." She paused. "Is that what you think of me?"

"I don't know what to think of you, Miss Pickford. Is that your real name, by the way?"

"What? Oh…well, no. It's actually my mother's maiden name." He slid the question in so neatly Thea answered before she realized it. But unless Mr. Stone frequented the tawdry depths of New York City's Bowery he would not associate her with Hetty Pickford. "Please don't ask for my real name. I don't want to lie to you anymore."

"Ah." Another one of those flicks of blue light came and went in his eyes. "We're in accord, then. I don't want to be lied to. Now, it's getting late. Is your companion— Mrs. Chudd? Is she likely to be concerned about your whereabouts?"

"Well, if I don't turn up by midnight, she'd notify the front desk at least."

"Not a very efficient companion."

"No. She's mostly for appearances. I'm supposed to be a wealthy heiress, engaged to an earl. A chaperone's expected. Mrs. Chudd's former employer just passed away. She said she'd always wanted to see upstate New York, but after we arrived she developed an aversion for crowds."

"I see." He rubbed his palms together. "All right, then. What say we return to the village? Can you walk, Miss Pickford, or shall I carry you to my buggy?"

"I can walk," she answered too quickly, and in the sunset's glow she caught his ironic smile.

In her haste to scramble to her feet a wave of faintness almost contradicted her words. He put his hands on her waist to steady her, and though the courtesy was brief, almost impersonal, Thea's limbs turned to sand.

"Shall I carry you after all, then?" he offered after her first few steps.

"No. It's just a silly weakness, already passing." More a weakness of her mind than her limbs. "I could probably walk back to the village, but—"

"Don't be a goose, Miss Pickford. Pride's a useful commodity on occasion. This isn't one of them."

The sun slipped behind the mountains to the west as he handed her into his buggy. The contrast between this simple one-horse, two-seat runabout and Edgar Fane's waxed and gleaming omnibus harnessed to a team of four matched horses was as incongruous as the realization that, given a choice, Theodora much preferred the former. Confused, she watched Mr. Stone light the single carriage lamp, and give the horse an affectionate pat.

Who was this man?

# Chapter Eight

She looked like a woebegone waif sitting beside him in the gathering darkness, smelling of peppermint and illness. Strands of hair hung limply around the pale oval of her face and dirt smeared over her yellow shirtwaist. The floppy hat rested forgotten on her lap. For the first mile Devlin fought a battle with his conscience. Fortunately Miss Pickford herself broached the subject.

"I don't suppose you'd consider forgetting everything you saw and heard," she said, her grimy hands smoothing in ceaseless circles over the equally grimy hat ribbons.

"Not a chance." He paused. "Especially the scene on the pier. Your staging and timing were impeccable, Miss Pickford. However, compared to Edgar Fane you're a very small minnow tempting a shark."

She groaned. "You saw that?"

"From start to finish. If it's any consolation, I think the tactic worked. Humor can be a powerful weapon in a woman's arsenal. The shoe definitely captured Fane's attention."

"Only for a moment. I wasn't expecting to be fobbed off on a personal secretary."

"A dinner invitation will be forthcoming, Miss Pickford. Count on it."

"That's what I'm afraid of."

She spoke so softly he barely caught the words, but a chill spiked down his spine. Snug cottages whose windows glowed with lights had begun to appear on either side of the road; in moments they'd be back in the village, and Dev would have to let her go. An opportunity would be forever lost. Off to the right, a grove of shade trees offered privacy and without a qualm he turned the horse off the road and into their concealing darkness.

"What are you doing?"

"Nothing sinister. I just want us to come to a better understanding of one another before I turn you over to Mrs. Chudd."

"There's no point. I don't think I can…" A long hesitation was followed by an unraveling sigh, then, "I promised myself I could do this, vowed I could ignore my conscience, and all the doubts. But it's not working. The attacks of dizziness…they're getting worse. Stronger." She turned to face him, the fuzzy light from the carriage lamp illuminating a face taut with misery. "You told me you knew of Edgar Fane. Could you…would you tell me everything you know, without asking why I continue to pursue this man?"

Her sincerity disarmed him; he didn't want to believe she was being honest with him, because it would corroborate his perception of her true character—and reinforce the dangerous attraction that intensified with every encounter. She was an admitted liar, with trouble and secrets stamped all over her face. Yet her vulnerability appealed to every one of his protective instincts.

Compassion might kill him yet.…

"*Horses are prey animals,*" Uncle Jay counseled often enough to annoy when Dev was growing up. "*Humans, now—we're predators. But that don't mean we never feel threatened, 'specially women. A mean woman, or a threatened woman, can kick you with words, trample your heart. After Sylvia and your mother, it's possible you may never trust another one. I don't look to forgive your intended myself—so can't blame you none for feeling the same. That don't mean all females deserve the scorn I hear in your voice these days. Regardless of their behavior, like horses a lady never deserves the back of your hand, or a fist. Always be a man instead of a two-legged mongrel, lad, so's you'll sleep at night."*

"How about we trade information?" he began, slowly. "You tell me about these 'spells,' and I'll tell you what I know about Edgar Fane."

In the darkness Dev heard her exhale a long wavering sigh. "My grandfather warned me about rogues and knaves. He never warned me about someone like you."

"Well, if I'm not a rogue or a knave, what does that leave?" *Keep it light,* he ordered himself. *Go gently. You can lead a horse to water, but if you want him to drink, feed him something salty to whet his thirst.* "Or perhaps I shouldn't ask?"

"Grandfather also warned me about men who think too much. Shakespeare had the way of it—such men *are* dangerous. I should be afraid of you. I don't trust you, but you've been…kind." A beat of silence hovered before she continued slowly, "Ever since I was a girl, I've had occasional spells of vertigo. Sometimes they're debilitating. Since last year they seem to be worsening." Her voice thinned. "But there's no other course. I have to do this."

The last declaration was scarcely above a whisper. "What is it you have to do?" Dev prompted after a while. "Does it concern Edgar Fane?"

Her hands crushed the hat. "Yes."

"Ah." Since he wanted answers, not another episode of vertigo, he told her what he could. "Edgar Fane is a wealthy, likable fellow who enjoys the company of others, particularly attractive women. His father made a fortune, the older brother's expanding it and his other brother is marrying a French countess next year. From what I've gleaned, Edgar's decided his role is that of charming wastrel—one of those men your grandfather *would* have warned you about."

For a moment he silently studied her. "Is your family in dire financial straits, Miss—I can't continue to call you Miss Pickford, now can I? Will you tell me your name? I haven't personally met Mr. Fane, but I know enough to question certain aspects of his character. Of course, it doesn't seem fair to confide my observations unless you're equally candid." He paused. "For instance, when he asks you to dinner, how do I know whether you might decide to warn him about a certain Mr. Stone, and the rumors he's bandying about?"

This time she refused to rise to the bait. "Your observations about Mr. Fane must be highly salacious."

Night had fallen, covering them in a soft matte darkness. The carriage lamp threw out enough light to illuminate the intelligence glittering in the coffee–dark brown eyes. So. She had recovered. It was to be a battle of wits to the end, then. Strangely pleased, Devlin affected a shrug, then gathered up the reins and smoothly backed horse and buggy onto the road, all without saying a word.

She lasted until a block before the Grand Union Hotel. Garish electric lights strung on ugly poles shone down on crowds of laughing people. A loud burst of masculine laughter startled the livery horse; Dev automatically soothed the animal, then turned onto Broadway into a sea of gleaming carriages and buggies.

"You really do have a way with horses, Mr. Stone."

Dev pulled into a vacant spot a block from the Grand Union Hotel. "I love them," he replied simply, wondering at the undercurrent of longing in her voice. "If you treat horses with affection and respect, you'll earn their loyalty until they die. Yes, they're animals, and occasionally unpredictable. But if I had to choose between a horse and a human being for companionship, I'd stick with a horse."

"Then why are you here, at one of the most crowded hotel resorts in the world?"

Her astute question jabbed him square on the chin. He deflected it with some questions of his own. "Perhaps to rescue you from whatever harebrained scheme you've concocted? There's no titled duke, is there? Where did you get that ring? At a pawn shop?"

"The ring was my grandmother's," she retorted in a tone frosted with ice. The wobbly-kneed girl he'd ministered to had metamorphosed into the most dangerous of all species: an angry woman. "You made me want to trust you, and I'm ashamed of myself for that. Thank you for your kindness. I won't trouble you further. If we have the misfortune to meet again, I promise to ignore you. And for your information, Neville was an earl."

She made as if to leap from the cart. Dev grabbed her arm. "Sorry."

"You ought to be. Let me go."

"Not until you accept my apology." Beneath his fingers her arm tensed. In a soothing motion he slid his hand down to her wrist, keeping the grip gentle, yet unbreakable. "Besides, I would never abandon a lady I'd just rescued until she was safely home."

"Even if the lady wishes otherwise?"

"A dilemma, to be sure, Miss—what did you say your real name was again?"

"Lang—" Her lips pressed together.

A glaring beam from a nearby streetlight illuminated her face, allowing Devlin to witness the battle of emotions. *Lang...* Something tingled at the back of his neck, an elusive fragment of knowledge that vanished when her pursed lips softened in a *Mona Lisa* smile. She was disheveled, her attire wrinkled and soiled; dirt was smeared across one cheek. Yet that half smile somehow captured his heart and it swelled like a hot air balloon.

Panic skittered through him. "Ah. So it's Miss...Lang. Strange. Neither name really fits you." All the newly restored color leached from her complexion. *Insensitive clod,* he reprimanded himself. "I'll escort you to the lobby. Shall I have a bellhop fetch Mrs. Chudd to help you to your room?" He distracted her with verbal rambling while casually monitoring the pulse in her wrist. "How about if I call on you in the morning, say ten o'clock? I believe the band is scheduled to play a medley of popular tunes. Have you enjoyed the pleasures of Congress Springs Park?"

"Yes, I love the park. It's very peaceful, even with all the other people. Mr. Stone, I accept your apology. But I don't think it's wise for us to meet again. I don't want to encourage your false impressions of me, and I don't want to—could you please let go of my wrist?" She waited, her dark gaze unwavering, until Dev complied. The *Mona Lisa* smile flickered, then she passed her tongue over her lips and cleared her throat. "Thank you. I wish...I wish we'd met under different circumstances."

And before he could think of an appropriate response, she jumped out of the runabout and marched off toward the hotel. Though she garnered several strange looks from evening strollers, she sailed past with the regal poise of a duchess.

A man was in a wheelbarrow full of trouble when watching the back of a woman made his pulse rate spike and his fingers tingle.

## Chapter Nine

The invitation from Edgar Fane arrived two days later. Thea read the lazy scrawl of words, with every breath a dull spike lodging deeper in her chest. So. Her wish had come true at last, but the fulfillment was tinged with the taste of gall: Dinner at Mr. Canfield's Casino was not the scenario she had envisioned.

The Casino might enjoy a reputation for first-class cuisine, and it might be patronized by the country's wealthiest and most powerful personages. But for Thea the dignified red brick building also housed a glittering palace of iniquity, a den of vice, preying upon weak minds with more money than common sense. From local gossip she'd learned that reformers had managed to close down the gambling there for a couple of years, but like the racecourse it had reopened for this summer's season.

She should have known a wretch like Edgar Fane would entertain guests at a gambling palace.

Her father loved gambling more than anything else on earth, including his family. He'd been playing roulette the night he'd met Thea's mother. After winning a small fortune, he convinced himself, and her, that together they'd change the course of each other's lives. In a way, he was right. The unwelcome appearance of a baby nine months later introduced an equally unwelcome dose of reality.

Her father dumped Theodora with a letter of apology on her grandparents' doorstep, then disappeared for three years. Only the infrequent postcards reassured the family that he was alive. Charles and Mathilda Langston loved her as their own; until she died Mathilda never gave up believing the prodigal son would see the error of his ways. But some of Thea's earliest lessons, learned snuggled in Grandfather's lap, included the evils of gambling.

Apparently she had shed that particular lesson along with her conscience. Life, she reminded herself defiantly, *was* an uncertain stew of happenstance.

So for thirty-six hours Thea suffered a Coney Island roller-coaster ride of elation, fear, guilt and determination. Now the time was at hand, and she would not, *would not* permit the shy, morally upstanding little girl she used to be to dominate her thoughts. Tonight she planned to practice every feminine wile she'd gleaned from years of reading literature and talking to many of the authors of it who enjoyed "rusticating" on Staten Island. By the end of the meal Edgar Fane would…he would—

Mrs. Chudd poked her head through the door to Thea's room. "Bellhop's here. A Mr. Simpson is waiting for you in the lobby," she announced in her flat nasal voice.

"Have the bellhop tell Mr. Simpson I'll be right down." Nerves cramped her stomach and chilled her skin. "Mrs. Chudd? Won't you come along? It would be more appropriate."

"Got no use for rich food." She skimmed a long look at Thea, her pale eyes briefly flickering with curiosity. "You been fine all month, ferdiddling on your own. So I'll stay here, same as usual." Jaw jutting, she nodded twice, started to turn away. "Not having a spell, are you?"

"No." Thea forced her lips to stretch in a rubbery smile, and beneath the satin-and-lace evening gown locked her knees. "I'm fine."

"Humph. Then I'll fetch my knitting, finish this sweater for my grandnephew. You might want to be careful what you eat."

"Ah, Miss Pickford. You're a vision to behold," Mr. Fane declared upon meeting her and Mr. Simpson at the entrance to the Casino's dining room. He himself looked very much the wealthy gentleman in his black evening suit and blinding white waistcoat. "Quite a dramatic change from the intrepid angler who reeled in a shoe." Mischievous brown eyes twinkled; to avoid looking at him Thea glanced around the crowded dining room.

"I've ordered us filet of sole for the entrée," he continued easily, a secret laugh embedded in the words. "I hope you approve."

Thea finally managed to tear her awestruck gaze away from the rows of stained glass ceiling panels, and the equally glittering rows of tables full of guests, all of them staring at Thea and Edgar Fane. *Either win him now, or justice will be denied forever.* She squared her shoulders, lifted a hand to lightly brush her grandmother's cameo brooch, a steadying touch to bolster her resolve. "I trust all the laces have been removed from my catch so they don't get caught between our teeth," she replied.

Mr. Fane threw back his head and laughed out loud. "I think I'm going to like you very much, Miss Pickford. Who knows? You might turn out to be the catch of the day."

"Mr. Fane, I might say the same about you."

He laughed again, then led her between rows of circular tables to the back of the room, where a party of ten—six ladies, four gentlemen—watched their approach with the intensity of a pack of jackals about to tear into the carcass. "I've asked some friends to join us," Mr. Fane explained. "Less…intimate, and safer for you at this stage of our acquaintance." With a flourishing bow he pulled out one of the empty chairs. A folded card with "Miss Pickford" written in formal script sent an oily shiver down Thea's spine. He gestured to the woman seated beside her place.

"This is a very dear friend, Mrs. Cynthia Gorman." As Thea gingerly sat down he leaned close enough for his breath to stir the fine hairs on the back of her neck. "If she takes a liking to you, you'll be able to learn anything about me good manners prohibit you from asking." He straightened. "Mrs. Gorman, Miss Theodora Pickford." Thea angled her head toward Mrs. Gorman, away from Edgar Fane.

"I asked Simpson to find out everything he could about *you*," Edgar next informed Thea without a shred of remorse. "I have to be careful, I'm afraid. Women can be fortune hunters, the same as men. Can't they, Mrs. Gorman?"

"As you can see, Edgar loves to torment, and call it teasing," Cynthia said. With her long narrow face, worldly green eyes and golden hair, she reminded Thea of a beautiful but restless lioness. "I understand your fiancé is a British earl. Lovely engagement ring—antique, is it? I adore jewelry. We can talk about your fiancé and jewelry if you like, Miss Pickford. Or the charms of a season at Saratoga. Edgar of course will want to confine the conversation to himself. But whatever you do, please refrain from asking about his paintings."

"Paintings? I've heard he enjoys working with oils and watercolors. Why wouldn't I ask about them?" Thea returned, artfully lifting one eyebrow.

"Dearest Cynthia, is your nose still out of joint?" Edgar

sat down on Thea's other side, and without a word the waiters began to serve crystal compotes full of fresh peaches, strawberries and grapes. "She wanted my latest work of art, but I gave it to a lonely old gentleman who owns a couple of quaint old bookstores in Baltimore. He was most appreciative."

"So appreciative he checked out of his room at the United States Hotel the next day," a round-cheeked man with a spade-shaped beard chimed in. "Last I heard, he was planning to auction your landscape to the highest bidder, to avoid the bank foreclosing on his stores."

"What must he be thinking?" Edgar popped a strawberry in his mouth and chewed it with unselfconscious enthusiasm. "I'm no Rembrandt. But if someone's foolish enough to spend their well-earned dollars on dabbling I give away for free, I'll not put a crimp in their style."

Everyone laughed, and as the rhythm of the courses moved in watchlike precision from fruit to oysters on a bed of crushed ice, to a delicate clear soup, Thea's nerves settled into quiet determination. Mrs. Gorman spent several moments deliberately prying, but when Thea remained charming but vague the other woman turned to the man seated on her right. Conversations swirled over and around them; Edgar Fane, she discovered reluctantly, made for a thoughtful, entertaining host. By the time the fish was served—and she laughed with everyone else when the waiter presented her with an exquisitely prepared filet of sole—Thea was almost enjoying herself. The vertigo remained in abeyance, and beneath the table her knees had finally quit shaking.

But she had not forgotten her mission.

Find a weakness. Find evidence. Expose Edgar Fane as a liar and a thief.

"Is Saratoga Springs your favorite destination for the

summer season?" she asked Mr. Fane during a conversational lull.

"Certainly has been a wise choice this year," he replied, smiling at her. "When I heard the prim-mouthed do-gooders had failed in their attempts to keep the Casino closed, I decided to signal my support by spending the season here at Saratoga. I've rented a cottage a few blocks away. When not entertaining friends there, I invite them to superlative suppers here at the Casino, to help Mr. Canfield keep his coffers full." Something in the way he studied Thea set warning bells to clanging. "A lot of my friends enjoy the game room upstairs. In fact, several acquaintances have won and lost considerable fortunes. You look disapproving. Tell me your opinion toward gambling, Miss Pickford. Is it a tool of evil, or the engine that keeps not only Canfield Casino but this little community from sinking into oblivion?"

Thea took several sips of water, but her palms dampened inside the doeskin evening gloves. "I don't care much for gambling away monies someone else has earned by the sweat of honest labor. If those men lose a fortune they earned with their own hands, that's their choice. But men who gamble away food from the table or the roof over their children's heads are dangerously irresponsible."

"Mmm. A well-thought-out response. How about ladies, Miss Pickford? Are you aware that Mr. Canfield has altered the old restrictions and now allows ladies to indulge? Gave them their very own gambling room. There's now a betting ring at the racetrack for them, as well. I believe Cynthia actually won herself a tidy bundle a few days ago." Edgar picked up his wineglass and touched it to Thea's as though to let her know he'd noticed she hadn't taken a single sip. "So you pass judgment on *ladies,* for gambling food from the table and the roof from over their children's heads?"

"I'd say either gender is equally vulnerable to the risk of gambling, Mr. Fane."

"You snagged yourself one of those religious reformers, Fane!" Smirking, a needle-thin man with a monocle surveyed Thea. "Miss Pickford doubtless attends church every Sunday, praying for fire to rain down on the rest of us heathens."

"I don't have the right to pass judgment on anybody." Thea leveled the oaf a look that made him drop the monocle. "Neither, sir, do you. I was asked a direct question. I answered honestly. If my sense of right and wrong differs from yours, perhaps the matter would best be addressed someplace other than a dinner party."

Cynthia Gorman clapped her hands. "One for you, Miss Pickford. Geoffrey, stop needling her. Besides, if I recall my distant childhood catechism, God Himself does not approve of gambling, which is why I only indulge once or twice a year."

Mr. Fane emitted a loud groan. "Cynthia, dear, must we introduce religion? Almost as taboo as politics, is it not?"

"You started it, *dear.* And controversy certainly livens things up a bit. Don't you get tired of trivial gossip, Edgar?" She made a moue, shrugged her shoulders. "Of course, none of it matters to me."

"Ah. Trivial gossip." Still smiling, Edgar turned to Thea. "She wounds me with words, Miss Pickford, though she's one of my oldest friends. Tell me, since you seem to be fearless as well as honest, do you think God will strike me dead because I'm one of those who enjoys gambling large sums of money I haven't earned?"

## Chapter Ten

The clinking of glasses and the scrape of cutlery against china stilled. Once again all gazes fastened onto Thea, including the sideways flash of sympathy from a waiter removing her plate. "If you prefer honesty," she returned, picking her way through a mine shaft of volatile responses, "I'd have to say I agree with Mrs. Gorman about God's view of gambling. I can't quote a precise verse of scripture. On the other hand, I do recall a verse where Jesus instructs His disciples to *'Judge not, that ye not be judged.'*"

"Told you she was one of those reformers."

"Shh!" someone hissed, then added, "Let her be. Noose is already around her neck...."

"Jesus ate with sinners, didn't He?" A greyhound-thin woman sitting opposite Thea leaned over the table. "You think you're being Jesus, Miss Pickford, surrounded by so many evil people? Got to warn us about our wicked ways?"

"That's enough!" Edgar Fane half rose. "Miss Pickford is *my* guest."

Thea shivered a little at the possessive tone but managed a reassuring smile. "It's all right, Mr. Fane. Truly. I'm not offended. I've attended many dinner parties where the conversations broke every social rule in the book, and frankly, found them stimulating."

Mr. Fane sank back down into his chair. "Stimulating?" He shook his head, laughed. "You're…quite the lady, aren't you?" His hand came down over hers and briefly squeezed.

Quick as a terrified mouse who just realized the tickly feeling was a tom cat's whiskers, Thea whipped her hand away and thrust it out of sight beneath the table. For a moment the room shifted off balance…or was she tipping sideways?

For some reason an image of Devlin Stone popped into her head, auburn-tipped brown hair windblown over his forehead, lake-colored eyes intent as he washed her hands with a gentleness she'd never experienced from a man. "I was reared to be a lady," she murmured. "As for faith, I haven't talked much about God or Jesus with anyone lately. I haven't made up my mind what to think, until now." She lifted a stubborn chin and faced them all. "Now I see that most people, whether they call themselves Christian or heathen, are quick to judge, and slow to understand opposing viewpoints. I have compelling personal reasons that govern my views on gambling, but I ask forgiveness for any offense I caused in stating them."

"Dessert, miss?" the waiter's voice inquired at her elbow.

Startled, Thea glanced up. His face was expressionless, but admiration briefly lit his eyes. "Thank you," she said. The icy ball in her stomach thawed as the rest of the waitstaff efficiently drew attention away from her.

Another lady made some remark about the superb quality of the meal and queried if anyone planned to attend the concert at Convention Hall the following night. Someone else across from her responded, and the atmosphere smoothed into gaiety once more.

Later, while coffee was being served, Edgar Fane leaned over to Thea, his voice pitched so only she could hear. "I have obligations for the rest of the week, but I must see you again. Will you join me for a private dinner, next Tuesday night? Just the two of us this time?"

Another eddy of dizziness warned Thea to stall; she ignored it. She had survived an evening with Edgar Fane and his friends, so the worst of the attacks must be under control. "I'd be honored—as long as you fetch me yourself, and leave Mr. Simpson to whatever other duties he performs for you."

"Ah. Humor, principles and pride. Miss Pickford, I just might come to find you irresistible."

Panic leaped through her like a sword flashing in moonlight. "Then beware, Mr. Fane," she retorted, and tossed her head. "At the moment, I am not inclined to reciprocate."

Devlin loved rainy days. He could think better, more clearly, on days when rain drummed on the roof and splattered on the earth.

Or at least he could until Miss Pickford-Lang erupted into his life. Something about the elusive lady didn't fit, either her dogged pursuit of Edgar Fane, or the secrecy and lies. All clear markers of malfeasance, yet Devlin was ready to stake his reputation on her innocence. Restless, he prowled the two-bedroom suite he'd rented in the Cottage Wing of the United States Hotel, alternatively casting glances through the windows at the rain and the writing table covered with documents, reports and reams of information he'd been analyzing for—he tugged out his pocket watch—for six tedious hours.

Dev wearily plowed a hand through his hair. *I could resign, turn the Hotel Hustler case over to somebody else.* Despite pouring heart, soul and a significant stash of his own money into this case, Operative Stone had precious little to show for his efforts.

The fleeting impulse to quit trampled him like stampeding hooves. Dev rolled his head to relax the knotted muscles in his neck and shoulders.

"You're such a sap," he muttered aloud. Then, jaw set, he picked up the daily report he'd been working on for the last few hours. *"...concluded the female Miss Lang, aka Pickford, in need of closer surveillance, due to unflagging interest in E. F. Will await instructions while maintaining present persona."*

Was it possible to sound more priggish? With a muffled imprecation Dev tossed the weekly report back on the heap of papers, snagged his umbrella from the stand by the door then strode from the room. Back in Virginia he never used the contraptions; here they offered a valuable aid to anonymity.

When he reached the entrance to Congress Park he realized it had been his destination all along—a place to satisfy his hunger for green spaces, for a patch of earth that retained at least a partial resemblance to nature as God created it. Dev paid for his ten-cent ticket, skirted the elaborate Arcade and the few visitors sipping hot coffee in one of the colonnade cafés and headed toward the center of the park. Due to the rain, pathways and lawns were deserted. He might have been tramping across a wooded meadow at StoneHill, except for the blurred outline of the music pavilion with its quaint domed roof. Weather permitting, the band played concerts there every afternoon. Today, happily, weather did not permit. Unable to resist the novelty of having the space to himself, Dev headed for the ramp over the pond.

Then between the decorative cast-iron posts, he spied a solitary figure seated in one of the band chairs. Disappointment ripped through Devlin. Confound it, was it too much to ask, a half hour of his own, without tripping over some—

The figure turned slightly and he stopped dead, his disbelieving gaze on the profile of the face that had haunted his dreams for weeks now.

Dev set the umbrella aside, a dangerous sense of jubilation coursing through his veins. "Seems I'm not the only one who enjoys a good rain. We seem to have cultivated a habit for unexpected meetings, Miss Lang."

Slowly she rose to face him. Hatless and gloveless, today she wore a narrow pin-striped shirtwaist and plain navy skirt, which gave her the look of a schoolteacher as opposed to a well-turned-out heiress. "If I'd known in time it was you beneath the umbrella, I would have left before you saw me," she said.

*Not a chance,* Devlin thought, though he nodded agreeably. "I experienced a similar reaction when I realized the gazebo was occupied. Since the rain's picking up anyway, we may as well allow ourselves to enjoy a bit of natural drama, together. Is that what you came out here to do? Enjoy the rain?"

A shawl was draped over the back of her chair; averting her gaze, Miss Lang wrapped it around her shoulders. "I suppose you think I'm even more of a peculiar sort of female than you already did, for seeking an isolated spot outside in the middle of a rainstorm."

"No more peculiar than a man after the same thing." He sensed her wariness and arranged a pair of the spindle-backed chairs where he could not only watch Miss Lang but prevent her from bolting across the ramp. "Mrs. Chudd's warm and dry in her room, I take it?" A wisp of a reciprocal smile fluttered before she nodded. "Good." He rubbed his palms together. "Then there's no reason we can't make the most of our opportunity to share what we've been up to this past week."

Between droning raindrops, turgid silence fell until Devlin plowed ahead. "I've only caught a glimpse of you once, outside a tearoom with several other ladies." And experienced far too much relief, because for the past several days he'd been shadowing Edgar Fane in an exhausting round of shopping, dining, solitary painting expeditions and noisy group excursions to every tourist attraction within ten miles. Not once had Miss Lang been part of his entourage.

"I didn't think you'd care to associate with a woman who makes a public fool of herself," she finally murmured.

"Oh, I don't know. I've seen a quite a bit of foolery over the years. Perhaps you don't care to associate with a man who's witnessed human behavior at its worst, and too often been unable to correct it?"

"Well, when you put it like that." Solemn-faced, she sat back down. "Your phrasing is intriguing. You sound like either a preacher or a policeman."

Fortunately a lifetime around horses and several years as a Secret Service operative had taught him not to betray strong emotion, particularly anger, fear—or surprise. "An intriguing analysis. Well, despite the unpleasant price you paid later, you were pretty entertaining the other day, there by the lake." He twitched a chair around and straddled it, propping his forearms over the back. "Was it worth being sick in the bushes? Did you receive your invitation?"

"Yes." A fleeting sideways glance. "Dinner at the

Casino. I was offered, like bait to a bear, to a table full of his acquaintances."

Rage prickled his careful equanimity. "I'm sorry. Are you all right? Did the vertigo—"

"They made me angry. I didn't have a spell. The anger might have helped, but I've thought about it a lot ever since, and I think there's a more practical solution."

"And that is?" he asked when she seemed hesitant to continue.

"When you were a child, were you ever afraid of monsters hiding under the bed? And when you finally found the courage to check, you discovered your fear was the product of a too-vivid imagination?"

"So you no longer believe Edgar Fane is a monster."

"Let's just say I've come to understand that some monsters know how to disguise themselves more discreetly than others. His friends are mostly sycophants. A few tried to be kind. I can hold my own with them."

"Ah." This time they watched the rain in companionable silence. "Something's still troubling you," Dev eventually observed.

"Yes." Her shoulders lifted in a nervous shrug. "You really are very perceptive. Um…would you mind if I ask you something?" When he hummed a lazy sound of assent Miss Lang cleared her throat, fiddled with the ends of her shawl, then shared softly, "I don't know why, but for some reason it matters that you not think the worst of me. A month ago I didn't know you existed, but now…" She ran her finger over the chair finial, color staining her cheeks. "Never mind. This is silly. It must be the weather. Rainy days have always made me introspective. But that doesn't mean I should—"

"I feel the same way, about rainy days," Dev interrupted. Reaching down, he let his hand hover over hers for a moment, and when she didn't flinch away he gave her restless fingers a reassuring squeeze. "We have more in common than you realize, Miss Lang. Come now, tell me what's troubling you. Today I promise not to bite."

# Chapter Eleven

Only a flicker of a smile appeared. "My last name isn't really Lang." Above the white collar of the shirtwaist her throat muscles stretched taut. "I would prefer to not reveal my surname right now. If you…could you call me Thea? That's my Christian name. I—it's unconventional, but here at Saratoga the unconventional seems to be the accepted standard of behavior. My name is really Theodora, but most times I prefer Thea. Theodora sounds too formal, when the man I'm talking to has…seen me at my worst."

In the muted, rain-drenched world her brown eyes had darkened to the color of wet pine bark. Automatically Dev registered the subtleties of her body that conveyed truth telling—slightly expanded pupils, crinkly eyes accompanying her shy smile, leaning slightly toward him—even as he filed away the revelation that she was afraid to tell him her last name. "Thea. It suits you. A strong name, and a deep one. Family name?"

"No."

He lifted an eyebrow. "Hmm. Touched one of those chords you don't want to play, did I? No, don't turn all tense on me…Thea. Yeah, that fits, much better than Miss

Pickford, or Miss Lang. To even things up, call me Devlin. My grandmother was Irish. You may have noticed when the sun shines on my hair there's a wee bit o' red? But that's all the Irish heritage I received, besides the name. My grandmother died when I was two so I don't remember anything else about the woman responsible for naming me."

"Your parents didn't choose your name?"

"They couldn't agree, so they asked her to." He could hear the curtness in his own voice, but Thea merely nodded her head, that wistful aura hovering around her again, twisting his heartstrings. "What else did you want to ask me about?" he added quickly. Let it be Edgar Fane, or something about the vertigo. Or the weather, for crying out loud. Just—no prying questions where too much honesty might be demanded.

With this woman, he should have known better.

"Have you ever made one mistake," she said, the words emerging pensive and slow, "and no matter how hard you try to make up for it, the rest of your life crumbles a piece at a time, until you're left with nothing but wreckage?"

For a moment Dev scrambled for solid footing in a mental quicksand. "Everybody makes mistakes," he finally ventured. "It's the price we pay for being human. Some mistakes have lasting consequences, some pass into oblivion. I try not to dwell on mine more than I can help. I like to think I've done the best I can, to make a good life for myself." Fine words, from a man who an hour earlier had been halfway ready to hop aboard the first southbound train. "What mistake do you believe has destroyed your life, Thea?"

"Sometimes…being born?" A hollow laugh did little to ease the uncomfortable pall that descended between them. "I beg your pardon, Devlin. My grandfather scolds me about my propensity to talk before I think about how the words will sound aloud. It must be a family trait."

He barely heard the last sentence, since she'd mumbled it beneath her breath. "You've had some troubles, haven't you?" He kept his voice gentle. "This fiancé from England. He's a fabrication, right?" She nodded, but when she would have responded Dev shook his head. "It's all right. I've known almost from the first. You have your reasons, same as how you don't feel you can share your real surname. You asked me once if I'd ever been desperate. Are your parents trying to force you into a marriage you don't want? Is that why you came to Saratoga with a false name and a manufactured betrothal in your trunk, to chase after one of the country's wealthiest bachelors without looking... desperate?"

"If only it were that simple." Shifting on the chair, words abruptly burst forth in a passionate gush. "I'm not chasing Edgar Fane in hopes of a proposal. I despise him. He's a cad, and the only reason I'm 'chasing' him is because I want to find the evidence to stop him from ruining some-one else's life. But nothing I've planned is turning out the way I expected. Nothing. Tuesday night is my last chance—he's leaving next week. One of his lady friends, a Mrs. Gorman, told me. And it's Sunday...." She stared through Devlin as though peering into a lake filled with monsters. "I don't know if I have the courage. I'm afraid I'll have an attack, I'm afraid I'll make a mistake and he'll know I'm a fraud, I'm—" her voice dropped to a broken whisper "—I'm afraid, and I'm ashamed of it. But I have to do this. Have to..." She pressed her lips together until they turned white.

The skin beneath her eyes looked bruised; above the tattoo of rain on the roof Devlin could hear the labored rasp of her breath. Without a qualm he mentally laid aside badge and credentials, and focused all his skill on coaxing back the woman who had faced down a crowd of bored sophisticates at the Casino.

"Don't be ashamed of fear," he said, leaning closer until their heads were inches apart. "It's an instinct, designed to protect you. If you're afraid to share a meal alone with Edgar Fane, perhaps you should heed those instincts, and call it off."

"I can't. I won't."

"Mmm. Which one, Thea?"

Some of the wildness dissipated, and the white slash of her mouth softened. "Won't. Grandfather tells me I'm more stubborn than an ink stain. My friends are kinder. They call it resolve. Mr. Stone—I mean, Devlin? Do you believe in God?"

What in the—? "You want to know if I believe in God?" Confound it, but her mind swished about like a horse's tail chasing off flies. She nodded. Dev sat back in the chair and studied on the question for a moment or two. "Well, yes, I suppose so. Most people do, I reckon. My dad was a praying man. But he died when I was six. I guess I've been looking ever since for what he found. Why do you ask, Thea?" There. That was better, him asking the questions. "This shame you're feeling. You think God's punishing you?"

"I don't know. I was sort of hoping you would. I used to say my prayers faithfully, at mealtimes and bedtimes, when I was a girl. But God never answered. When I was older, everyone I asked seemed to think God was whoever or whatever we created in our minds, as a way to cope with life. For a while I guess I came to believe them, except…"

"Except what?" Abruptly Devlin turned his chair

back around and sat forward, his gaze never leaving Thea's face.

"Except my grandfather always believed God really was this omniscient Being, Someone who cared. Over the years we've attended many lectures by atheists, readings by naturalists or presentations by scientists, all of them trying to prove God doesn't exist. Or that we were all gods, ourselves. Grandfather always listened politely, always thanked them. Then on the way home he'd remind me that the greatest gift we enjoy as Americans is the right to believe whatever we choose to. He told me his choice was to place his faith in the God of the Bible, rather than human beings."

Incredible as the notion sounded, it was as though her words reached inside Devlin's own mind, releasing questions that had festered for years that he hadn't known how to ask. "And has he changed his mind?"

Shoulders slumping, she shook her head, started to speak, then her lips clamped back together.

"Lately I've been thinking about God more than I used to," he said, because those haunting eyes still begged for communion with another soul, and he wanted to be the person Thea communed with. He'd seen her at her worst, held her when she was too weak to stand. She'd allowed herself to be vulnerable with him.

Assuming for the moment God did exist, and did care, God would know this particular woman had stomped to dust all Dev's defenses against lying females.

"I was engaged once, years ago," he said. "Sylvia was a churchgoer. We attended services every Sunday for almost five years. Then she went to visit relatives in North Carolina, and I went to New York City. When I returned home to Virginia a few months later, Sylvia had eloped with a banker she met on the train."

"B-but you'd known each other for years. You were engaged." Her voice trailed away. "I'm sorry, Devlin. No wonder you didn't like me when we first met."

He managed a crooked smile. "It's a fact I'm not too fond of liars. Her being so religious, I couldn't understand how she could stab me in the back. For a long time I didn't have much use for God. Pretty silly, I guess, blaming God when it's a person who's at fault."

"You knew each other for *five years*."

Something inside Devlin relaxed. "Mmm. That's true. I'll put it this way. Back home, one of our neighbors owns an old plow horse, put to pasture years ago. I used to see old Betsy every time I drove to town, even stopped occasionally to give her a carrot. But that doesn't mean I'd walk up behind her and clap my hands. I can see what you're thinking. No, I'm not comparing Sylvia to a decrepit plow horse."

They shared a look of perfect understanding, and that unfamiliar sensation—soft, welcoming—uncurled even further. "You're a literal-minded soul, aren't you? Let's just say I knew Sylvia's outside, but I never saw her sick and afraid, never talked with her about God, or what went on inside her head." No weighty subjects like faith and fear. Good and evil. Hopes. Dreams. "In retrospect, even after 'knowing' her all those years I'd have to confess Sylvia and I never left the barn."

"I may be literal, but now you sound like a horseman. You wear a lot of hats, Devlin Stone." Her cheeks were flushed, her awkwardness charming. "See? I do know how to be metaphorical."

Unfortunately, her statement forced him to don his "professional" hat again. The woman seated beside him had not only lied to him, she was still hiding some monstrous secret; he knew little about her background, including her surname. She could still be a wanted criminal, even an accomplice of the Hotel Hustler, and Devlin Stone's profession as a Secret Service operative might be irrevocably compromised if he blindly accepted her innocence.

Yet Dev felt in his gut that he still understood Thea better than he ever had Sylvia. "Knowing" a woman must include more than the marriage bed. He swallowed hard as new truths tugged him completely out of the barn, beyond the pasture and into an unexplored forest: if he'd had to choose between the two women, Sylvia would have been left inside that barn.

But if the choice were between Thea and the Service?

Dev couldn't answer that question, so he shoved it deep out of sight.

Outside the gazebo, the rain abruptly dwindled to a misting shower. The air brightened, and a shaft of sunlight speared through the receding clouds, directly onto the chairs where Devlin and Thea sat.

Dev lifted his hand and watched the interplay of golden light transfuse the skin. "Do you think," he mused, watching the bar of light create a golden nimbus around her, "that after talking about Him so much, God might be trying to gain our attention here?"

Thea lifted her hand as well, holding it beside Devlin's, a slender-fingered, smaller and paler appendage bathed into transparency by sunlight. "If He is, I wonder what He's trying to tell us. I've been steeped in symbols and metaphors all my life. Frankly, I'm weary of them. I suppose I am a literal-minded soul. If the Almighty needs to send word to me, it will need to be something more tangible than a burning bush, or a sunbeam."

A warning chill brushed Dev's spine. "Have a care,

Thea. That sounded more like a challenge than a request. My theology might be sketchy, but I don't think God responds well to demands."

## Chapter Twelve

Thea sneaked sidelong peeks at Devlin as they strolled along the waterlogged path toward the entrance to the park. He moved with the unselfconscious power of a man comfortable enough in his own skin to not have to make an impression on others. Yet it was that unassuming confidence that had captivated her heart.

The tug drawing her to him strengthened every time they talked. She wanted to pursue their discourse about God; for months her hunger for meaningful conversation had remained unsatisfied because her thirst for justice was insatiable. But Devlin's caution about not tempting God, however well-intentioned, had effectively muzzled her mouth. For all of her life Thea had struggled with a feeling, however irrational, of inferiority. All right, so shaking a fist at God might result in eternal rejection. Until this moment, she hadn't really cared; the compulsion to avenge Grandfather had been her only solution to the ever-present memory of his gaunt face behind those iron bars.

Still, for a moment or two back in the gazebo Thea had almost yielded to the stronger-than-ever temptation to blurt out the entire sordid story to the only man other than Charles Langston who really *listened* to her.

"What is it?" His deep voice interrupted her melancholy; his warm hand pressed briefly at the small of her back, steadying her. "You're too quiet, and you look almost…" He halted on the path, stepping in front of her, his gaze searching her face, then lifting to scan the dripping shrubbery and trees. "I can't describe it," he finished slowly. "Not frightened, or angry, but something in between. It's a baffling expression. The first time I saw you, it was this expression that grabbed my attention."

Before she could frame an answer he shook his head and resumed walking. "It's Edgar Fane, isn't it? What has he done to you, Thea?"

"At the moment, he's done nothing. Devlin, I wish I could explain, but it wouldn't be fair to you. It means more than you can possibly understand, to have shared what I could, and that you…you've listened to me." She drew in a hard breath. "I'm having dinner with Edgar Fane tomorrow night because I have to, not because I want to. I'm telling you the truth, Devlin."

"You have to? Is he threatening you, Thea? Holding a gun to the head of someone you love?"

Shocked, before she could collect herself Thea laid a hand on his forearm. His head whipped around, scrutinizing her face with scorching intensity. Beneath her fingers and his damp tweed jacket, the muscles were hard as wrought iron fence posts. "Devlin—" her throat burned, and she passed her tongue around lips gone dry as dust "—I'm in no danger from Mr. Fane." It was the other way around, but she could not afford to confess. Not yet. "I'll explain, after Tuesday night. If you still want to hear."

Once again his hand covered hers, only unlike that brief instant in the gazebo, this time the fingers crushed hers in a bruising grip. "I'll want to hear. But if he hurts you, Thea, he'll have to answer to me."

The light eyes had turned dark as charcoal, with diamond-bright chips hard enough to shatter a bone—or break a heart.

"You mustn't talk like that," she managed unsteadily. "I don't want you to make an enemy of this man. He… Devlin, his family is one of the most powerful in America. He could ruin you."

"And you're immune?"

"He thinks I'm just a pretty new toy. A novelty to entertain him, assuage the boredom. If I'm careful—and I have been—he'll have no reason to think anything else."

Devlin's nostrils flared, and for a moment Thea wondered if his dark glower would turn her to a pillar of salt. Then he released her and folded his arms across his chest. "You're lying," he snapped. "You despise the man, and you're afraid of him."

"I haven't had a spell. How can you *know?* Nobody else—"

"Your eyes. The way your chin tilts upward, how your nose crinkles when you talk about him. That's the contempt." Without warning his arm whipped out and he snagged her hand again, holding it up in front of her face. "Cold hands, which you twine together to try and control the fear. Listen to me, Thea!" A single tug brought her close enough to feel the heat of his body. "Whatever you feel compelled to do, it's not worth your reputation, or your self-respect. Remember the lake, and stay away from Edgar Fane."

"What would you know about it?" she flung back, stung. "Or is it…you still think I'm a—a floozy. I shared my heart with you, I actually trusted you enough, I believed you'd changed your mind about me." Her voice rose; biting her lip, she hurriedly glanced about the rain-soaked park.

"Great glory, woman!" Devlin Stone muttered. "You don't know anything."

Suddenly his free hand cupped her chin, tilting her head back. Rough-tipped fingers stroked down the line of her jaw, brushed over the pulse throbbing in her neck. "You don't know anything," he repeated in a growling undertone. Then he dipped his head and kissed her.

Thea gasped against his lips, closing her eyes as a firestorm of startled wonder consumed her. Her hands fumbled for purchase until they found Devlin's shoulders, muscles rippling with an entirely different strength from the day he'd found her helpless in the bushes. He'd offered her tenderness then, a pallid shadow of the intense response she'd unwittingly provoked now.

His mouth slid a breathy path beneath her jaw, then trailed fleeting kisses to her eyes, her forehead. Goose bumps raced over Thea's skin. A soft sound, somewhere between a laugh and a groan, blew into her ear. "You taste of rain, and flowers," he whispered, and pressed his lips against her temple. "And temptation."

Then his head lifted, his hands curved around her waist and he firmly set her at arms' length. In the golden mist rising from the saturated earth he loomed over Thea like an ancient Greek warrior in a gentleman's clothing. Emotion throbbed between them, beating time between each labored breath. Finally Devlin passed a hand around the back of his neck, and heaved an explosive sigh.

"I won't apologize, because I wouldn't mean it." A crooked smile flickered. "Don't look like that. I might give in and kiss you again."

"All right. But I'm still eating dinner with Edgar Fane tomorrow night."

He groaned and flicked a glance heavenward. "Thea…is

that why you think I kissed you? As a diversion? Seduction as the weapon of choice to bend you to my will?"

"Well, how would I know?" she threw back crossly. "Nobody's ever kissed me like that before. I mean, I'm not a naive schoolgirl, I've been courted by several gentlemen...." A blush burned. "See what you've done? You've rendered me a featherhead."

"That makes two of us. I've broken every rule in every book, so I may as well do a thorough job of it." Grabbing her hands again, he lifted them to his mouth and pressed a kiss against the knuckles. "Tomorrow night? I'll be watching as well as waiting, Thea. Don't worry. Neither you nor Edgar will see me. You're not alone anymore, all right?"

"There's something you're not telling me, isn't there?"

One dark eyebrow lifted. "Did you think you were the only one with secrets?" He gave her hands a final squeeze, then released them. "I'll be watching," he repeated, then swiveled and loped off between a hedge of boxwoods.

Thea stood in the middle of the deserted path, one hand fisted at her midriff in a vain attempt to calm her stuttering heart, the other pressed against her mouth, in an equally vain attempt to hold the warmth of his lips against hers.

# Chapter Thirteen

"Take them into the room at the end of this hall," Edgar ordered the sweating laborers. "Carefully, my good fellows! The contents of those crates are invaluable to me." Chuckling to himself, he followed the two men down the rabbit warren hallways of the old house, noting the way they took care to lower the crates to avoid hitting the antique sconces on the walls.

After unpacking the crates, the laborer mopped his sweating brow and glanced at Edgar. "Where you want us to stack these frames, Mr. Fane?"

"Against the empty wall, to the right of the doorway. You'll see where I've rolled up the carpet and moved the furniture?"

"Yassir."

*Unobservant dunderhead,* Edgar thought. But then, most people were. After the workmen departed he rang for the butler. "Dodd? Please inform the housekeeper that I need a key for the door to the study down this hall. Tell her—what's her name again?"

"Mrs. Surrey, sir."

"Ah, yes. Tell Mrs. Surrey to instruct the housemaids to stay out of that room for now. I'll be gone for the night.

If Simpson arrives tomorrow before I do, direct him to the morning-room office. I've left the correspondence on the desk there."

"As you wish, Mr. Fane."

An hour later, when the house was empty of everyone but Edgar, he strode down the narrow hallway and into the study. The frames had been stacked, most of them carefully, against the wall. Smiling in satisfaction, Edgar ran his fingers along heavily ornate gilt edges, polished cherry… ebonized wood that gleamed in the gaslight. *Which one?* he thought, in his mind's eye filling out the frame with a picture. A fruit study, perhaps for the cherry. An African village for the ebonized wood. Quietly amused, he turned off the wall lights and left, rubbing his hands together in anticipation.

Now he could focus all his attention on Tuesday evening, and the surprise he'd planned for Miss Pickford.

"Don't know why ya turned so particular," Mrs. Chudd grumped as she and Thea waited in the lobby for Mr. Fane's carriage. "M'rheumatism's acting up. And he better not serve shellfish. You know I don't eat shellfish. Gives me hives."

"You know quite well I can't go to a strange house, for a private dinner with a gentleman unknown to the family, without you," Thea repeated, not for the first time. "Some proprieties are common sense, even here in Saratoga Springs."

"Humph. No need to get on a high horse. I know my place." Her double chins quivered. "Your grandpapa ought to be 'shamed, agreeing to this twaddle." The heavy walking cane she'd produced to aid her with her "rheumatism" thunked dourly on the tiled floor. "But you needn't fret. My mouth won't be catching any flies."

By the time the shiny black coupé drew to a smooth halt in front of a large rambling house, Thea's nerves had dissolved into a gummy mess lodged beneath her breastbone. Light ripples of dizziness washed over her at odd moments, but she was able to ignore them, offering Mr. Fane a dazzling smile when he opened the carriage door himself to help her out.

"I appreciate your keeping our dinner engagement, since I was unable to obey my marching orders to pick you up myself." He greeted her with a bow. "An unavoidable telephone call. May I compliment you on your lovely costume? That shade of pink—mauve, I believe they call it—suits you."

His deft compliment flustered her. Evil villains weren't supposed to be so amenable. "Thank you. This is my companion, Mrs. Chudd."

"You are both welcome."

By the time dinner was served, Thea had almost relaxed enough to taste some of the food. Mr. Fane made no untoward remarks, instead offering almost courtly discourse devoid of sarcasm or scandal; after several attempts to include Mrs. Chudd in the conversation, however, he left her companion alone, giving Thea a conspiratorial wink.

"You say this house belongs to friends of your family," Thea ventured toward the end of the meal. She glanced around the cluttered dining room, suppressing a shudder. Pictures hung on every inch of wall space, and the massive table could have accommodated thirty guests. The walls were papered a dark red color that reminded her of calf's liver.

Edgar laughed. "Monstrous, isn't it? I believe the furniture in this room hasn't been moved in a hundred years. Don't worry, we'll have dessert in the morning room. It's one of my favorite spots, tucked away at the back of the house. Lots of windows, with a peaceful view of a pond, complete with ducks. The sun sets directly over it. I've been meaning to paint the scene. Perhaps," he added, idly tracing his index finger around the rim of his water glass, "you'll provide me with sufficient inspiration."

Thea almost choked, and hastily lifted her napkin to dab her mouth. Apparently the wolf had decided it was time to discard the sheep's clothing. "Everyone talks about your paintings—when you're not around, of course. But I've never seen one of your efforts. Does that mean you're a serious artist, or a dilettante, Mr. Fane?"

"When I decide, I'll let you know." Shifting, he scooted his chair a little closer to Thea's. "What about you, Miss Pickford? While pining for your English aristocrat, how do you entertain yourself, aside from reeling in gentlemen with your fishing pole?"

Thea wondered if this was how a fish felt, when the shiny bug gave way to a sharp hook. She laid the napkin by her plate, and ordered her face muscles to smile. "I enjoy fresh air and vigorous exercise, Mr. Fane, so I go for lots of walks. Back home I own a safety bicycle. I also enjoy meeting and talking with people." Always tell the truth whenever possible, she'd learned. Worming in a lie or two between made them more believable. "And I share everything I do, everyone I meet, with my Neville, in long weekly letters. We're thinking of spending every season in a different spa resort. How about you, Mr. Fane? Do you have any preferences as to locale? I've heard Newport has become a fashionable destination, with first-class beaches. Have you ever been there?"

"Several times." Toying with his earlobe, he leaned closer and continued in a lowered voice, "If you plan to extend your season there, perhaps I could change my itinerary."

Shock almost made her jump. Boys had teased her, gentlemen had flirted, a few here at Saratoga had been a trifle forward. But Mr. Fane was neither a boy, a boor, nor she well knew, a gentleman. Given the circumstances, she should have anticipated such remarks.

"How flattering, Mr. Fane. But you're a little more forthright than I'm comfortable with, even with the presence of a chaperone."

"Agreed." He quit fiddling with his ear, studying her for a moment before he rose lithely to his feet. "I have just the solution. Mrs. Chudd? May I show you to the library? There's a comfortable chair, with a gout stool, which will be more comfortable for you. The Daubneys have wide and varied tastes. I daresay we can find you a good book to read while Miss Pickford and I stroll by the pond."

## Chapter Fourteen

**M**oments later, her traitorous chaperone was happily ensconced with Tolstoy, her leg resting on the gout stool. Mr. Fane led Thea down several bisecting hallways into a large, airy room with wicker furniture and Boston ferns. Two paddle fans lazily moved the air. "Over here," he said. "We've missed most of the sunset, but there's still enough light to appreciate the view."

She approached warily; he had placed himself between a side table and a corner, leaving Thea little room. "Very serene," she agreed. And very isolated. "Um...I believe it's too dark for a walk."

"Possibly. I wouldn't want you to be nervous, so..." He took a step toward her, his mouth twitching when Thea stiffened. He reached past her and tugged the chain to a Tiffany floor lamp. "There you go. A bit of artificial light, to help you relax? Tell me, Miss Pickford, what really prompted an engaged lady to accept a private dinner invitation with a man like me?"

"A man like you? Heavens, Mr. Fane, have you crafted some nasty plot to drug the coffee, sell me to the Arabs? Or—" she darted around him, over to a floor globe situated between a revolving bookstand and a chair "—are you deliberately trying to fluster me?" With a flick of her wrist she set the globe awhirl and prayed her internal spinning would remain stationary for one more hour. She needed places, names—any clue, however oblique, to Edgar Fane's private life. A chink in his impenetrable armor. "I would like to know why one of the richest men in the country would ask a lady engaged to another man to have a private dinner with him."

"Irrepressibly impertinent. I think I like it." Mr. Fane ambled toward her, head cocked to the side and a brooding expression hiding his thoughts. "Would you believe me if I said loneliness?"

"No."

"Are you always this forthright, Miss Pickford?"

Her conscience winced, but Thea answered steadily enough. "I'm not going to hang on your every word, or offer flattering sobriquets in the hope you'll offer to drape me in jewels. On the other hand, I would like to understand the man hiding inside a crowd of hangers-on. Do you have a—a real job, Mr. Fane? Or do you merely enjoy spending the family fortune?" She stopped, biting her lip. "I beg your pardon. That *was* impertinent of me."

"You know, Miss Pickford…I wonder about you. I really do. I'm not sure you want to understand me as much as you want to—how shall I phrase it? Test the waters? See if I'm a better catch than your English earl?"

"I'm sorry an impulse to attract your attention led you to believe I could be that sort of woman."

"You already know I'm a wealthy man, Miss Pickford. Your fiancé might be an earl, but that doesn't mean he's well-heeled. I'm used to people who hope to benefit from my, I believe *largesse* is one of the press's favorite descriptions. Of course, many of them are the women who hope for a marriage proposal."

"I do not want to marry you, Mr. Fane."

For the first time a flicker of surprise cracked his set features. "You actually sound as though you mean that."

"Whatever else you believe or your secretary spy reports about me, you can count on my complete disregard for such an alliance." A stew of vicious emotions bubbled inside. She was a bat-brained idiot, to think she could pry information from a man sophisticated enough to convince bankers and government agencies of his innocence. "Mr. Fane, I think we should—"

"Well, well, well…what have I interrupted?" Cynthia Gorman emerged from the shadowed hall. Lifting a graceful hand, she flicked on an electric light switch, and green-gold light illuminated the morning room. "Forgive me, my dears. And here I thought *I* was the only woman to enjoy a cozy tryst with Edgar."

A flash of rage, quickly banked, darkened Mr. Fane's eyes but he recovered rapidly. "Cynthia, don't be more catty than you have to." He met the other woman in the middle of the room, effectively blocking her from Thea. "What are you doing here? I'll have that butler sacked."

"Oh, stop sputtering, darling. I told him I stopped by to fetch my parasol. I left it yesterday, in one of these private tucked-away rooms. The ones you like to hide people in. Forgive me, Miss Pickford. No offense intended. Edgar and I are forever teasing each other."

"None taken." Eyeing the doorway into the hall, Thea inched toward a sitting area behind Cynthia Gorman. "I should go anyway. My companion is elderly, and doesn't need to stay out too late."

Cynthia gave a peal of laughter. "The old woman in the library? She's snoring like an elephant with a cold. Please. I'll fetch my parasol, whisk myself out. Carry on with your evening together, and pretend you never saw me."

"I'm almost to a point where pretending won't be necessary," Mr. Fane said.

The caustic retort wiped the smile off Cynthia's face. "I've apologized. Nicely. Don't turn into an oaf, Edgar." Long, elegant fingers stroked down his sleeve. "I promise to be gone before you've taken a first sip of the coffee I smelled perking. Is it from those Jamaican beans you like so much? You'll enjoy it, Miss Pickford. Make sure you ask for some of the English biscuits to go with your brew. Mayhap it will remind you of your earl, loving you from afar." Smiling like a mischievous cat, she engulfed Thea in a quick hug, then disappeared in a froth of white lawn and lace.

"Ah, Cynthia. The air is rife with shiny knives when she doesn't get her way." Mr. Fane reached Thea's side. "You needn't glare at me accusingly. I did not invite her to be part of a ménage à trois."

"I beg your pardon? A what?"

Chagrin softened the thick ridges scoring his forehead; in all the weeks she'd been following him, Thea had never witnessed a display of such rancor. "Never mind," he said, but his smile looked forced. "I shouldn't have mentioned it. Let's have some of that coffee."

Her insides felt as though she were squeezing them through a wringer washing machine. Time was evaporating, the mood darkening, and she was…desperate. Perhaps she could bait him with words, goad him into an unguarded response. "Only if you tell me why the son of one of the most influential men in the country spends most of his time doing…nothing useful. Along with healthy activities and socializing, like my companion I read a lot, Mr. Fane. Since arriving at Saratoga Springs I've discovered you're a favorite topic of conversation among people and newspaper articles, yet I still know very little about you. And your manner to Mrs. Gorman just now…I'm wondering if I made a mistake, accepting your dinner invitation." Invisible pressure against the side of her head gave an ominous push, and she surreptitiously gripped the curved back of a wicker chair.

"I was concerned her remarks had offended you. We've known each other for years, remember. Sometimes she abuses our friendship and I call her hand. Don't allow her jealousy to—"

"This has nothing to do with Mrs. Gorman. It's late, and I think I should leave. Can you direct me back to the library, please?"

"Are you all right, Miss Pickford?" Frown deepening, he studied her. "You're not acting like yourself." Slowly his hand closed around her elbow in a light grip, and it took the last of Thea's dwindling courage not to jerk away. "Very well. I'll take you to Mrs. Chudd."

Tension vibrated in the press of his fingers, and the way his gaze seemed to dart about every room they passed. Or perhaps she was superimposing her own nerves over his? He left Thea seated in the entry hall while he went to wake her companion and summon the driver; within moments he was handing her and a querulous Mrs. Chudd into the carriage.

"An interesting evening," he said, bowing over her fingers, which unforgivably trembled. "With an interesting woman. What a shame circumstances forbade the opportunity to get to know each other better. Mrs. Gorman has a lot to answer for."

All the way back to the hotel, with Mrs. Chudd glowering and silent on the opposite seat, Thea wondered at those parting words, and cursed herself for her ineptitude.

She hadn't even discovered Edgar Fane's pending destination, much less a crumb of condemnatory evidence.

The vertigo hit with the force of a nor'easter while she plaited her hair for bed.

"What are you doing here?" Edgar stalked across the room to Cynthia, who was sitting on a Turkish divan while she smoked one of his Cuban cigars. The affectation disgusted him, because whenever he smoked around her she taunted him about the filthy habit and vile odor.

"Saving you from yourself." She stubbed out the cigar and stood, idly waving the smoke away with her hand. "Why the interest in that girl, Edgar? You know she's only after your family fortune."

"You know less about her than I do." He went to stand over her, but Cynthia merely lifted her brow. Edgar took her chin in a forceful grip. "But I do know you, and this cat-and-the-empty-birdcage look. What have you been doing in my house, hmm? Tell me, my dear. I'm in no mood to play games this evening."

"Too bad." She shoved his hand away. "You play them so well. All right, I can tell you're in a beastly mood. I did forget my parasol, but I was at loose ends this evening so decided to prowl around this ridiculous pile of bricks while I waited for Miss Prim to decide whether or not to stay for coffee." A nasty smile curled her lips. "I found a locked door, in the opposite wing? And you know what they say about curiosity."

A sense of inevitability settled over Edgar, and he turned away from her until he could school his face to a polite mask. "I take it you charmed my soon-to-be-former housekeeper into unlocking the door?"

"Of course. I'm not stupid, my dear, and neither are you. I've wondered, for quite some time now, what you were doing with your many peregrinations from city to city, like Diogenes looking for the light. You're a very clever man, aren't you?"

"Yes. Why don't we go for a moonlit walk by the pond, and discuss the terms of your silence? It wouldn't do for Mrs. Surrey to overhear anything."

Cynthia tossed her head. "I don't mind filling in for Miss Pickford. But if you try to kiss me to seal the deal, tonight I might be inclined to bite first."

"You'll probably do more than that," Edgar replied, and tucked her hand through his crooked arm.

A thunderbolt of anticipation tightened his muscles, while every nerve tingled over the bold step he was about to take. How…fortuitous?…that Cynthia turned up earlier in the library. He'd grown tired of her possessiveness anyway, and had actually toyed with the idea of quelling it through a genuine pursuit of the intriguing Miss Pickford. On the other hand, he would still pursue Theodora, though the outcome for both women would be quite different from what they hoped.

"What are you smiling about?" Cynthia grumped beside him. "Now *you* look like the cat by the empty birdcage."

Edgar patted her hand. "All in good time, my dear. All in good time."

Devlin waited until Thea and Mrs. Chudd entered the Grand Union Hotel before he stepped out of the shadows and followed them inside. *She'd looked pale, and drained, as though the evening had sucked color and life from her.* The open rotunda stretched all the way to the top floor; balconies on each level allowed guests to peer down into the lobby. Dev unfolded the newspaper he'd been carrying and leaned against one of the marble columns, watching with relief when the two women trudged along the second floor landing without glancing down. Just before they disappeared down a hallway Thea seemed to wobble, and one hand braced against the balcony railing until she recovered.

Moving rapidly, Dev mounted the staircase after them, gliding with soundless step to the corridor they had entered. A moment later he heard the sound of a key rattling in the lock, and a low murmur of voices.

For the moment, Thea was safe.

He padded to the end of the hall, where he discovered a small open parlor. Excellent. Relieved, Devlin stationed himself so he could see if anyone else followed Thea back to the hotel, or showed untoward interest in her hotel room. At a little past midnight a noisy family tromped back to a room two doors down from Thea's, and a half hour later the night watchman wandered past the parlor for the second time.

"Still here, eh?" Bald and potbellied, the guard smiled sympathetically. "Fight with the missus? She lock you out of the room?"

Devlin yawned. "Worse. Insomnia," he said. "She snores."

Nodding, the watchman moved on. At two o'clock Dev concluded Thea was safely asleep. No suspicious strangers lurked outside her room. And if she'd suffered an attack of vertigo, she and Mrs. Chudd were handling it. For now, the need for vigilance was over.

Back in his own rooms, after writing his report Devlin passed the rest of a miserable night tormenting himself with images: Thea, dining with Edgar Fane; Thea falling ill and *Fane* holding her close, bathing her face with a cool cloth. Thea and Fane, laughing because the Hotel Hustler was not one man, but a team, and Devlin Stone had been duped by another woman. All her self-conscious ramblings had been designed to learn *his* soft spots, and fool that he was, Dev had handed her a cartful of them.

No. Call him arrogant, or duped, but he refused to believe Thea was a criminal, devoid of a conscience. He'd met enough of those over the past two years to tell the difference. Theodora was a woman in trouble, and she needed his help.

He hoped.

## Chapter Fifteen

Dawn found him at the racecourse stables, helping the grooms ready their charges for the day. Over the past weeks his willingness to shovel manure, groom dust-coated hides and clean tack had earned him a free ticket to wander wherever he chose. Some of the owners even unbent enough to ask his advice, especially when one of the grooms announced that Mr. Stone had "the touch" with the creatures. Didn't matter that he owned and trained draft horses, not Thoroughbreds.

By the time the noon hour rolled around, the sanity of a sunny summer morning had dispelled some of the night goblins, and the physical exertion had cleansed his mind. He ate lunch with a pair of crinkle-eyed Irish lads, sifting through tidbits of possibly useful information, then wandered over toward the grandstands to catch a couple of races. Somewhere the ringer clanged the bell, signaling the minutes to post time, and Dev absently counted rings while he made his way through hurrying race goers. Thirty yards away from the betting ring a ruckus seemed to have erupted.

Dev wandered over to investigate. "What's going on?" he asked an onlooker.

"Fracas in the betting ring. Something about passing phony goods to the bookie. Someone fetched a copper. Just goes to show, don't it?"

"That it does. Thanks, friend." Without waiting to hear more Dev wove his way over to where avid witnesses circled the knot of red-faced, shouting men.

His big feet solidly planted on hundreds of discarded betting tickets, the policeman clamped a hand on one of the troublemakers' shoulders. When his call for order was ignored, he pulled out his billy club but achieved no noticeable effect, as all three men continued shouting threats and imprecations.

"...and if you don't release me this instant, the mayor will hear of this! I'm a guest and a law-abiding free citizen—"

"...know queer money when I sees it! Them hundred-dollar bills he tried to give me are bogus goods! Ask my sheet writer! He seen 'em, too!"

"Well, he paid me twenty-thousand dollars in bills that look just like those. If they're all fake, I want my money back—my real money, before they throw his carcass in the big house."

"I tell you, I have done nothing wrong. Officer, you are making a grave mistake here."

Every one of Dev's senses heightened when he caught a glimpse of the man in a neat gray suit and top hat being held by the policeman—Randolph Lunt.

After following him for weeks, Dev had been ready to scrub Lunt off the list, a discouraging admission, which did not bode well for his professional reputation. What a piece of luck, to happen along the very moment Lunt made his move. Too bad he'd have to identify himself to the policeman as a U.S. Secret Service operative in order to verify fraudulent bills. Too soon, too public—too much of a risk.

More troubling, even if the bills in question proved to be counterfeit, at the moment the man could only be charged with passing bogus goods. With his connections, Lunt would be back on the street and out of sight before the ink dried on the order to release him. The previous autumn, a clever New York lawyer and an unimpressed judge had made mincemeat of the Service's case after Charles Langston was arrested on the same charge Lunt now faced. Langston claimed Edgar Fane had fleeced him, so Fane had been questioned, as well. But ultimately all charges were dropped for insufficient evidence. Langston and Fane walked, the case once more hit a dead end—and here Devlin stood, on the same precipice as his hapless fellow operatives in the City last fall.

Of course, if Lunt also had ties to the Hotel Hustler…

*Not yet.* The order whispered through him as clearly as though the words had been voiced aloud. Something— some blink of an instinct, something more forceful than a hunch, shut Devlin's mouth, held him poised and watchful, muscles bunched. A second thought crossed his mind that perhaps his presence here at this particular moment was something other than mere "luck."

Cautiously he inched around to better analyze Lunt's face and body movements. The man repeated his protestations of innocence, all without contractions, the timbre of his voice growing more elevated; his left hand was stuffed inside his pocket and bulging outward—all signs he was lying. Mr. Girard and the bookie, on the other hand, both radiated honest outrage.

"You're a liar, that's what you are!" Girard said, jabbing a finger toward Lunt's chest. "A cheat, and a liar."

"I won that money fair and square over at the Casino,

not two hours ago," Lunt protested, his voice hoarse with outrage. "As for your libelous claim, Mr. Girard, I have paid you what was owed, and will see you in court, sir."

"Maybe, maybe not," the unflappable policeman returned. "Best all you gentlemen come with me. These here are serious charges, and I'll do my duty as I see it to keep all activities at this racetrack legal. Tully?"

"Yessir?" The bookie removed his flat cap and wiped his sweating forehead.

"Bring all them bills to police headquarters, every one of them. Right now, eh? We'll sort things out there, right and proper."

Two more policemen arrived, forming a wall of brass-buttoned resolve. Randolph Lunt, along with Tully, his sheet writer and Mr. Girard, were escorted from the betting ring and off the racecourse. Dev, unnoticed, followed them into the village, down Broadway to the stately brick Town Hall, which housed the jail and police headquarters. Pedestrians scattered out of the way, staring after the procession as the police ushered the three men up the steps and through the arched entryway into the building. On the opposite side of the street, Devlin paced as he waged an internal debate—telegraph headquarters? Reveal himself to the police? Or wait for that mysterious unseen Voice to give him further direction?

Either the God his father had believed in was revealing Himself to Dev in an unexpected manner, or lack of sleep had induced some form of cerebral delusion.

Nearby strollers were suddenly jostled aside by a woman who darted between them and passed Devlin with arms thrust skyward. Skirts and petticoats flared wide, she stumbled across the cobblestoned curb into the street, barely dodging a passing buggy in her erratic flight.

"Help!" she cried brokenly. "Help! P—police! We need a policeman!"

A portly man had followed on her heels, but he stopped on the sidewalk, right beside Devlin. Breath sawed from his lungs, and his eyes stretched wide and unblinking in a darkly flushed face. One hand went to his chest.

"Easy," Devlin said. "Here, I've got you. Lean on this hitching post. Catch your breath."

The man shook his head violently, tried to speak and finally braced one shaking hand against the empty post. His white-eyed gaze latched onto Dev's at the same time his other hand grabbed Dev's sleeve. "Dead," he got out. "She's dead." Damp patches darkened the armpits of his blue blazer and large droplets of sweat rolled down his beet-red face. "A woman. Dead. Woodlawn Park. We found her, my wife and I...we found her, in some bushes. Out walking. I—we didn't know what to do, so we..." His lips turned an alarming blue tint. "We couldn't find...a policeman."

"Calm yourself, sir. Your wife's reached Town Hall. Catch your breath, hmm? I'll see that your wife is informed of your whereabouts, and promise her you'll join her soon. You, lad—" he caught the eye of a gangling young man wearing a cobbler's apron "—could you fetch this gentleman some water? Is there a place he could sit for a few moments, inside your shop? If you think it's necessary, go for a physician." He pressed the winded husband's shoulder in a final gesture of reassurance, then dashed across the street after the wife.

*A dead woman in the park.*

As he ran, a brief arrow of anxiety found its mark too close to his heart for comfort. For the first time in years a particular woman's well-being mattered, triggering irrational thoughts born both of too much knowledge—and too little. Surely, out of thousands of women who visited or lived in Saratoga Springs, surely the victim wasn't Thea. Devlin blanked the unwelcome conjecture from his brain.

But sure would help if he knew where she was at the moment.

Inside police headquarters, all attention had momentarily focused upon the two policemen with set faces who hovered over the distraught woman. Neither Lunt, Girard nor the bookie Tully and his helper were in sight.

A sergeant glanced up at Devlin's approach. "You the husband?"

"No. He's across the street, catching his breath. I told him I'd check on his wife, let her know he'll be along as soon as he can."

"I'll pass along the message." When the officer brusquely ordered Dev out of the way, he complied without protest. An unknown woman's death was after all none of his business. *It is not Thea, Stone. Concentrate on your own job, you tomfool chump.* Somewhere in this building Randolph Lunt was being held, and the charge against him *was* Devlin Stone's business. Thinking rapidly, he marked the presence of the Police Chief, whose double rows of buttons signifying his position gleamed dully against his uniform jacket. He was engaged in deep conversation with a gentleman dressed in a funereal three-piece black suit, probably a lawyer. They stood behind a waist-high railing, ignoring the furor taking place on the other side of the room. Dev waited until the black-suited man turned away to gather some papers off a desk, and the Chief set off toward the woman now quietly weeping into her handkerchief.

Decision made, Dev quietly moved to block his path. "Chief Blevins? My name is Devlin Stone. I'm an undercover operative with the United States Secret Service. I'll provide badge and credentials later. I know you have an unknown dead woman in a park, and a possible high-profile counterfeiter in your custody. Both require immediate investigation. I'd like to offer my assistance with Randolph Lunt. I witnessed most of the altercation at the racetrack, and am willing to testify under oath that Mr. Lunt was not telling the truth. With your permission, I can also determine whether or not the bills in question are bogus."

He paused for emphasis, then added, "But I need one request granted. It is imperative that my identity remain absolutely secret from everyone but you."

With an effort that threatened to crack his jawbone he managed to shut his mouth, before he included an *un*professional request for the identity of the murdered woman.

As soon as he could grab ten minutes, he'd verify Thea's whereabouts for himself.

*She's fine,* he repeated silently. *She's safe.*

# Chapter Sixteen

Thea's latest spell of vertigo gave her no respite until lunchtime the next day. Mrs. Chudd ministered to her efficiently but without warmth, dosing her with cool sips of springwater or draping her face with damp, mint-scented cloths until Thea drifted off to sleep. When she woke, her companion silently helped her dress in a loose-fitting house gown and ordered a light brunch for them both.

"I'm better," Thea pronounced with relief when she managed to sit up enough to finish a bowl of soup by herself. Slowly she turned her head from side to side, smiling when the room did not dip and sway. "I think it's over."

"Humph. Bad one, this time."

"Yes, it was. But as you see, I'm quite recovered."

"Still planning to chase after that Mr. Fane?"

Thea laid her soupspoon down, stood and carefully walked over to the window, which overlooked the garden court. Near the center of the lawn, a group of children and their nannies were being arranged by a photographer for a group picture. Sunshine poured through the trees in golden streamers, birds flitted among the branches. A block away, a train whistle blew and on the piazza directly below, the hotel band warmed up its instruments. It was a lively, cheerfully *normal* scene, and bitterness coated Thea's throat like ashes. For the first time she couldn't banish a niggle of doubt about the ultimate nobility of her mission.

Devlin might be right: instead of making herself God's instrument of justice for Grandfather, she'd been challenging the Almighty of the universe to do something about Edgar Fane. On Thea's terms—not the Lord's.

"I don't know what to do about Edgar Fane," she said. Turning, she added slowly, "But I can't give up." Not yet, not now when she was finally making progress. "What did you think of him?"

Mrs. Chudd sniffed. "Too much teeth in his smile. Knows his manners, though. Not my business, but you weren't reared this way, missy."

"No, I wasn't. Times change. So do circumstances." Resolute once more, Thea headed toward the large armoire in the corner of her room and flung it open. "I think I'll go for a walk, clear my head. I don't need any further help, Mrs. Chudd. Perhaps we can dine al fresco for supper when I return."

With a short nod the woman departed into her own chamber. Moisture burned Thea's eyelids. More than anything, she would like to have buried her head in Mrs. Chudd's shoulder, given and received a hug and thanked her for her help. But Mrs. Chudd cared little for affectionate displays or words of praise, having rebuffed Thea sufficiently their first week at Saratoga to ensure the distance between them was firmly established.

Swallowing hard, she changed her attire and left the morbidly quiet room. As she wandered downstairs to the main level, she entertained a fledgling hope that Devlin would be waiting in the lobby. He'd promised to watch over her, whatever that entailed. Thoughts of him set her pulse to galloping like one of the racehorses. *Devlin*.

All right, these hopes were for giddy schoolgirls, but for an hour of her life she was going to be one. She had survived the disastrous dinner with Edgar Fane and the misery of a vertigo spell, and now she planned to savor every memory of the previous afternoon with Devlin. The words he'd spoken. The clasp of his hard hand. The creases in his cheeks when he smiled that smile.

Most of all…that kiss, and the heated warmth of his lips. Her palms tingled even now from the memory of his broad shoulders and strong arms, corded with muscles so unlike any of the pallid, intellectual young men she'd known back home on Staten Island. However, Devlin had awakened shrouded chambers of her heart not merely because of his masculine physique, but because he'd looked at her as though…as though she were someone precious, someone desirable.

Nobody had ever looked at Theodora the way Devlin Stone had, that afternoon in Congress Park. Many had praised Thea for her agile mind and her business acumen, her hostess skills and her cordiality. And if Charles Langston insisted on training his granddaughter to do so, why of course she could run a publishing company as well as any man, they told her.

Until Devlin, not a single gentleman ever thought to remark on her desirability as a woman.

Devlin thought she was *tempting*. Thea hugged the word, and the incandescent memory of their kiss. After this walk she would address the consequences of her evening with Edgar Fane, analyze the few bits of information she'd gleaned, then decide the most judicious course to follow. But for one golden moment of time, she wanted to forget everything but the man who was dangerously close to capturing not only her imagination but her heart.

Late in the afternoon, she returned to the hotel, weary but refreshed in spirit. Devlin had not popped up at the Columbian Spring Pavilion to share a cup of water, or the Indian Encampment, where she'd peered at native bead-work, pawed at trinkets and souvenir glasses, watched tourists miss most of the shots at a target shoot. After a wistful hour, Thea bid the schoolgirl daydream farewell and simply embraced the freedom of enjoying herself. She didn't dwell on Devlin's absence or Edgar Fane's perfidies, or her doubts. For the first time in over a year, she dabbled without guilt in the trivialities of life.

Her heart, on the other hand, had been firmly leashed and muzzled. Thea Pickford was an illusion, a will-o'-the-wisp destined to die like the last of the summer roses. Charles Langston wasn't the only one who had lost every-thing. Courtesy of Edgar Fane, Theodora Langston had nothing to offer an honorable man like Devlin Stone. Her family's reputation was irreparably tarnished, her inheri-tance was gone, along with the small publishing company Grandfather had owned for half a century. The company Thea had been trained to run when he retired.

In fact, the next time she and Devlin crossed paths, if they ever did, it would be a kindness to confess the depth of her iniquities. He'd already suffered enough from the betrayal of his fiancée. *God…if only You kept Your prom-ises like Grandfather used to believe, then I wouldn't be in this imbroglio.*

If only He would administer justice to Edgar Fane, and grant her a droplet of peace.

Somewhere a clock bonged the hour of five o'clock. Thea quickened her pace, aggravated with her inability to control this obstinate pining to believe in the God who loved humanity enough to sacrifice His Son for them. *Her present conduct precluded mercy.* So why appeal to the Almighty in the first place? He had never invested a presence in her life. From a theological perspective, her willful choice to hound Edgar Fane until he was behind bars pretty much guaranteed God would turn His back on Thea altogether. Certainly Jesus never stalked villains to proclaim their villainy.

But somebody had to do something about Fane. Thus far he spread his evil wherever he chose, claiming victims like wooden ducks at the shooting gallery in the Indian Encampment.

Evil. It was an old-fashioned word, difficult to apply to the debonair gentleman with his dark eyes and easy charisma—until Cynthia Gorman's interruption in the morning room. Shivery foreboding jigged down Theodora's spine. For over a year she had devoted every waking hour to a course of action, but not once had she seriously considered the possibility of personal danger. Then she'd glimpsed the look in Edgar's eyes when Cynthia walked out of the room, seen the banked eagerness of a wolf waiting for the opportunity to slake its killing hunger.

The next time Thea inveigled an invitation from the man, she would armor herself with more than determination.

A policeman stopped her at the entrance to the Grand Union. Tall and gangly, with reddish sideburns showing beneath his policeman's helmet, he inquired curtly, "Miss Theodora…Pickford?"

"Yes? What is it, Officer?"

"Been waiting for over half an hour. You were to have returned by five."

Perplexed, Thea darted a glance behind him, into the hotel. "You've spoken to my companion, Mrs. Chudd? Has something happened to her?"

"No, miss. I need you to come with me to Police Head-quarters, at Town Hall. Right now, if you please." He lifted a white-gloved hand. "It's right down the street."

"All right." Thea paused, then added firmly, "After you tell me why."

The policeman's face darkened. "Chief Blevins's orders." He glanced around at the curious gazes of pass-ersby, then leaned down a bit, bringing a hand up to stroke his gingery red mustache at the same time he muttered out of the side of his mouth, "Miss, there's been an… incident. Your name has been introduced as a person of interest. I'd rather not say more, not here." He stepped back, somber and unflinching in his blue serge uniform and round policeman's helmet.

An incident? What did that mean? Obviously noth-ing good, or he wouldn't be so uncommunicative. "Very well." Thea thought about demanding that Mrs. Chudd be allowed to accompany her, but squelched the urge. Arguing with the police tended to achieve the opposite result one desired. "I do need to have a message sent to my chaperone so she won't worry."

"Already taken care of."

He gestured with his arm, and Thea fell into step a little ahead of him, uncertainty beating the air around her like thousands of bat wings. In her experience, the only reason for the police to demand your presence was because they believed you'd committed a crime.

By the time she and the impassive officer completed the two-block walk to Town Hall, uncertainty had meta-morphosed into fear, and Thea could scarcely feel her feet inside her dust-coated walking boots. The stone lions guarding either side of the building looked as though they were about to pounce upon her, and she climbed the shal-low steps on trembling legs. Heart racing, mouth dry, she suddenly realized in scalding clarity that this was how her grandfather must have felt when a New York City detective and two Secret Service operatives knocked on the door the previous autumn.

At the end of a long hallway the officer opened a door; Thea squared her shoulders as she entered a room crowded with sober black suits and blue serge uniforms, a rumpled clerk who gawked at her through wire-rimmed spectacles—and Edgar Fane.

A starburst of satisfaction spiked through Thea's fear. She inhaled a quick breath of relief, in her agitation completely forgetting the Theodora Pickford persona who knew nothing of Mr. Fane's perfidies. "You've arrested this man, then? You need me to testify? I'll be glad to tell you everything Mr. Fane—"

"My dear Miss Pickford," Mr. Fane interrupted, stepping in front of the speechless officer. The expression on Edgar's face belied the ice pick precision of his words. "More lies will only exacerbate your situation. You wove your web skillfully, and I'm deeply chagrined by my gullibility."

With the timing of a theater performer he waited until all gazes were riveted upon them. "I've abased myself before these officers of the law, honestly admitting my attraction for you. It's no secret I enjoy the company of ladies. But I have never misled a single one of them about my intentions, including you, Miss Pickford. Ah. Your look of shocked bewilderment is excellent, though a waste of time. Come now, let's be done with pretense. You worked so hard to gain my attention this past month, didn't you? Several acquaintances have remarked on your attempts. Well?"

"You're twisting the circumstances." Thea turned to the group of silent officials, but her tongue felt glued to the roof of her mouth. "He's…it's not what he's saying. I—I did try to attract him, yes. But—"

"But you discovered last night it was all for naught. If only I had known… Now my friend has paid too dear a price for your wicked schemes, for assumptions I never encouraged." His voice choked; he tugged a pristine silk handkerchief out and dabbed his temples.

"What are you talking about?" Thea cried, searching the grim faces gathered around her. "If anyone is guilty of deceit, it would be—"

*Guilty of deceit.* Further denials and charges died unvoiced. A chasm yawned at her feet; she tried without success to swallow a gelatinous lump threatening to choke her.

"You see?" Edgar Fane spread his arms in a gesture that triggered a groundswell of murmurs and foot-shuffling among the police officers. "Even now she seeks to spin her webs. Miss Pickford, or whatever your real name is, the game is up. If you'll confess at once to this heinous crime, and spare us all needless hours of suffering, I will in turn see that you are fairly treated."

"I've committed no crime." Her voice rose. "You're twisting everything around, just like…just like…"

"Silence!" A different policeman, older, with thinning gray hair neatly parted and authority stamped across his lined face, pointed an index finger at Thea. "You will have your day in court, Miss Pickford. For now, the magistrate deems probable cause, you are being charged on suspicion of murder and I am placing you under arrest."

## Chapter Seventeen

"I'm under arrest?" Thea sputtered. "For—for *murder?*" The words made no sense, as if the man had spoken them backward, with all the syllables rearranged. She swept a loathing glance over Edgar Fane. "This is ridiculous. Based on the testimony of one person? Of *this* man?" Across a waist-high railing, the clerk busily wrote something onto a piece of paper. The scratching noise of the pen hurt her ears. A sensation of unreality infiltrated her skin until she felt disembodied and stripped of all emotion.

Then she saw the smug triumph hovering around Edgar's mouth. Temper flared to life. "What have you done to corroborate his charges? Who is the victim? Exactly when was I supposed to have committed the crime? And for goodness' sake, why have you allowed Mr. Fane to poison your minds? If a murder has been committed, *he's* the person you should be placing under arrest! Why don't you question him?"

"Miss Pickford, you will please show respect, and moderate your tone of voice. Legal counsel has been notified on your behalf, and will arrive shortly. But aggressive displays of temper cannot be tolerated." The authoritative police-man nodded once, and before Thea realized what was happening another policeman took her wrists and fastened them together with a pair of heavy metal handcuffs. "Mr. Fane is present because he identified the victim, and after apprising us of pertinent facts issued his complaint under oath. Due to the gravity of this case, Chief Blevins further ordered that every word spoken in this room be faithfully transcribed, including yours, Miss Pickford. Mr. Fane is well-known hereabouts. Over the years he and the rest of his family have established many friends in the village of Saratoga Springs. You, on the other hand, cannot offer such a history."

Thea's outrage fizzled into silence. Until last year, she had believed truth always protected innocence. Truth, ha! Truth was a multifaceted prism of many colors and multiple sides, not a windowpane. She stood mute, teeth grinding, while this gravel-voiced officer of the law recited Edgar Fane's distorted version of events.

"At approximately ten o'clock last night Mrs. Cynthia Gorman interrupted your evening together with Mr. Fane, at the Franklin Square residence occupied by him for the season. Mr. Fane grew alarmed by your irrational anger over her brief appearance to retrieve her parasol." He cast a baleful look at Thea. "A behavior corroborated just now by your tirade, in full view of this department. According to Mr. Fane, last night without cause or provocation you threatened Mrs. Gorman with dire consequences if she did not at once leave the dwelling where Mr. Fane currently resides."

"Lies!" Thea exclaimed. "Those are bald-faced lies! She stopped by to fetch her parasol, but it was Mr. Fane who was angry, not me. You should have seen *his* face. Wait—no." Cold chills racked her limbs. She felt as though she were fighting her way through a thicket of needle-pointed briars. "Are you telling me that Mrs. *Gorman* is the victim? Mrs. Gorman is…dead, and the man who committed the deed is standing right here in this room, yet *I'm* the one wearing handcuffs?"

The room erupted in a barrage of angry orders and accusations and shouts for silence. But it was Edgar Fane, the epitome of wealth, power and gentility in his dove-gray morning suit and silk tie, who finally restored a semblance of order.

"It's quite all right. I am not offended, gentlemen, and appreciate your spirited defense of public order." He gestured to Thea. "She is angry because she's been caught. She's afraid of the consequences. Over the years I've had plenty of experience with her sort, I'm sorry to say. The picture of innocence, but it's all the act of an unstable, desperate woman who took advantage of my trust. I almost feel pity for her, except Mrs. Gorman was like a member of our family."

Thea lunged forward. "You monster! You're a liar. A *liar!*"

Rough arms hauled her back, squeezing her elbows in a painful grip that took her breath away.

Another officer approached, double rows of buttons gleaming dully down his uniform. "One more display of histrionics and I'll add defamation of character and attempted assault to the charge of murder," he warned. "Do you understand?"

Chest heaving, Thea managed a nod. Abruptly her legs began to tremble and she swayed. The policeman holding her up shifted his grip until it supported, rather than restrained. "What about the defamation of my character?" she asked in a soft but clear voice.

A tornado of silence sucked all the air from the room.

Then Fane laughed. "You see why I was captivated by her? Impulsive, passionate. Cheeky, and courageous.

I admired you, Miss Pickford, but you never should have allowed greed to blacken your soul beyond redemption."

Anger and a thirst for revenge had blackened her soul, not greed. But what did it matter now? "I didn't kill Mrs. Gorman," she stated dully. "You have no proof. I have a companion who can vouch for me. Why haven't you questioned her?"

"A companion who until last night never accompanied you anywhere," Mr. Fane murmured. "Chudd's her name. There is a possibility Miss Pickford hired this woman off the street—she's a sullen, unsuitable creature who deserted her charge immediately after dinner, by the way. In fact, Mrs. Gorman saw her in my library, where she was sound asleep. Such a woman's word is worthless." Shaking his head, he rocked a little on his feet before adding, "There's also the matter of Mrs. Gorman's jewelry, all of which is missing. Perhaps if we searched Miss Pickford's and this companion's rooms at her hotel?"

"The chaperone will be questioned, the room searched once a search warrant has been issued. Mr. Fane, with all due respect we must wait for—"

"Sorry." He smiled, that charming, oh-so-convincing smile to which not even police officers were immune. "I appreciate your duty, Chief Blevins, and in no way wish to trample upon it." Fingers steepled, he added lightly, "However, do not forget that I am the one who made a gift of her to you, saving this department time, expenditure of funds, correct? The need for manpower is already stretched to the limit at the height of the season, is it not? Mrs. Gorman's death is a terrible blow. I merely need to see for myself that Miss Pickford understands she cannot escape the consequences."

The chief cleared his throat. "I have allowed you license, Mr. Fane. But I cannot permit further badgering. Miss

Pickford is entitled to legal counsel, and will have her day in court."

"Of course, of course. By the way, if money is an issue, I am willing to pay her legal fees. As you say, she is entitled—"

"I refuse to accept a nickel of financial assistance from that man, nor will I accept the services of any attorney he hires. Any money he offered would be as—" Barely in time Thea managed to choke back accusations concerning counterfeit money. Who would believe her?

She was innocent, yet about to be dumped in a jail cell. Just like Grandfather. Not fair. Not right. *Not right!* She longed to hurl the charge at every one of these blinded, unreceptive faces. Where was justice? Where was…God? No, why ask? She was the one who had turned her back on God.

"Could we let her sit?" the officer who had escorted her to police headquarters asked. "She looks a mite unsteady on her feet."

A chair was produced, and not unkindly, Thea was pressed down onto the hard wooden seat. Someone thrust a tin cup of water into her hand. Her teeth chattered against the rim, but she managed to choke down a sip.

And Edgar Fane watched, satisfaction stamped over his handsome face. "Not so confident now, are we?" he said, the hard brown eyes boring into hers. "You believed Cynthia to be your competition, even though she went out of her way to treat you with kindness. Secretly you hated her—I witnessed it all, remember. Your hatred, and the fear when you finally realized the depth of my affection for her and that all your schemes had failed."

He surveyed the circle of stolid faces surrounding them. "I realize now I shouldn't have tried to befriend a young woman out of kindness, nor confided to her my true feelings for Mrs. Gorman. There's not a man among us who hasn't shuddered before the wrath of a woman scorned. Admit to your crime of passion, Miss Pickford, and let's be done."

Mutely Thea shook her head. Edgar leaned over her, his low voice an undertow that sucked her into a whirlpool of horror. "I'll never forget the sight of her lifeless body, and the marks on her neck," he said. "Paid some cutthroat to garrote her, right? Did you use some of the jewelry you stole from her body to pay him?"

"All right, Mr. Fane. That's enough, eh?"

Abruptly he swiveled on his heel and stalked away. "Almost, Officer. Almost enough. Chief Blevins, I appreciate your bending the rules. If there's any other paperwork you need me to sign, you know where to find me."

"You're leaving Thursday, for Boston?"

"The clerk already has the address where I can be reached. But first I'll make a trip down to New York City, where Mrs. Gorman's mother resides. Oh—one last thing. You'll want to talk to my secretary, Simpson, about the 'Pickford' name. He did some preliminary investigation on the girl and found some discrepancies, though regretfully I told him not to bother with a more in-depth search. She looked so innocent. Even now, it's hard to believe...."

Vaguely Thea listened to the steady tread of footsteps fading into the distance. She heard a door open and close. He was gone, but his taint still coated her in its deadly mist.

Edgar Fane was gone, and she had no one to blame but herself for the willful self-destruction that might end with her own neck in a hangman's noose.

# Chapter Eighteen

It was a little past five o'clock. Devlin paced the train platform, checked his watch for the third time in five minutes
and suppressed the need to kick the depot's brick wall.
Fortunately from down the track the shriek of a whistle
finally pierced the air and a moment later the train chugged
to a hissing standstill by the covered platform. Shortly
thereafter Dev greeted Operative Brian Flannery, from
the New York City office. The operative grabbed a bulging Gladstone bag from the baggage cart and flipped the
handler a quarter. On the short walk from the depot to the
jail, Dev supplied details of the case Flannery hadn't heard
via telegram and telephone.

"...and while I'm not prepared to say Lunt's the Hotel
Hustler, he's definitely been passing bogus bills, mostly
twenties and hundreds. Wish I'd been able to nab him
earlier, but at least the timing finally worked out. He made
a mistake. I happened to be in the vicinity."

"Better to be lucky than wise, my granny used to
say."

Dev nodded, though he still wondered privately if
there was something other than coincidence at work here.
His father once told him that God's ways were like the

air—largely unseen, but always at work, even when a body didn't feel the current. "Police confiscated another two hundred thousand in counterfeit bills from Lunt's hotel room. I haven't interrogated him myself." He exchanged a rueful look with Flannery. "Chief Hazen agreed with my decision to identify myself only to the Chief of Police. Keep my cover intact. Chief Blevins secured a room for me in the basement of the Town Hall to examine the bills, and promised nobody would bother me, or know I was there." It had been a strange, lonely feeling, sequestered in a silent room while above and all around him people went about their business and, please, God, discovered the identity of the dead woman.

It was irrational, but until he could snatch a moment to talk to Thea…

"And?" Flannery asked impatiently.

Dev pinched the bridge of his nose. "Sorry. Long night, longer day. Over the past three hours I've examined about half the bills he tried to pass at the racetrack. Superb quality forgeries, but so far none of them bear the Hustler's mark. A couple with marred head vignettes, some where the Treasury seal is off a hair." He grimaced, flexed his stiff shoulders. "We're close, but not close enough. I haven't had enough experience to be able to tell where the paper came from, but even if Lunt's not the Hustler I can prove they're counterfeit, and that Lunt knew it."

Flannery swore cheerfully and clapped a freckled paw of a hand on Dev's shoulder. "You've done better than the rest of us, boyo. Uncanny, they tell me, after only a couple years' experience how you sniff out fakes and liars. This time we're that close. I feel it in me bones. Y'know, for someone who enjoys shoveling horse manure, you ought to look happier, not like a bloke on his way to a funeral."

Devlin's heart gave a quick flip. "Manure makes good fertilizer, and clean stalls make for healthy horses."

"You're a cipher, Devlin me boy. A regular cipher," Flannery said, sky-blue eyes alight with sympathy. "Say, you're not planning to up and quit over this Hustler business, are you?"

"No. I plan to get that boil on the Treasury's backside behind bars, whatever it takes, Brian." He smacked a fist against his open palm while he talked, hoping to relieve some of the internal pressure. "Arrogant peacock of a man. Those little clues he leaves on some of his work are nothing but jabs at the Service."

"Still on c-notes or tenners? Same mark, but never the same place?"

Dev gloomily nodded. "Before I came up here I spent a week examining two dozen different bogus bills recovered from the New York job so I'd at least know what to look for. I thought I'd come up with a good scheme, hunting in his own turf, so to speak, without draining the Treasury coffers. But unless Lunt ponies up some names…" There was little value in self-flagellation, so Devlin shut his mouth and shrugged his shoulders.

"Gotten a few stinging telegrams and a letter or two from Washington, hmm?"

Brian's easy sympathy soothed, lightening the yoke of too much responsibility and too few results. "I'm not the chief's favorite operative at the moment. He's wanting Lunt to be the Hustler, and I wish I could agree. But I don't. The Hustler's too smart to be caught publicly in a lie, with the goods scattered for all to see."

They paused in front of the Town Hall, and Brian glanced at the two stone lions. "I like your guard dogs. We could use a pair of 'em downstate, somewhere in our little village."

For the first time in days, Devlin laughed. "I'm sure the architect would be flattered by the prospect." A noisy party of tourists was approaching; the two men exchanged looks. "I'll leave you here," Dev said in an undertone. "I have an errand to run. Good luck with Lunt."

"Aye. Don't you worry, lad. You might be the best at sniffing out a liar, but I'm the best at the art of nonviolent, perfectly legal interrogation." With a wink and jaunty tip of his bowler, Brian Flannery strolled up the steps into the building.

The hands of the clock in the bell tower read seven minutes past six. *A quick quarter of an hour,* Devlin thought. That's all he would allow himself to focus on something other than a table piled with counterfeit bills. Long enough to make sure Thea had survived the aftermath of her evening with Edgar Fane. She'd be wondering where he was, because he'd promised to watch over her. A man ought to keep his promises…especially when the man's honor slipped its leash and he kissed an innocent woman without asking permission.

*She'd kissed him back, melting against him, holding him with fervent abandon. And her eyes…dark, mysterious and luminous—the expression in those lovely eyes would be lodged forever in his head.* A need he'd ignored for twenty-four interminable hours slammed into Dev. Need, mixed with that pinprick of fear. Inside the hotel, he bounded up the stairs two at a time.

Mrs. Chudd answered his knock, her countenance as welcoming as a hailstorm.

"I'm here to see Miss Lang."

"Wrong room." She started to close the door in his face.

"Wait. You are Mrs. Chudd?" As a precaution he planted a large booted foot in the doorway.

"Who's asking?" A tall, spare woman with mouse-brown hair and a formidable Roman nose, Thea's chaperone eyed the foot in the door, then favored Devlin with a disapproving scowl. "Your name?" she repeated, crossing her arms.

"My name is Devlin Stone, and I've had the pleasure of Miss Lang's company on several occasions these past weeks. Could I—"

"Don't see how, when you don't even know her name."

"Ah." Jaw muscles clenched, Dev fought for patience. However rude her manner, this woman was doing her best to protect Thea. "How about I stopped by to inquire about Miss Theodora Pickford?"

Relief flickered across her face before suspicion returned. "Police send you?"

*The police?* He felt mule-kicked, breath backed up in his lungs and ringing in his ears. "No, ma'am. I'm just a friend." He finally noticed the signs of strain in the lines on either side of Mrs. Chudd's mouth, and the beads of perspiration dotting her upper lip. "I'd like to think I'm a good friend, someone Miss Pickford trusts. Where is she? What's this about the police?" Foreboding stirred greasily in his gut. "Mrs. Chudd, I know Pickford isn't her true surname, and I know she had dinner last night with Edgar Fane. I know she hates him as much as she fears him. I want to help her, I promise. Just…let me see her. Please." *The police?*

For an interminable stretch of time Mrs. Chudd contemplated the floor, one bony-fingered hand rubbing circles over her elbow. Finally she lifted her head. "You wait here. I've got a note. I'll just fetch it and you can deal with the mess," she muttered, shaking her head. "Girl's got herself in trouble, I say, and only herself to blame."

Five minutes later Devlin left her standing openmouthed in the doorway as he sprinted back down the hall.

A crowd had gathered outside the Town Hall, with a line meandering up onto the piazza. Most of the men wore black tie and tails, and the women's costumes were frothed-up creations of silk and lace with jewelry sprinkled from head to toe—something going on in the opera house on the upper floor, Devlin remembered, slowing his step and pasting a bland smile on his face to deflect curious eyes. Urgency pounded with a heavy fist but he sauntered, absently nodding as he made his way down the hall to police headquarters.

He opened the door.

Thea, her wrists handcuffed, was being led by a police-man toward the doorway to the cells.

If she focused on minutiae she could survive—the heavy weight of the handcuffs, the Wanted posters on the wall, the brass doorknob. A battered spittoon. Panic swelled when a large-knuckled hand closed over the knob and turned it. *They were going to put her in a cell, a dark cell devoid of light, like her grandfather.* He'd been a broken man ever since. No matter how hard Thea tried, she hadn't been able to piece him back together. If she couldn't help the only person in the world who loved her, how could she hope to help herself?

"This way, miss."

She jerked, staring up at the flushed freckled face. "Won't be so bad," he said. "See, I'm putting you on the end, in a cell by yourself. Only got two other inmates, see—and one o' them's being interrogated elsewhere." He paused, adding in a gruff rumble, "Sorry, miss."

"Not your fault." Her limbs might rattle like skeleton's

bones but at least she managed to keep her voice free of tremors. "I am innocent, you know. I didn't kill her."

"Ha! They all say that!" the incarcerated man in the other cell called. He shook a fist through the bars. "What kind of copper are you, locking up a pretty little thing like that?"

"Shut yer trap, Girard, or I'll feed ya some brass knuckles."

Thea shuddered; a strange buzzing filled her ears. When the door clanged shut and locked her inside the cell, her mind went sheet-blank. She stood in the middle of the floor, terrified to move because if she moved everything would be real, she would understand that she'd just been arrested for murder and nobody...nobody on earth or in heaven was going to stand up for her. She had been efficiently erased from life. Hope? Hope had shriveled into a dry husk.

Devlin had made her a promise. Like every other person in her life except her grandfather, Devlin Stone had let her down. They had exchanged a kiss and she'd made the mistake of allowing herself to believe. To hope she was someone of value.

Now she knew the truth: Theodora Langston should never have been born. Her life was a mistake, created from a moment or two of carelessness, and nothing she had done her entire life could atone for that inconvenience.

Belief in someone or something—love, hope, purpose— hurt too much.

Each movement was an effort; like a mortally wounded animal, Thea crept to the darkest corner of the cell. Back pressed against the unforgiving wall, she huddled in the arid wasteland of her misery.

# Chapter Nineteen

The door to the outer offices opened; Thea didn't bother to lift her head. A low rumbling of masculine voices ensued, followed by the scrape of hurried footsteps.

"Miss Pickford? Thea? For the love of Pete, man, how could you do this to her?" Keys rattled in the lock and the cell door swung open. "Thea? It's all right, now. You're free. Officer, stand back, please. Last thing she needs is crowding. Blast it all, she's shaking like a leaf." Unlike the anger-riddled words, warm hands closed gently around her arms, tugged her up, led her forward into the garish light and loud masculine voices. She winced away. The angry words softened to a coaxing drawl. "Shh, now. Don't struggle. I've come to take you out of here, Thea. Do you understand? The charges have been dropped. You're free."

Thea blinked slowly, lifted her head. A man's face swam above her, a blur of angles and planes with unruly locks of hair that reminded her of Devlin. *God? Help me, please?* Fear had finally tipped her mind into hallucinations. She didn't believe in dreams with happy endings. She couldn't....

Yet the hands propelling her forward didn't feel like

a delusion. *Devlin?* Could this really be…? Somehow he had found her. He had kept his promise. The truth trickled through, dim but persistent. She tried to say his name, her voice a hoarse whisper. "D-Devlin?"

Somehow he heard. "Yes. It's Devlin." He shifted, wrapping one arm around her shoulders in a comforting grip. "I didn't know you were here until I talked to Mrs. Chudd. I'm sorry, Thea. But it's all right—you're all right." A husky note deepened his voice. "You're alive.…"

"They think I killed Mrs. Gorman."

"Not anymore they don't. Here we go, that's it, through the door. I've got you, and I won't let go."

His hand closed over her fingers, which she belatedly realized had dug like frenzied claws into his forearm. "Sorry."

Devlin whispered something she didn't catch, because the Chief of Police suddenly loomed in front of her and reflexively Thea shrank against Devlin.

"Miss Pickford." Hands clasped behind his back, Chief Blevins regarded her in ponderous silence, then shook his head. "Mr. Stone has signed an affidavit. In it, he states that after your dinner with Mr. Fane, he observed Mr. Fane handing you and your companion into his carriage at approximately twenty minutes past ten. Mr. Stone followed the carriage back to the Grand Union Hotel, then followed you and your companion until both of you entered your room. At this point Mr. Stone kept watch in a small lounge with a view of your door. A private night security guard employed by the Grand Union has corroborated Mr. Stone's presence there on two separate occasions as he made his rounds, until approximately 2:15 a.m. this morning."

"I don't understand." Thea passed her tongue around her rubbery lips. She'd doubted, when all along, unknown and unseen, Devlin had in fact been her bodyguard. Thinking hurt her head as well as her heart; sighing, she tried to focus on Chief Blevins. "I could have left my room, after two-fifteen."

A glimmer of some emotion lightened the police chief's tired eyes. "Yes, you could have. But not, I think, for the purpose of committing murder. The physician who examined Mrs. Gorman's remains has determined that death occurred well before midnight. You're free to go, Miss Pickford. I'm sure you and Mr. Stone wish to discuss his reasons for standing guard over you. Before you leave, however, please accept my profound apologies for your ordeal."

"Policemen don't apologize," she murmured.

Chief Blevins stiffened, but he answered equably, "This one does." His gaze shifted to Devlin. "You'll see to her care? When she's sufficiently recovered we might need to question her further about her last encounter with Mrs. Gorman." He paused, adding heavily, "But without Mr. Fane present. Try to understand, see. He and his family are well-known in these parts. Their generosity and affection for Saratoga has long been enjoyed by all. There was no reason to doubt the authenticity of Mr. Fane's shock, or his accusations. I allowed him to question this young woman against my better judgment. It won't happen again."

Tremors started inside Thea despite Devlin's comforting hold, which tightened further when she couldn't control the shakes. "Understood, Chief Blevins," he said. "We'll discuss it in more depth later. Right now, I'm taking Miss Pickford to her hotel room. Could someone provide a buggy?"

Moments later Devlin lifted her inside a run-down piano box buggy. Fervently Thea rubbed her fingers over the worn seat, inhaled the odor of old leather and stale perspiration, which smelled like a bouquet of roses because it meant she really was no longer in a cage. She was free. Safe.

Despite the mild summer night, after raising the top, Devlin tucked a scratchy woolen blanket around her, and only then did Thea realize she was still shivering. *Devlin came,* she repeated to herself over and over, struggling to believe the nightmare had ended. Struggling even more to comprehend that this man cared enough to bother.

He sprang into the seat beside her and lifted the reins. "Five minutes," he promised. "Mrs. Chudd can fetch some hot tea and toast. Can you hold on that much longer?"

"Yes. But I don't need tea or toast. I need to talk. It's just…I can't seem to stop shaking." A watery laugh trickled out, and she clutched the rough wool fabric, wishing it were his arm. "You came…you came for me."

"Would have a lot sooner, had I known." The buggy lurched into motion. "Thea…I really am sorry."

"Don't apologize. Please." She choked back tears. "I'm the one who needs to apologize to you, Devlin. I should have told you days ago who I am, and why I'm chasing Edgar Fane. But I was stubborn and foolhardy and…and afraid. If you knew who I was, if you knew my family, I was afraid you'd disappear. It's what I deserve, but I—I—"

"It's all right, sweetheart." With disarming swiftness he shifted in the seat and leaned to brush a kiss against her snarled hair. "Rest. Later you can tell me whatever you need to. I'm not going anywhere."

"You might change your mind, and I wouldn't blame you." Her voice broke at last but shock and relief and terror finally undermined the last of Thea's equanimity. "Devlin, I need to tell you the truth. The truth. Have you ever thought about truth? Is there a truth that stays the

same, and no matter how a person twists and turns things
about, the truth remains? Some of what Edgar told the
police was true, but he—he twisted it into lies yet the
police believed him. I told the police nothing but the truth,
only they didn't believe me because I've told so many lies.
Not because I wanted to deceive them, or all the people
I've met here, or you. Most especially you. Devlin…" She
covered her face with her hands. "God help me, I'm no
different from Edgar Fane. Do you think God can forgive
a liar? Can you?"

"Thea…" He spoke her name on a long, tired sigh. "For
most of my life, I've hated liars. When my father died,
my mother wanted to return to New York, but she also
wanted me to appreciate my father's heritage—StoneHill
Farm. She promised that if I waited in Virginia until I was
eighteen, then I could come to New York, and choose for
myself the life I wanted. She promised to write. Only I
never heard from her again. Then there was Sylvia. After
that, I pretty much funneled everything into a blind hatred
for liars."

He pulled the buggy up in front of the hotel.

They were both lost souls, but knowing brought desola-
tion, not comfort. "I don't want to go inside yet," Thea
admitted. "I can't face other people, even Mrs. Chudd."
Couldn't face the self-excoriation, couldn't face Mrs.
Chudd's indifference that contrasted too sharply with Devlin's solicitousness. "I…can we walk? I need to feel—"
Her mouth worked, but she couldn't explain the atavistic
need to at least reassert her physical freedom, to know she
could walk or run or skip anywhere she pleased without
fear a policeman would haul her off to jail.

Penance, however, still shackled her mind. "I need to
ask your forgiveness," she finally said, unable to look at
him. "Even though I don't deserve it." After this night

was over, he would vanish from her life because he hated liars.

"If you want to walk, we'll walk, sweet pea," Devlin drawled, the lazy Southern voice wrapping Thea up like a hug. His movements unhurried, he helped her down. "Sounds like we both have some millstones to lay down, hmm?"

They wound their way through the night, around guests enjoying their own perambulations, past the brightly lit restaurants and hotels where music from the nightly ritual of hops and dances drifted through opened windows. Eventually they reached a quiet residential street, where Thea could feel the cool night breeze on her face. Above them, a star-spangled sky and a fingernail moon dispelled much of the horror of the last hours.

"I'm ready now," she finally said. "I won't blubber all over you anymore, nor ask philosophical questions you don't want to answer."

"Mmm. How about if I find your tears and questions irresistible, almost as much as I do you—no matter who you are? Which, by the by, I'd really like to know before I kiss you again."

Thea stopped dead in her tracks, her heart rhythm bumping painfully against her ribs. "You're going to kiss me again? Why? I'm a liar, just like Edgar. You hate liars."

"Absolutely we're going to share a kiss. As for the rest… well, you never let me answer your question."

"What question?"

He laughed, and before the sound died his head lowered, his warm breath gusting against her cheek just before he pressed a light kiss against her lips. "The philosophical one. Where I try to explain why I'm thinking that God wouldn't be God if He didn't forgive a liar, when Jesus reportedly forgave a murdering thief from the cross. If He could do that while dying in agony, well…I need to rethink my own attitude. Mostly I'm trying to change it because of you. While we're on the subject—don't ever compare yourself to Edgar Fane again. Unlike that double-tongued cur, you're not a liar by inclination, Theodora. I saw that, weeks ago. I just didn't understand the 'whys.'"

"I don't know anymore." The nearest streetlight was a block away. In the darkness, that brief kiss had taken on a life of its own. Thea wanted to lay her head against Devlin's sturdy shoulder and cling; she wanted to grab the lapels of his jacket and press her mouth against his for another kiss; more than anything, she wanted to be free of Theodora Pickford.

And she wanted to know if God could accept her as compassionately as Devlin.

Only one way to test them both…

## Chapter Twenty

Resolution pushed through her in a furious gust. "My name is Theodora Langston. My mother's maiden name is Pickford. She's a vaudeville singer, and I have no idea whether or not she's still alive. I live on Staten Island with my paternal grandfather because my mother deserted my father a month after I was born. My father didn't know what to do with a baby, so he dumped me on Grandfather and left, too. His name is Richard, and he's a professional gambler now. Nothing matters to him but the next hand, or the next roll of the dice, certainly not his daughter. So you might say I understand better than most how you felt when your mother abandoned you."

"You might say that," Devlin responded after a prolonged tense moment. "So…your grandfather reared you? His name was Langston, I take it?"

"Yes. Charles Langston." Most men were awkward with female emotions, particularly dramatic displays of it. Thea shrugged aside his curt tone, her relief over finally sharing the truth filling her with giddiness. Confession apparently *was* good for the soul. *All right, Lord. I'll try.* "My father used to send me souvenir cards from wherever he happened to be. Grandfather was ashamed of him, but never

gave up hope that one day his son would return home."
She chewed her lip a moment. "I did. The last card arrived
two months after my tenth birthday. But at least I knew
my grandfather loved me. Then Edgar Fane entered our
lives."

"Ah. The serpent in the garden. Why didn't he recognize
you here, Thea?"

He still spoke in that strange, carefully neutral tone,
perhaps to calm her? Grateful, Thea struggled to emulate
it. "He'd come to the island to visit one of his friends, met
my grandfather at a lawn party. Grandfather liked him.
*Everybody* always likes him. I never met him or I'd probably have been equally gullible. But I'd been trying to
take over the reins of the publishing company Grandfather
owned. I spent all my days in the City. The imprint was
prestigious, but small. Times were bad—we still hadn't
recovered from the Panic of '93 and Grandfather was concerned for my future."

Her voice wobbled, and without comment Devlin
wrapped his hand around her forearm in a warm clasp.
"There was the threat of bankruptcy. That we'd lose everything. There's no other family—Grandfather lost his wife
and three other children in a ferry accident when I was
three. Edgar Fane persuaded him to sell a piece of land
Grandfather owned near Central Park—promised him top
dollar. He also persuaded him to sell Porphyry Press. 'It
will still be your company,' he promised. And he told
Grandfather not to worry, he would take care of everything. His father is one of the richest men in America.
Our lives, and our financial security, would be safe. We
believed him!"

"His stock-in-trade," Devlin said. Shifting, his arm came
around Thea's shoulders, a sturdy buffer despite the anger
rife in his voice. "I understand, Thea. Try to relax."

"Not the worst!" she cried, twisting free of the comfort she craved but wouldn't accept. "You still don't understand the worst of it. Devlin, Edgar Fane is not just a criminal. He's *evil*. He paid Grandfather in cash, told him that way Grandfather would know the money was real. But it wasn't. It wasn't real!"

Arms wrapped around herself, she hurled each angry word. "He paid with counterfeit bills, and when Grandfather went to deposit the money the police and S-Secret Service arrested him. They arrested my grandfather and put him in jail. And now Edgar Fane has done the same thing to me and he's the one who's guilty. He's a filthy counterfeiter, and a liar. And if he's responsible for what happened to Mrs. Gorman then he's a murderer, too. I wanted to catch him, wanted justice! Why couldn't they see…" Her voice thickened, and in an outpouring of impotent rage she suddenly turned to pound her fists against Devlin's chest instead. "I loathe Edgar. *Hate him*. Him and the police and the Secret Service because they should have known. They should have known he was a liar. Nobody believed me, because I turned into a liar, too. I hate myself.…"

"I believe you, Thea." Dev folded his hands over hers, stilling the blows, prying open the fists. "I believe you."

Thea continued to struggle, and Devlin reacted instinctively, stanching the anguished fury of words with his mouth. "I believe you," he whispered again and again against trembling lips, his voice hoarse. "I believe you.… I need you to believe in me." When at last she melted against him, her arms lifting to slide around his neck, Dev forgot about the danger, forgot about circumstances, forgot everything but the incendiary joy consuming him.

This woman was meant to be *his*.

He kissed her eyelids, tasting the bittersweet saltiness of

her tears, her hot damp cheeks. Heard the soft gasps, felt the frantic need in her that met and matched his own.

In the darkness behind him the faint sound of clip-clopping hooves and the soft sputter of buggy wheels rolling along the street drifted into his ears. When the horse snorted, Devlin jerked his head up, then on a muffled groan yanked himself free of Thea's embrace and took two backward steps.

By the time the buggy rolled past, his head was almost clear enough to manage a single sentence. "I didn't mean to do that."

In the starlight he watched her blink rapidly, watched the incandescent softness freeze into a brittle woman with haunted eyes. "I didn't either," she said, but she touched her lips with fingers that trembled.

Watching her, Devlin inhaled a sobering breath of night air. "If I can keep my hands to myself, will you listen to me?" he asked. "It's important."

He felt like a man on a rack. For most of his life nothing, not even StoneHill, had filled that misshaped, ill-defined piece of Devlin that forever seemed to be…listening. Waiting. Searching for whatever it was that would fit itself into that misshapen piece, and make him whole.

Uncle J. told him more often than Dev cared to hear that likely the "feeling" would pester him the rest of his life. "You'll always have a home, and the horses, and I know you love 'em as much as a man can. It's a crying shame you lost your folks when your head weren't no higher than a Shire's knees. The thing is, lad, you can't spend your life looking for 'em."

And just when Dev thought he'd finally found the missing piece, he learned that the woman he'd passionately kissed was the granddaughter of Charles *Langston*.

When Thea learned Dev was an operative for the

organization she hated probably as much as Edgar Fane, he would lose her as surely as the sun rose in the east. If he couldn't convince her to trust him now, and she ran for the sanctuary of Staten Island, she might unwittingly run into the arms of a murderer.

Thea wanted to know if God would forgive a liar.

*Are You teaching me a lesson here?* Or was this one of life's crueler ironies, that the woman with whom he was falling in love would never be able to return it?

Grimly he tried to think of a solution other than the perpetuation of his own lie by omission. Couldn't let her go—couldn't share his own deception. *Is there a truth that stays the same, and no matter how a person twists and turns things about, the truth remains?* Thea had asked. Dev didn't have an answer she'd like, but it was the only one he had to offer: he'd do whatever he had to, including withholding his identity as a Secret Service operative, to keep her alive.

Watching her, he ran a hand around the back of his head, then gave her a crooked smile. "Remember the first time we kissed, and I said you tasted of temptation?"

Solemnly she nodded.

"Well…now more than ever, I want to give in to it." He held his hand in front of her face to show her the tremor in his own fingers. "See? But I can't give in. I know I have a lot of flaws, but I wasn't raised that way, Thea. You're a lady, and you're in more trouble than I think you realize. I want to help, not take advantage of you."

"I'm the one who's been taking advantage of you. That first day, when I chased you down, I—I wanted to use you, to get close to Edgar Fane." She focused on some distant point over Dev's left ear. "I might have been a lady once, but not anymore. Perhaps I should try out for the stage."

"Don't be—" He swallowed the words then, impatient

with them both, glared at her. "We'll discuss this, thoroughly, later. Right now we don't have the luxury of time. When Edgar Fane learns you've been released, do you think he's just going to dust you off like a piece of lint on his suit coat?"

"He's leaving day after tomorrow. He thinks I'm in jail. By this time next week he'll have forgotten I exist."

"Not likely. As I heard it, you more or less engaged in a slanging match in front of the entire Saratoga Springs Police force. Why did you do that, Thea? You believe him evil, then why provoke him?"

"I hadn't found another way to convince people who he really is. Why else would I risk my reputation and my future? It's imperative to find proof that will hold up in a court of law. Don't you see? At the very least, he's a counterfeiter, Devlin, and there's no telling how many other lives he's destroyed like he did my grandfather. But he may be guilty of worse. He said I hired someone to murder Cynthia. What if that's what *he's* done? We have to find out, Devlin. We have to."

Her voice had risen; quick as a blink Devlin covered her mouth with his hand. "Shh. Sounds carry at night." Touching her was a mistake. His palm felt branded by the imprint of her lips, and leashed desire strained to stifle further words with another kiss. In the blink of an eye his pale, defeated waif had once again transformed into a fire-breathing dragon. She was also using her agile brain and reaching the same conclusions as Devlin.

He was proud of her—and terrified for her. "Come over here, under this tree. The trunk should muffle some of our words, and we'll be better hidden from those houses." Once there, he planted both hands against the rough tree trunk, trapping Thea without touching her. "At this moment you have no evidence to prove he's a counterfeiter, and no proof other than instinct that he killed Mrs. Gorman, right?"

"No." A long sigh stirred the air. "Devlin...I'm not going to run away. Do you need to stand so close?"

"It's the best I can do, when I promised not to kiss you again." With a rueful half smile he dropped his arms. "Listen. We don't know everything that happened today, but while I was at the station, in between explaining why you couldn't have been party to a murder, I listened, analyzed reactions. I'm quite renowned for my observation skills, remember," he added, hoping to coax at least a small reciprocal smile before he had to whip up the fear again.

"I haven't thanked you, for saving me."

"Shh. I promised I'd be watching, didn't I?"

"Promises are usually only words."

"Not," Dev said, "for me. I spent a score of years, waiting for what turned out to be an empty promise, as empty as the word of the woman who was supposed to be my wife. I bear the scars of betrayal as much as you do, Theodora. So hear me when I tell you I don't make very many promises. But those I do—I keep."

Thea reached out and brushed light fingers over his bicep. Devlin twitched in surprise. "I'm sorry. I didn't mean to hurt your feelings," she said. "But I still need to thank you." And there came the smile, when he least expected it. "I'll listen now, and keep quiet. I believe you were bragging about your gift for reading people?"

Amazing, when he was terrified for her life and weighted with guilt, that she could make him feel lighter than a handful of sun-warmed hay. "Good with people, better with horses," he qualified. "Let's see, where was I? Oh, yes, while, ah, giving my deposition I...um...overheard Chief Blevins order one of his men to initiate a watch on Fane, but to be discreet about it. Do you understand the significance? The police were supplied with sworn testimony that legally required them to arrest you. But that doesn't mean they believed every word Fane told them, even though he's the son of Thaddeus Fane and could raise an almighty stink. They'll be risking their own livelihoods, maintaining surveillance."

"Even so, they won't stop him from leaving. He's guilty, Devlin."

Frustrated because she was right, he nonetheless pushed his point home. "You have to let the law do its job, Thea. It's an imperfect system, and yes, mistakes are made. But your one-woman crusade can also be perceived as vigilante justice."

"I don't want to hang him myself. I just want—" She stopped. "It's not fair. I waited for months, but—" Again she stopped midsentence, once more wrapping her arms around herself in that heartbreaking posture of defensiveness and insecurity.

"You've accomplished more than you realize, but you must consider the consequences of your actions. What might Fane do to the woman who's out to prove him a liar, a cheat—and a murderer?"

"He doesn't know who I really am." The words emerged haltingly. "We never met on Staten Island, remember. To him, I'm just another avaricious skirt out to snare him for a husband. He believes the police didn't listen to me at all—he was gloating about it, Devlin. Why risk harming me when he's already beaten me?"

"When he learns you've been released—and he will—he won't feel victorious. He'll be enraged. Now we have an arrogant, angry man convinced he can do anything he wants. Anything. And the second killing will be easier."

# Chapter Twenty-One

Unable to resist the need, Devlin unwrapped her arms from their protective shield. Urgently he rubbed his thumbs over her knuckles. "You can't stay here any longer. You're in too much danger. Yes, Fane is leaving Saratoga—but his absence makes for a good alibi. One evening you'll be strolling along—and the next morning your body will be found in the bushes. Wherever you go, Fane can have you followed. If you retreat to Staten Island he'll connect you to your grandfather in a heartbeat, and learn your real name. You've already discovered this man will stop at nothing to achieve his ends."

"I hadn't thought that far ahead," Thea admitted, her fingers nervously flexing in his.

"Mmm. You haven't been able to. I have." The possibilities frankly terrified him. "Thea…I don't want anything to happen to you." Nerves, hot and sharp as nails, blistered his spine. "Here's what I've come up with. I want you to come home with me, to StoneHill. Mrs. Chudd, too. And of course we'll arrange for your grandfather to come down. He and Uncle J. would have a grand old time together. My aunt loves to cook for crowds—it's one of her few vanities. And I'll introduce you to the most magnificent horses and the most beautiful piece of land on God's green earth. Most important of all, you'll be safe. Even with all his money and power Edgar Fane won't know how to find you. He won't even know where to look because he doesn't know I exist."

"I—I…what are you saying, Devlin? This is too much." In a frantic motion she tugged her hands free, then abruptly grabbed his again, clutching them with fierce strength. "You can't just sweep up my whole family and our problems and deposit us in the middle of your life. Despite what you say, what's to keep Fane and his band of hired henchmen from learning about you? Someone could follow *you* to StoneHill as easily as they could follow me to Staten Island."

"Chief Blevins has assured me today's events are vaulted within the walls of the Police Department. Nobody else will know I was there at all."

"I don't trust them." Shrouded in the night shadows beneath an old oak tree, all Dev could see was her poignant silhouette, resolute and alone.

"I know you don't. But I do. Trust *me,* Thea." He invested every ounce of confident authority he could muster into the words. "You and Mrs. Chudd will travel to Virginia in perfect anonymity."

"I think I could trust you, Devlin. I do. It's just…" She hesitated, then finished awkwardly, "Going to Virginia wouldn't be, well, proper."

Proper? *Proper?* She'd been arrested and tossed in jail; he'd jeopardized the entire Hotel Hustler operation for her sake and she was turning prudish? Hampered by the one secret he was honor bound to maintain, Dev's frustration got the better of him. "Ha! When have you ever been proper? If I were a wagering fellow, I'd bet your grandfather's had his hands full over the years."

"You'd lose." Her head drooped. "Growing up, I always tried too hard to make people like me. I tried, endlessly, to please them, especially Grandfather. I've spent my entire life atoning for the prodigal son who never returned home, and the tawdry actress daughter-in-law from the Bowery who never wanted me." A wavering catch-breath seared Devlin's ears. "I've never behaved like I have with you, not for my entire life. As for Fane, apparently I'm almost as good an actress as my mother. Now Grandfather might spend the rest of his life being ashamed of his only granddaughter."

"Sorry," Devlin said after a moment. "I'm a cad, I spoke out of turn. What you think about yourself—it's not true about the Theodora I've come to know. That woman is admirable. She's strong-minded, idealistic, principled— No, don't shake your head. You've been playing a part, yes. But from almost the moment we met, you tried to tell me as much of the truth as you felt you could." His mouth was dry as the dust on his boots, but he'd talk the rest of the night to undo the mess he'd made with his thoughtless words. "Let me finish telling you about this woman. She doesn't cower from her fear, she faces it head-on. She fights for what she believes. Your grandfather will be proud of that woman, Thea. He deserves the opportunity to meet her. Come to StoneHill. I can keep you safe—it's the only place where you'll *be* safe, until we—" he barely caught the slip "—until the authorities can deal with Fane."

To distract them both he gave in and slid his hands up her arms to her neck. Tenderly, he stroked the soft skin as he tipped her chin up with his thumbs. "I don't want to lose you, Thea," he whispered again.

"Devlin, please don't say things like that," she said, and faint starlight shone on fresh tears welling in her eyes.

"You don't understand. I don't want to dream, to hope. It hurts too much."

Groaning, he cupped her face. "Do you think I don't know that? We're both of us two abandoned strays, fearful to trust an outstretched hand. But I'm willing to risk another smack, because it couldn't hurt worse than your ending up like Cynthia Gorman."

Her forearms rested lightly against his chest, her palm directly over his heart. "I agree I'm a threat to Edgar Fane. I know I can't stay here. But I can't let him walk away, free to destroy someone else's life. For me that would be an act of cowardice."

"We've talked the subject to death. *Stalking Edgar Fane is not your job.* Leave him to the authorities. They want him off the street every bit as much as you do. I know you've little use for them but the Secret Service's mandate is to track down counterfeiters, and—"

"I will not talk about the Secret Service!" Before he could react, she'd ripped herself away and walked several paces down the street before whirling back around. "I told you, you don't understand! How would you feel if your uncle went into town one day and didn't come back, because some officious lout from the U.S. government had had him tossed in jail? My grandfather is seventy-four years old! But until last November he'd been as strong as you or I, full of vigor and confidence. Now he's a broken man, and it's all because the Secret Service didn't care about the truth."

"Thea…" Dear God, it was more than a man could take. Dev stood, every muscle taut, while the woman he'd fallen in love with verbally assailed the agency he'd sworn an oath to defend and serve. An agency he'd pledged his loyalty to, regardless of the personal cost. *God? I don't know what to do….*

"Devlin, forgive me." The words bridged the broken glass distance between them, but with every soft syllable, more shards punctured his heart. "You can't possibly understand what I'm talking about. You…I never believed a man like you existed. I'd give anything—almost—to accept your offer, and come to StoneHill. But I—I can't."

*A man like him.* Trapped, defensive, for the first time he could remember Devlin couldn't think his way out of a predicament. "Can't, or won't?" he repeated the question he'd tossed at her once before. Only this time the answer mattered, too much. "What will it do to your grandfather when he receives an impersonal visit from one of those operatives you despise, whose sad duty it is to explain how his stubborn, headstrong granddaughter got herself murdered? I can't follow after you indefinitely, like a shadow with strings, trying to protect you from yourself *and* Edgar Fane. I have a life, Thea, and people who depend on me. Horses who trust me to take care of them."

Except all of them had fended quite adequately for themselves without him.

Thea was not the only one with a choice to make. *If he told her he was a Secret Service operative, he'd have to turn in his badge.* The prospect no longer made him flinch, but the illumination smeared Devlin's spirit like soot.

"All right." The statement floated across on a sigh. "All right, Devlin."

"No, it's not all right. Nothing's right about this whole infernal situation."

"I'll come with you to StoneHill."

Devlin's jaw dropped. He shook his head. If a dozen rocks had rattled loose from his brain and rolled onto the ground he wouldn't have been more incredulous. "You'll… come? Just like that, you change your mind?"

"A woman," Thea replied with knife-edged sweetness,

"who upon reflection doesn't change her mind, doesn't possess much of a mind at all. Although, given your response, I have to wonder if I'm losing mine altogether, agreeing to your quixotic proposition. I'm sure Mrs. Chudd will—mmph!"

He silenced her with a kiss.

Some things in life you learned to live with, some things you stood your ground. And some things you held on to, any way you could, regardless of consequences.

"And leave tips for all the household servants with Mrs. Surrey," Edgar instructed Simpson.

The secretary nodded his head while simultaneously slitting open the afternoon mail with an ivory-handled letter opener. "Unused frames were packed up this morning, except for one." Simpson finished opening letters and arranged them in a perfect stack, then glanced up at Edgar. "Do you have further instructions for that frame, sir?"

"We'll deal with it later." Tired of it all, he waved a dismissive hand. "Do you have our train tickets? Verified that one of the family's rolling stock has been added?"

"I have the tickets, and received confirmation while you ate lunch that your father himself arranged for The Wanderer to be made available."

"Good." Abruptly he dismissed his secretary to focus his attention on the Saratoga Springs Police Department, who had proved to be most cooperative.

He must remind Simpson to send along a memo to his parents, requesting them to send another expression of gratitude. Humming beneath his breath, he placed a call to headquarters. "Good afternoon, Chief Blevins," he said cordially some moments later. "My train leaves in a couple of hours. I won't have the opportunity to do so in person, but I wanted to thank you again for your handling of Miss

Pickford's interrogation and subsequent arrest. I've had my secretary draw up a list of local attorneys, should the— What's that? I'm afraid we have a bad connection."

"…and the matter of Miss Pickford…you must understand…no longer at liberty…discuss…"

A moment later Edgar banged the telephone receiver down, kicked over a nearby spittoon, then stalked out into the hallway. A maid dusting furniture squealed in fright when he approached, ripped the dusting cloth from her hands and threw it across the room, then lifted her completely off her feet. "Get out of my way!" he snarled in her face. "And shut up."

"Mr. Fane," Simpson spoke somewhere behind him, "two Jockey Club members have arrived to wish you farewell. Dodd has seen them to the formal parlor in the south wing. Shall I inform them you'll join them in…a quarter of an hour?"

Edgar dropped the paralyzed maid, who gathered her skirts in bone-white fingers and fled for safety. A moment later a door slammed. Slowly Edgar turned around to his blank-faced secretary. "You're a good man, Simpson. How long have you served in your current position?"

"Three years and five months, sir."

"Find the maid. Extend my apologies. Offer a month's wages as compensation. Is that sufficient to retain your loyalty as well as your services?"

"Yes, Mr. Fane."

Edgar nodded. "I'll see the Jockey Club gentlemen. And Simpson? After you soothe the maid, I need you to run one final errand for me. It concerns Miss Pickford."

# Chapter Twenty-Two

*StoneHill Farm, Virginia*

Thea spent much of her first week at StoneHill Farm in a daze. Forty-eight hours after their arrival, with no reports of strangers lurking in the area, Devlin decided Thea could safely wander the property on her own. She sensed his reluctance, but embraced the freedom to explore, especially since she seldom saw Devlin. He rose at dawn, and for the past three nights tramped back to the house after everyone else was in bed.

Both of them were determined—at least on the surface—to put Edgar Fane in the back of the larder. Devlin was utterly absorbed in taking control of the business of the farm once more. Whenever they did have a private moment or two it consisted mostly of a quick smile of apology on Devlin's part, a reassuring murmur on hers that she was perfectly fine, and for him to reacquaint himself with his horses. Much to her surprise, Thea was enjoying serene days, and the most restful sleep she'd experienced in months.

All right, yes. She missed Devlin, yearned for the solicitousness he'd offered at Saratoga and over their long trip south to Virginia. But she was pragmatic enough to know the difference between a summer season at a famous resort and the gritty essence of real life: Devlin was not a gentleman of leisure like Edgar Fane, but a horseman, trainer, breeder.... The more Thea learned about his life at StoneHill, the more she puzzled over why he'd hared off to Saratoga Springs Resort. When an opportunity arose, she planned to ask his true motivation for a summer sabbatical in upstate New York.

The dreamy little girl wanted to beg God's forgiveness and resurrect her faith in a loving heavenly Father, Who by divine design brought her and Devlin together.

The wiser woman was unwilling to lower her guard because, still lurking in a dark corner of that larder, the stubborn avenger refused to give up her quest for justice.

Most days Thea focused her time on exploring Stone-Hill. Devlin had not exaggerated the magnificence of his domain—the main house sat on the crest of a small hill surrounded by three thousand acres of prime bottomland and a view of the Blue Ridge Mountains that brought tears to her eyes, particularly at sunset. To the south, a sweeping panorama of blue sky, broad valley and hazy mountains made her feel paradoxically insignificant, yet able to breathe more deeply than she ever had in her life, secure on a tiny island in the Hudson River.

In green pastures, immense horses grazed in the shimmery heat of late summer. Hired workers gathered hay into towering stacks, while dragonflies and butterflies darted among late-summer wildflowers. Someone had planted hundreds of pink spider lilies and yellow black-eyed Susans around the dry stack stone walls which surrounded the dignified stone-and-brick house. Their sunny colors brightened the sultry air.

StoneHill charmed her with its storybook splendor; Thea

stubbornly refused to fall completely in love with Devlin Stone, but she was utterly captivated by his home.

"Explore all you want," Devlin's Uncle Jeremiah told her in that slow cultured drawl that reminded her of Devlin, "but always wear boots and carry yourself a stout walking stick. Down here in Virginia, we got snakes. Mostly they'll leave you alone, but you have to watch out for the no-legged kind same as you do the two-legged. We got our share of both. Myself, I'd rather deal with a rattler."

Jeremiah possessed a dry wit along with his slow smile. Devlin was right about his uncle—when her grandfather finally arrived the following day, he would like Jeremiah, very much.

A clump of flowers peeking through the grasses at a bend in the creek beckoned. Thea swept her walking stick in front of her, then knelt on the damp earth beside the blossoms. "Look at you," she murmured, feathering her index finger over white-tipped petals, the center of which deepened to rich magenta-colored streaks. "So lovely, yet hidden away by this little creek." It seemed unfair, somehow, for God to have created such a stunning variety of flora most human eyes never beheld.

Apparently her soul still smarted, if she could hold a grudge against the Almighty for his placement of wildflowers.

"They're water willow, but still not as lovely as you." Devlin said behind her. "Here, now!" He lengthened his stride, grabbing her arm just before she tumbled backward into the creek. "Sorry I startled you."

"Well, I was having a private conversation with those flowers." Thea's gaze wandered over his cuffless and collarless lawn shirt, streaked with dirt smears. He looked as different from the urbane gentleman of Saratoga as a farm wagon from a barouche. "What are you doing here? I thought you had a yearling to train."

"I did. She behaved like a little lady, and I wanted to keep it that way. She's back frolicking in the pasture now, but she'll retain a positive memory of our time together."

"I'd like to watch, someday, unless…I'd be too much of a distraction."

"Well, you're a distraction no matter what."

They smiled at each other, and Thea realized only then how lonely she'd felt. "So you hunted me down because you were in need of a diversion?"

His smile deepened, forming the deep creases in his cheeks that never failed to weaken Thea's knees. "I'm headed to the hardware store. Ordered some new harness brackets a while back, and got word the shipment finally arrived. We've had too little time together, so I thought you might like to come along?"

"I suppose I can fit you into my crowded social calendar."

Sunlit sparkles danced through his eyes before they darkened to charcoal. "Do you have any idea how unique you are? I didn't realize until I walked into the barn, the night we arrived, how much I've missed this place, the horses. Thanks for understanding. For not…" He stopped, shaking his head.

"For not whining? Pouting? Making life miserable for you and everyone else?" Thea shrugged, though what she yearned to do was give him a comforting hug. "Of course, if you'd spirited me off to a rickety row house that leaked, with a curmudgeon of a housekeeper—"

"Bessie is a curmudgeon."

"But a lovable one. Believe it or not, she and Mrs. Chudd have formed a bizarre friendship. Bessie tempts her with Southern cooking, and Mrs. Chudd turns her nose up.

Then they both cackle." She yielded to the temptation and brushed a dried clump of mud off his sleeve, just so she could touch him. "I'm at peace here, Devlin, I promise. StoneHill is even more breathtaking than your descriptions. Don't worry about me. I plan to savor every moment, including the few I can share with you." *Especially those,* she admitted silently.

As they walked back down the path, shoulders brushing, hands swinging inches apart, Thea sneaked sidelong glances, and told herself she was seven kinds of a fool to pretend their lives could last beyond an announcement of Edgar Fane's arrest.

"Something on your mind?" Devlin asked softly just before they left the woods. "The smile has left your eyes. You seem…preoccupied. Not afraid of going for an outing, are you? No dizziness?"

"I haven't been afraid since the train pulled out of Saratoga Springs, Devlin. Not a dizzy spell in sight."

"Good." His hand descended onto her arm, bringing her to a halt. "But I'm still sorry I haven't been able to keep you company, show you around. Once I catch up, I promise things will change."

"This is your home, your life. You love it, that's all. I don't know how you were able to leave it for so long." Or why…

The creases in his cheeks disappeared, and a shadow darkened his eyes. "I'm wondering the same thing," he said. "Human nature, I suppose, to not miss something until you don't have it anymore."

Abruptly he released her and resumed walking at a ground-eating pace. "We'd better hurry if we're going to make it to town and back before dark. Bessie's not shy about her feelings when someone's late for supper. And Mrs. Chudd's silences fill in the rest."

An hour later they rattled into the small community of Stuarts Crossing, a one-street assortment of aging brick buildings shaded by huge old trees. The hardware store was situated between two massive sycamores. A general store sat on the corner across the street, and a little past the hardware a post office had been built the previous year, Devlin told her. "We're on the map now," he said as he helped Thea down. "Bessie doesn't have to wait an extra week when she orders something from the Sears Roebuck catalog." He ran an affectionate hand over the sweating flanks of Dulcinea, the placid Percheron whose gray color just about matched Devlin's eyes. "I need to talk some business for a few moments, as well as pick up my order. Instead of perusing rows of tools, turpentine and nails, you might prefer Gilpen's Mercantile. We're not New York City here, but—"

"Neither," Thea interrupted him levelly, "am I."

A farm wagon rumbled past. Devlin stood, chagrin in his eyes and annoyance thinning his mouth. "I don't know what I'm going to do," he finally muttered half under his breath. "Thea…"

"You're going to take care of business," Thea told him, "and I'm going to go find a hostess gift for Bessie." With a firm nod and a hand wave, she hurried away before her resolve wilted like the sad row of asters drooping from twin flower boxes in front of the post office.

# Chapter Twenty-Three

Devlin watched her stroll across the packed dirt-and-gravel roadway, his pride and his heart smarting. Didn't matter which hurt worse. How was a man supposed to accept spiritual guidance when life was a confounded mess? If God chose to soften his heart with an irresistible woman, He could at least have chosen one who didn't despise his current profession. If only—with an impatient swat at a hovering bee Devlin cut off the litany of "if onlys."

As soon as Thea disappeared inside the mercantile he grimly focused his gaze on the end of the street, and the dust-coated surrey slowly making its way toward him. Lawlor was late; Devlin had expected him to be waiting inside the hardware store. They could have shared their brief reconnoiter in relative privacy. Then he noticed two other men in the surrey with Lawlor. Fellow agents? They looked familiar. Devlin's jaw hardened. He went into the hardware to pay for the harness brackets.

Ten minutes later, after stacking a half-dozen boxes in the buggy, he straightened to scan the street. Conscious of the possibility of curious eyes, especially Thea's, he noted the location of every person in sight. Footsteps scraped on the walk outside the Post Office, and without haste he strolled over under the shade of one of the sycamores to meet the trio of men. He never should have yielded to his need and invited Thea to accompany him to town.

Three pairs of narrowed eyes monitored his approach, but it was the gent wearing the navy striped suit, liberally coated with road dust, who stepped forward.

"Good afternoon. We're reporters from the Washington *Evening Star.* M'name's Lawlor. Other two gents are Mr. Wolfred and Mr. Amos. We're looking for a Devlin Stone, of StoneHill Farm?"

"Reporters, hmm? And why would three gentlemen of the press travel all this way to see a farmer?"

Amos, a slight young fellow with wire-rimmed spectacles and a severe case of acne, unwound the string from a portfolio and withdrew a newspaper. "P-perhaps this will explain." Splotches of red stained his cheeks as he held out the paper, but the mild brown eyes stayed steady on Devlin. "P-page eight, right column."

"So you know Stone's a farmer?" Lawlor said. "We'd appreciate your help in locating him, or his farm."

"You were the one who indicated he lived on a place called StoneHill *Farm.* Why are you looking for him?" Devlin countered without looking up from his perusal of the underlined article. "What does the murder of a society woman at Saratoga Springs Resort in upstate New York have to do with Devlin Stone?"

"Well, rumors are spreading thick and fast that Mr. Stone is a person of interest in this case." The third man, Wolfred, lifted a bushy black brow when Devlin made no comment. "He was seen at the Saratoga Springs police headquarters the same day the body was discovered, but then he disappeared. Police and an untold number of other private investigators from Boston to Richmond are eager to learn his whereabouts."

"I have an acquaintance in the D.C. Detective Bureau," Lawlor added casually. "When we…ah…discovered Devlin Stone was purportedly from the state of Virginia, only a day's train ride away from Washington, well, we thought we'd see what we could find out."

"So you're after a story, hoping to track down this man. Sell papers with whatever you discover?" Devlin folded the newspaper and tucked it under his arm. "I think you gentlemen have made a long trip for nothing."

"Maybe so." Wolfred pursed his lips, his index finger rubbing up and down his striped suspenders. "But there's another rumor floating south, one all three of us decided deserved closer investigation, as well. Has to do with one of the richest men in the whole blamed country, or at least the man's son—Edgar Fane?"

"Heard the name in passing," Devlin commented, every muscle in his body tensing when, from the corner of his eye, he watched Thea exit Gilpen's Mercantile. Her face lit up in a smile until she caught sight of the three men, who from her angle probably looked as though they'd surrounded Dev. His mind spun out a list of possible consequences of hastily spoken words on her part, none of them good.

Still he had to say something, anything, but even as he opened his mouth it was too late.

"Who on earth are these men, Lemuel?" Thea called in a Southern accent thick enough to suffocate a bull. Smiling prettily, she sashayed right up next to Devlin, and gave the others a blinding smile. "Y'all look like you've been drug through a plowed field. Come a long way?"

"Yes'm. We…ah, p-p-perhaps you know…" Amos's

stutter trailed away as he darted quick looks at the two other men, then Devlin.

"We're looking for Mr. Devlin Stone. Do you know him?" Lawlor's blunt statement didn't faze Thea, who tipped her head to one side as though she were thinking hard.

"Name's familiar," she offered with an apologetic fluttering of her eyes. "Is he from hereabouts?"

The men exchanged looks, while Devlin struggled to keep his expression suitably noncommittal. "We think so," Lawlor finally admitted. "Heard he owned a horse farm."

"Well, if y'all don't know, then you must not be friends." Thea shrugged. "Sorry we can't help, but it's getting on for suppertime, so we best be heading for home." She nodded to the men, then turned to Devlin. "Don't stand there gawking. We need to go, Lem." She flashed the three flummoxed-looking men a final smile. "I hope you find Mr. Stone."

"If we don't, others might have better luck," Wolfred said. "All right, then. Let's go, boys. I don't much fancy taking this road back up the hill after dark." He touched the brim of his homburg. "Ma'am, sir."

The three men trudged past Devlin without further comment, though all of them slid heavy-lidded looks Thea's way as they piled into the surrey. Lawlor jumped into the driver's seat, then paused, fishing around inside his jacket. "One thing, Mr.—I'm sorry, I don't believe I ever caught your surname."

"Didn't give it," Devlin shot back, one hand lifting to Thea's shoulder, gripping it with enough force that she pressed her lips together and kept silent. "Don't see the need. I don't much cotton to nosy reporters from Washington, or anywhere else, poking their noses in a man's life."

"Freedom of the press." Lawlor pulled out a small card and thrust it toward Devlin. "It's true enough, there's those who don't care overmuch for myself and my colleagues. But they still buy newspapers—and read every word. If you hear anything of interest about Mr. Stone, I'd appreciate it if you'd let me know. Address is right there on the card."

Devlin nodded. So. Three bodyguards would now be prowling the sylvan vales of northwestern Loudoun County, ears and eyes perked for anyone interested in Devlin as well as Thea. Deep in thought, he stood without speaking by her, though he softened his grip, surreptitiously stroking the taut tendon connecting her neck and shoulder. Only after the buggy turned onto the road that wound its way up to the turnpike did he look down at the amazing woman beside him. "A performance worthy of Miss Pickford. What made you pretend I wasn't Devlin Stone, Thea?"

"I could tell you were discomposed, and I didn't know if it was because those men were threatening you—or because you were scared I'd say something you didn't want them to hear." Eyes dark, she searched his face. "I thought you might not want them to know who either of us were. You say they were reporters? Are you in danger because of me, Devlin?"

"What," Dev managed when he could find his tongue, "made you think I was…ah…discomposed?"

"You're not the only one who notices things, Devlin Stone. It's the way you held your shoulders, how your head was up and back—and there's an expression, actually it's more of a complete absence of expression, like you're trying very hard to keep any emotion from showing on your face. You looked at me like that, the day I stumbled over you in the Saratoga stables."

There was no help for it. Devlin slid his hand down to her wrist, tugging her until their noses bumped. "If we were anywhere but here," he murmured, the words low but gruff, "I'd have to kiss you." He rubbed the pad of his thumb in small caressing circles over the interplay of veins in her delicate wrist. "For now, this will have to do."

What he really needed to say, desperately, was that regardless of torturous inner conflicts he loved her. That with every passing hour he grew more convinced God really was more than a noncorporeal Being to say a blessing to before a meal, or to curse when disaster happened. That God, for whatever reason, had known exactly the sort of woman Devlin needed to open the rusted gate to his heart.

Sometimes a man had to trust without understanding.

Most people called it faith.

But the appearance of three of his fellow operatives made a declaration of love impossible right now, possibly forever. Devlin might submit to the need for God's will to supersede his own. But others were not so inclined, and Dev's personal decision could not alter an unpalatable truth.

Edgar Fane knew Devlin Stone's name—and planned to hunt him down.

If Fane succeeded, he would also find Thea.

# Chapter Twenty-Four

Overnight the wind shifted to the northwest, sweeping in cooler temperatures and the deep azure skies of approaching fall. Hugging a shawl around her in the pleasantly cool morning air, Thea shifted from foot to foot, anticipation crawling over her like ants.

Today she would see her grandfather.

She was about to start toward the neat brick carriage house to fetch the carriage herself when the extended brougham rolled into view, pulled by two stately bay Holsteiners Devlin had imported from Germany. "I took a chance," he'd told Thea. "They're primarily coach horses, great bones and natural balance, yet mostly unknown in America." He grinned. "Uncle J. groused for months about the expense."

Nab pulled the team to a dignified halt at the front door. StoneHill's coachman and stable manager was dressed for the occasion in a hunter-green frock coat and top hat; when Thea told him he looked splendid a self-satisfied smile beamed from the coffee-colored face, still smooth as a river pebble even though he'd passed three score years the previous week.

"Mister Stone'll be along in a jiffy, miss," he said. "He's

jawing with Jeremiah about Percy. Old boy's off his feed again, and you know Mr. Stone. Don't matter none that horse is older'n dirt, and if he takes a notion to pick at his feed a bit, why, leave him be, I say."

Oh, dear. Percy. Devlin and the Appalousey spotted horse had grown up together, and Devlin loved the animal with a devotion that moved Thea to tears.

"Nab, Mr. Stone doesn't need to accompany me." She buried the spur of disappointment deep, reminding herself that in a few short hours she would have all the company she needed. "Come on, let's swing back by the barn, and I'll insist."

Nab hopped down to hand her up into the carriage. "Miss Langston, you a mighty fine woman. The Lord took His time about it, but He finally gave Mr. Devlin what he's been missing for more years than I like to count."

Embarrassed, Thea busied herself with smoothing her skirt. "Thank you, Nab. But until the Lord sees fit to inform Mr. Devlin, I don't think I'll bring the matter up."

When they reached the stables, Nab darted inside. A short while later he returned with Devlin, who climbed inside the carriage, tossed jacket and homburg down on the seat beside him, then with a long sigh sat down across from Thea.

"Devlin, you don't need—"

"I'm coming with you," he cut across her protest. "I know you'd be safe with Nab, and are quite capable of traveling on your own. That's not the point. I'm coming because I want to be with you. Besides, it's the right thing to do, meeting your grandfather at the depot." He glanced down at himself and grimaced. "I did wash my hands and pick out the worst of the straw."

The odor of horse and hay and some stringent medicinal

smell wrapped around Thea. Devlin's thick mahogany locks fell in haphazard disarray, and streaks of perspiration marked his temples. His blue shirt was wrinkled and streaked with dried horse saliva. But he'd cleaned up as best he could, just to be with her and show respect to her grandfather. The spiny knot in Thea's chest slowly dissolved. "Grandfather used to spend most of his days with printer's ink smeared on his face and shirt cuffs. Thank you, Devlin. Since you insisted on coming along, I'll confess how glad I am." She hesitated, adding hesitantly, "How's Percy?"

"Holding his own. Uncle J. and I have finally agreed it's either the sprained ligament that holds the ball of the femur in the hip socket, or a diseased stifle joint. I've placed a telephone call to a veterinary surgeon friend. I know Percy's past his prime, but I can't..." His eyes clouded over. "We've tethered him in his stall to restrict his movement. He's alert, no signs of sweating or agitation. I got him to eat a little more of his breakfast. He's not in severe pain. I'd know if he were, he'd tell me—" He stopped and momentarily closed his eyes. "You must think I'm a softheaded crackerbrain."

"I think—" Thea leaned across and took one large fist, still damp, in both her hands "—that you're the most compassionate man I've ever known, and you have a way with horses I've come to believe is a gift. I mean...oh, padiddle. Now I'm going to tear up."

She blinked rapidly, feeling silly until Devlin reached across and brushed away the welling tears with his thumb. Thea's breath backed up in her throat. While the carriage rattled down StoneHill's long drive, for a span of unmeasured time the two of them swayed with the movement in a silence fraught with feelings too fragile to be acknowledged.

But when Devlin's steady appraisal of her persisted, his eyes gone dark as a late-summer thunderstorm, the words finally broke free. "Devlin, you are…a very special man. And I think more than ever I want to believe what my grandfather used to believe, about God. You do have a gift where horses and people are concerned that can't be learned through studies, or thoughtful dissertations or reasoned thinking. I think God gave you this gift." She laughed, a soggy, self-conscious sound. "Now I'm the one who sounds like a crackerbrain. Grandfather would say I'm thinking too much. Probably talking too much, as well."

"Not for me." Without warning the carriage jolted, pitching Thea sideways. Before she blinked her startlement, Devlin's arms shot out and he grabbed her shoulders. But instead of settling her back against the seat he pulled her across the space separating them and into his embrace. "Never for me," he whispered hoarsely in her ear. "Thea, what you said, about God? What would you think if I told you I've been thinking, too? That maybe our meeting in Saratoga Springs wasn't happenstance, or fate, or luck?"

Crushed against the solid muscles of Devlin's chest, her heartbeat thumping in her ears, Thea wriggled her hands around his back until she could lay her head against him and hear the thunder of his heart. Incredulity fought against fear, and a lifetime of disillusionment. Was he sharing his feelings—or his faith?

Finally the weight of his arms gentled, but instead of the kiss Thea secretly hungered for, he eased her back across the carriage, onto her own seat, then sat, elbows propped on his knees, his hands worrying his hair. "God," she heard him murmur, "what am I supposed to do?" Even as she sucked in air to offer something, anything, he lifted his head and gazed across the space separating them. "I can't tell you everything I want to—need to. Not today, not like this. I know it's not fair to you, but Thea? Will you be patient with me, for a little longer?"

In dawning wonder, Thea read in his eyes everything for some reason he wouldn't verbalize, and a wash of golden light seemed to flood her heart. For today, she decided, she could return to this man one of the gifts he had given her when he led her out of that jail cell into fresh air, and freedom. "Patience isn't my strong suit," she admitted, "but for you, Devlin, it's not difficult at all. Whatever you need to say to me can wait. After all, you did save my life. In some cultures, that means I'm bound to you, for the rest of it."

The lines of tension bracketing his mouth eased, and a slow smile spread across his face. "I like the sound of that," he said. "I like the sound of that very much, Theodora Langston."

Two weeks later, Thea and Charles Langston stood by the fence, watching Devlin work with Percy. The gallant old horse moved smoothly, with only a slight hitch in his black-spotted hindquarters. With each passing day, like the aging Appalousey stallion her grandfather had regained much of his former strength as well. Instead of the gaunt, defeated creature Thea had kissed farewell in June, he now stood tall and dignified. Courtesy of Bessie's cooking, he'd gained several pounds, and after the first two days had shed frock coat and bow ties altogether. He and Jeremiah acted more like long-lost brothers than two strangers.

StoneHill Farm, Thea decided, offered far more potent elixirs than all the springs in Saratoga.

"You love him very much, don't you, Taffy T?" Charles affectionately tugged a strand of hair that had slipped free of pins. Though now late September, a sultry summer haze still lay over the farm, and humidity had coiled the errant lock into a loose curl.

Absently Thea tucked it behind her ear. "So much it frightens me." Gaze fixed upon Devlin, she waited until the tremulousness that shadowed every waking hour subsided. "I think Devlin feels the same. But we haven't spoken the words." She laughed a little. "Do you see how wonderful he is with Percy? Infinite patience, gentleness—never a harsh word or sudden move? When Devlin and I are together, he treats me the same."

Charles snorted, then coughed to mask the ungentlemanly noise. "Can't think of a single woman I've known, including your grandmother, who wanted their man to treat them like his horse. That's a banal cliché straight out of Western pulp novels."

"Not when the man is Devlin." She glanced sideways. "On occasion he's displayed other emotions as well, Grandfather."

"Good." Beneath his neat iron-gray mustache the corners of Charles's mouth tipped upward. "I trust his intentions are as honorable toward you as they are toward his horses. I'm not sure I make as capable a chaperone as Mrs. Chudd, especially since I don't plan to give up my evenings playing chess with Jeremiah." A deep chuckle rumbled in his chest—a sound Thea hadn't heard in months. "I beat him last night. Plan to do so again. All I have to do is bring up the War. So if you and Devlin want to slip out to enjoy the moonlight, have no fear of your grandfather interfering. Frankly, I'm enjoying the two of you trying to pretend you're not in the throes of a courtship."

A twinge of guilt nudged Thea. She had not confided *all* details of her sojourn in Saratoga. "Well…at least you're more agreeable to be around than Mrs. Chudd." Five days after Charles's arrival, Nab had driven her former chaperone off to the depot; she'd endured quite enough Southern cooking, she informed Thea, and too much Southern humidity. Her services hadn't been needed since their arrival at StoneHill anyway. "At any rate," Thea finished, "I don't need a chaperone. I am almost thirty years old, remember."

"Ha! Look more like a sweet young miss to me. Let's see what Master Stone has to say about it. He appears to be headed our way."

Heart racing, Thea nodded absently, unable to tear her gaze away from Devlin. Shirtsleeves rolled to reveal tanned forearms, thick hair gleaming in the morning sun, he flashed her a grin that oozed contentment. Halterless, Percy clopped along beside him, ears pricked forward, his speckled muzzle just brushing Devlin's shoulder.

"Your horse is certainly looking more lively than when I first arrived," Charles said to Devlin when they reached the fence. "You say you've had him since you were a boy?"

Devlin nodded. "My grandfather was out in the Oregon Territory back in '76, searching for land because he was afraid we were going to lose StoneHill. He saved a family of the Nez Perce tribe from slaughter, along with a half dozen of their spotted horses. In gratitude, they presented him with their best foal, a colt my granddad named Percy, in honor of the tribe."

"He grew up some." Uncomfortable around horses, Charles stepped back when Percy thrust an enquiring head through the fence rails. One striped hoof pawed the dirt—his way, Devlin had informed Thea, of demanding attention. "Based upon my very limited knowledge of horseflesh, he acts surprisingly vigorous for twenty-one years old."

"A whole lot of love and a little bit of—" Devlin hesitated "—what I used to call luck. These days I'm thinking

I might call it something else." He stroked Percy's ebony withers, then ran his hand along the speckled rump. "Either way, he's been a faithful companion. It's a relief, seeing him improve daily."

"My granddaughter's perked up, as well." Charles winked at Devlin. "Does my heart good, seeing *her* daily improvements. She's needed to put this whole business with Edgar Fane behind. With that in mind—" he dropped a kiss on Thea's forehead "—I think I'll retire to a shady spot on your back veranda, and see if I can coax Bessie out of some of that apple strudel I smelled baking this morning."

# Chapter Twenty-Five

"Subtle as an Appalousey's spots, isn't he?" Thea kept her gaze on one of the striped hooves, a characteristic of this particular breed. She seemed to be learning a lot about the equine species these days, she thought, scratching behind Percy's ear.

"I see where you inherited your predilection for speaking your mind. Well, since he's provided the opportunity, why don't you come along to the barn, help me get Percy settled. Then we'll go for a walk." His voice turned sober. "I've been thinking."

*I never stop,* Thea wanted to say, her pulse still settling after her grandfather's throwaway remark about Edgar Fane. But with a newfound patience—or was it the old fears?—she maintained her silence, and followed Devlin and Percy to the barn.

An hour later, they left the worn path toward the woodland to stroll alongside the two-foot high stone wall that for over half a century had marked the boundaries of Stone-Hill Farm. Tufts of Queen Anne's lace and bunches of goldenrod brushed their clothing as they passed, while a warm southern breeze caressed the distant treetops.

Then Devlin enfolded Thea's hand in his, and began

to talk. "All my life, I've known this was home, and my responsibility," he said, trailing his fingertips over the wall as they walked. "Yet all my life, I've wondered who I might have been, if I'd followed in my grandfather's footsteps and headed west instead of going to college. Or if my mother had taken me back to New York City when she left after my father's death." The hand holding hers flexed, a restive movement quickly stilled. "These past weeks, I keep thinking that if she had, I might have met you earlier, before life got so complicated."

"Or we may never have met at all." Dread curled into a tight hot ball in her middle. "Devlin, if you brought me out here to tell me something unpleasant, I wish you'd go ahead and get it over with, particularly if you're trying to find a polite way to say my grandfather and I have trespassed on your hospitality too long. I've suffered through about all the suspense I can handle." Especially when a letter with a news clipping, freshly arrived with the morning mail, was now burning a hole in the pocket of her dress.

Devlin stopped and faced her directly. "I should have remembered. Your mind is prone to dark musings, and your imagination is stronger than a team of Percheron." When Thea opened her mouth to object, he kissed the tip of her nose, then cupped her cheek. "I love your mind, and have a healthy respect for your imagination. Which is why we're a perfect match. I can't hide what I feel any longer, Thea. Every day, those feelings dominate my day, no matter how hard I try to keep them stabled in the barn."

In one of the intimate gestures she'd grown to cherish he cupped her other cheek, holding her transfixed within a gentle cage. She could have broken free and run away— this man would never use force to bend her to his will, or trap her into listening to words she couldn't bear to hear.

And because of it, she'd given him her heart as well as her trust.

"I can't hold the words inside any longer. Whenever you look at me," he finished in a ragged whisper, "I see the same feelings in your beautiful eyes. You dread suspense. So don't you think it's time we shared those feelings with each other?"

Thea swallowed hard. "Yes. No." He was close, too close. Her head swam; she twined her fingers to keep from touching him and losing the battle with inevitability.

Abruptly, the warm hands encasing her cheeks dropped away. She heard the rustle of his clothing, opened her eyes in a panic, to discover him standing a yard away, watching her. Thea suddenly discovered a costly mistake was easier to bear than the long-suffering kindness blazing forth from those eyes.

"I wish I were a horse," she blurted, almost as angry with him as she was with herself. "They don't need words. You know already by their responses how much they love you. You don't make demands of them they're incapable of meeting. You just care for them, and allow them to be… to be horses," she finished, adding grumpily, "Don't say it. I'm not a horse. Grandfather already reminded me."

"And here I am, hiding a specially made halter just for you underneath my shirt." His absurdity made her laugh, and Devlin's whole body seemed to relax. "I'm willing to do just about anything, you see, to keep you at StoneHill," he said. One long step brought him back to her side, close enough to count his eyelashes. "Since we're not horses, I suppose we're stuck with words. I've tried not to say them because I'm just as afraid as you are. What if your feelings are mired in gratitude? What if your heart is irrevocably tied to Staten Island?"

"It's not. They're not. It's just that—"

"Good. No more excuses, then. Close your eyes if you need to, but unstop your ears, and your heart." He watched her, the irises expanding in his pupils until the black completely crowded out the gray. "I love you, Theodora Langston. I love you, more than I can explain. If you tell me you could never be happy here at StoneHill Farm, I don't know if I'd survive."

Nerves roughened his voice, and Thea realized in misty-eyed astonishment that he was shaking. As though a warm gust of wind swept over the mountain and shoved her with an impatient hand, she took one faltering step, then threw herself against him, wrapping her own shaking arms around his back. "I love you, I love you, too," she choked out against the salty dampness of his neck. "And I don't want to go back to Staten Island. You'll never have to be afraid that I'll leave you like your mother. Or Sylvia." Helpless against the emotions buffeting them both, she pressed fervent kisses against his neck and jaw.

All of a sudden rough hands slid beneath her arms and Devlin lifted her completely off her feet. "Yes!" he shouted the affirmation, his gaze more open and joyous than Thea had ever seen. "Thank You, God!" He whirled her around, then his head lowered and he kissed her.

The Atlantic Ocean churned, white-capped waves crashing onto the cowering beaches. Storm clouds scudded across a sky the color of iron.

Edgar Fane stood on the widow's walk of the seaside mansion he'd bought off a bankrupt shipbuilder three years earlier. Face lifted to the spitting wind, he allowed the fury of nature to batter away his own fury until, chilled and damp from salt spray, he returned to his study.

Simpson had left the latest reports tidily stacked on his desk. A muscle jumped over Edgar's left eyebrow as he picked up the one that had arrived yesterday. Most of the private detectives he'd employed over the past two months were as stupid as tree stumps, not worth the energy it would require to have them tossed into the surf. But this last fellow, fired by Pinkerton National Detective Agency the previous year for his questionable interrogation methods, was a gift from the gods. He'd have Simpson pay Hiram Witticomb a bonus, this time with real money.

Though rage still hummed through Edgar, he forced himself to sit down, suppressing the urge to sweep the rest of the folders to the floor again, just to torment Simpson.

Perhaps it was time to pay his secretary another bonus, as well. After switching on the banker's lamp Edgar read through Witticomb's report, this time with his temper firmly in check.

…and after extensive interrogation of all ferryboat captains, have been unable to verify date when Charles Langston departed Staten Island. I have, however, been able to verify the existence of a son, CL's only remaining progeny, briefly married to a woman whose identity I will endeavor to uncover by October 1. This union produced a female child, christened Theodora, as of this report approximately 27–30 years of age. Unmarried. Reared by CL, according to statements, having been abandoned by parents at time of birth. Also, according to three credible witnesses, in June of this year abovementioned granddaughter hired as a chaperone one Irma Chudd, purpose and destination unknown, though witnesses speculate either a) an elopement; or b) some form of travel which necessitated the services of a proper companion. Description of granddaughter is as follows.

As Edgar reread the detailed notes his mind tormented him with the mental image of Theodora *Pickford*. Witticomb's description of her couldn't be more accurate had she been standing in front of the man when he wrote it.

The chit had played Edgar for a fool, but she would pay for her temerity. So would the man named Devlin Stone, who had secured her release from Saratoga's jail, then vanished, probably with Theodora.

A satisfied smile gradually soothed the jagged edges of Edgar's anger; hands laced behind his head, he leaned back and contemplated the final revelation Witticomb had unearthed.

Name of CL's son is Richard. Lifelong estrangement from father due to addiction to gambling. Am at present following up on possible whereabouts of RL in Atlantic City, New Jersey.

"Every orphan dreams of a reunion with long-lost relatives," Edgar mused aloud to the ceiling. "It will be my pleasure to give you back your father, Theodora *Langston*." But not for long…

This time, Edgar would also ensure that no pesky lawyers or mysterious benefactors interfered. And an impotent Secret Service would continue to flail after shadow trails that led—nowhere.

As for Charles Langston, he'd always had a warm spot for the old man. But Langston was too naive for his own good. Another tidy moral lesson on life's disappointments needed to be delivered. Edgar would allow him to live out the remainder of his days, grieving for his son and, when the time came, his granddaughter.

# Chapter Twenty-Six

October arrived with a week of torrential rain, followed by skies blue enough to drown in, and air with an invigorating snap to it. Leaves lost their green luster, cloaking themselves instead in the first autumnal hues of the season. On a bright morning Devlin stood in the south pasture with Jeremiah, watching sunbeams dapple the hides of their small herd of Suffolk punch horses.

"Looking good, aren't they?" Jeremiah ruminated around a piece of straw he'd been chewing. "But I still miss the Clydesdales. They had…presence."

Stifling a smile, Devlin tucked his hands in the waistband of his trousers. They'd shared this conversation weekly for seven years. "Absolutely. But the country needs smaller horses for lighter loads, and logging." Starlight, one of the mares, wandered over; Dev fed her a carrot and idly ran his hand over her smooth chestnut belly and down her short sturdy forelegs. "At least nobody ever complains about leg feathers."

"Including me. Pain in the backside to keep clean."

They both laughed, then settled into companionable silence. Starlight wandered back over to the herd, and

Devlin allowed the freshness of the morning to settle his restless soul.

Then Jeremiah tossed aside the straw and looked him square in the eye. "Charles and myself had a long talk last night. He's wanting to know why there's no ring, and no talk of a wedding. He's also thinking it might be best if he and Thea returned to Staten Island while you make up your mind to ask the question."

The hairs at the back of Devlin's neck rose. For a week now he'd sensed a reticence in Thea, but he'd made the mistake of ignoring it. As a boy he poked sticks into ant-hills just to watch thousands of ants erupt in furious commotion, but he was long past the age where he invited turmoil. "That's probably just Charles's version. He's the one feeling restless. He's nervous around horses, so there's nothing much he can do around here except beat you at chess."

"He's turned into a gardener of sorts."

"So Thea tells me. She's tried her hand at hoeing and planting herself, when she's not helping out in the stables."

"Unlike Charles, she's a good instinct for horses, Dev. Amazing, when you study how things turned out with the pair of you. But something is plaguing her mind. Might be because the man she loves won't commit himself to her, for keeps."

The tranquil peace of the morning evaporated. "If I put a ring on her finger, I'll have to tell her I'm a Secret Service operative. When I do, I also want to be able to tell her I'm resigning. I can't do that yet, Uncle J."

"Confound it, boy, why ever not? You ought to have told her long ago, to my way of thinking. I've run myself to the bone these past couple of years, waiting while you chased after confidence men and worked the wanderlust out of your system. Now you're back home, with a good woman who won't up and skedaddle on you—"

"This has nothing to do with Sylvia and my mother."

"Bah! And the sky ain't blue today. Devlin, your place is here, and you know it. What's keeping you from sending in your resignation?"

Swiveling, Dev strode across the pasture, his thoughts black as Percy's ears. *Not much,* he wanted to yell. Just word from his "reporters" that a man's home in Philadelphia had been burglarized, and one of the stolen items was an Edgar Fane painting. Just that two days after the burglary, two Hotel Hustler C-notes surfaced in Steven Clarke's bank, though nobody knew who had deposited them so no charges were filed. Just that Fane still sought information about Devlin Stone so Dev had been "advised" to remain at StoneHill to avoid further jeopardizing the investigation. And the final gut-twisting news: an unscrupulous private detective now on retainer to Fane had bullied alarming tidbits about the Langston family out of local residents.

"Only a matter of time," Lawlor had warned him two days earlier, when Devlin was in Stuarts Crossing, "before he discovers your Miss Langston is the 'Miss Pickford' who was arrested in Saratoga Springs. Then, my friend, you'll both be frosted six ways to Sunday."

Devlin's choices might have put everyone and everything he loved in mortal danger, and his uncle wanted to know why he hadn't asked Theodora to be his wife?

Above him, the vast dome of an endless sky seemed to press down until he could hardly draw a deep breath; the soft outline of the mountains, worn to forested humps over tens of thousands of years, bore silent witness to pitiless reality—not even nature could halt time.

Over the past month Devlin had begun talking to God,

cautious, stumbling efforts that left him feeling foolish, yet strangely at peace. The thought came to him now that maybe trust in God was akin to Devlin's love for his horses. The animals trusted a two-legged creature who didn't speak their language but nonetheless intuitively knew how to communicate with them, using as the foundation patience, gentleness and love. He understood their basic nature was different from his own, and he respected those differences.

All right, then. He'd try—no sense shying away from the word—he'd try some more praying, this very moment, before Jeremiah's questions provoked Devlin into losing his temper. *God? If You understand, You need to find a way to let me know what I should do. I've dug a hole here, but I can't come clean and confess right now. Especially to Thea.* God might know for sure what her response would be, but Devlin didn't. He was terrified she would bolt— straight into Edgar Fane. The burden was Devlin's alone, and his knees were buckling beneath its weight.

For some reason his eyes stung. A whisper of wind whirled around him, raising goose bumps on his flesh. Then it infiltrated the pores of his skin in a scalding rush, scrubbing raw the pretenses of pride in which he'd clothed himself. He was afraid, and ashamed, because he felt like a failure. A failure as an operative, a failure as a man, to not protect the woman he loved and the home that had been his legacy. Thea's possible reaction to his identity was not the true reason he had kept his mouth shut.

If his uncle weren't standing twenty feet away Devlin would have dropped to his knees. Instead he stood, hands fisted at his sides, and suffered through the agony of self-condemnation. Yet even amidst the worst of it, some nascent core in his spirit flickered to life, a paradoxical awareness of power and humility that built into a steady flame. Like an unschooled horse, yielding his will was neither swift, nor simple. But when the yielding achieved mutual harmony instead of brutal dominance, well, the possibilities shook his soul.

"Dev? Devlin! You all right, son?" Jeremiah's hand clamped down on his shoulder. "Confound it, should've kept my mouth shut. Bessie's right. Might as well plow a field with my tongue."

For a moment Devlin was unable to respond; he could hear his uncle's voice but could not see him clearly. It was as though Devlin had emerged from the bottom of a rushing stream and water still blinded his eyes.

"Aw…" Jeremiah's voice deteriorated into mumbles. He wrapped a sinewy arm around Devlin's shoulders. "Never mind. We'll work it through somehow. That's the important thing here, Dev. We're family. We'll work our way through it, together." Jeremiah glanced behind Devlin, in the direction of the barn. "Your sweetheart's headed this way, carrying a basket. After we help ourselves to whatever Bessie's cooked up, how about if I help Nab with the training this morning? Good. Glad you agreed without an argument."

Without a backward look he headed across the pasture toward Thea.

"What's happened?" she asked, the moment Jeremiah was out of earshot. "Here. Bessie made something called johnnycake. Eat while you talk, it won't offend me. Were you and your uncle having a disagreement?" Hastily she added, "If you were, of course you don't have to tell me if— Oh!"

"Best way I know to hush up idiotic notions," Devlin said when he finally ended the kiss.

"Only temporarily," she answered on a breathless laugh.

His gaze caressed her glowing face, the love inside him inextricably tangled with the need to protect. This morning she wore a practical tweed skirt and shapeless corduroy jacket. She'd plaited her hair in a haphazard braid; already errant strands dangled everywhere. But to Devlin she was the most beautiful woman in the world. Ambivalence finally conceded the battle. His decision was after all the only one he could make and still call himself a man.

A man who had called out to God, and God had answered.

Things would work out, Thea would understand when Dev was finally able to explain.... *She had to understand.*

The glow had faded from her cheeks. "Is something wrong with Starlight? One of the other mares?"

"The mares are all fine." He plucked the basket of yeasty buns off her arm, then threaded his fingers through hers. "Let's go sit under that oak over yonder. Seems like ages since we've had an opportunity to enjoy a solitary moment together."

The shadows lifted from her face. "I think everyone else at StoneHill agrees. Grandfather claimed a twisted knee, Bessie refused to let me help with the laundry and thrust this basket in my hands. When I asked one of the stable hands in the barn where you and Jeremiah were this morning, he pointed out this pasture, and winked. And you saw your uncle, practically galloping away from us."

"Then let's not disappoint them."

They reached the shelter of a towering black oak, and Devlin spread his jacket over fallen leaves and trampled-down grass. Thea sat, arranging her skirt in a graceful circle around her as Devlin sank beside her, the wicker basket between them. Thea handed him a bun. "We better eat all this johnnycake I brought so Bessie won't fuss." Then she added, her tone a shade too casual, "I've been needing to talk with you about something anyway."

Devlin returned his square of the hot bread uneaten to the basket. "You can't return to Staten Island. I won't let you go. If that's what you needed to talk about, you may as well save your breath."

One mink-brown eyebrow lifted. "Now whose imagination runs away with them? *If* I chose to leave, you couldn't stop me."

"Not by locking you in a room, no," Devlin agreed despite the anvil crushing his chest cavity. "You won't go, because I love you, and you love me. And I think it's time we made it official."

He removed Thea's half-eaten johnnycake so he could hold her unsteady hands in his. "There are probably more romantic places, and a dozen more romantic phrases. But when I look at you, surrounded by everything else I love, I no longer believe our meeting was an accident. I can't imagine not having you in my life, and I should have asked this question weeks ago." Briefly the crease appeared in his cheek. "But I was more afraid of the problems than the promises we'd just made to each other. So...Theodora Langston, will you marry me?"

Inside his, her hands stilled, then clung. She swallowed several times, opened her mouth, then chewed her bottom lip instead. For Devlin, the whole universe halted its rotation. He could hear the pulse pounding away in his ears, all sensation drained from his limbs into the rich earth and a dozen anvils now squeezed his chest while he waited for her answer.

"Are you sure you trust me enough not to run back to New York, like your mother?" A single tear overflowed. "We haven't talked about it, since we...since the day we confessed our feelings to each other. But sometimes I still see what looks like fear in your eyes. I love StoneHill almost as much as I love you. But I need to know you believe that," she finished, adding hoarsely, "Please ignore these tears."

Devlin shoved the basket out of the way and hauled the maddening woman into his arms, where she belonged. When she laid her head against his chest he pressed one hand against the silken softness of her hair, holding her there. "Whatever emotion you thought you saw had nothing to do with comparing you to my mother, or Sylvia," he promised thickly. "I *love you*. Marry me?"

"I've discovered I'm entranced with horses. I want to learn everything about them. I want to be your helpmeet there, not take over Bessie's domain."

"You can dress in dungarees and currycomb every horse every day. Bessie can remain queen of the kitchen." He wrapped her braid around his hand and tugged, tilting her head back until their lips were inches apart. "First you have to marry me. Then you can make all the demands you want."

A delicious smile curved her lips, the dark chocolate eyes turned dreamy. "I've always wanted to wear a pair of dungarees and ride a horse like Annie Oakley." Abruptly the arms she'd wrapped around his ribs squeezed, then her lips pressed against his. "Yes," she breathed. "I will marry you, Devlin Stone."

For a golden hour, they sat beneath the grand old oak and dreamed.

And Devlin believed love was enough.

## Chapter Twenty-Seven

For Thea, October splattered over the Blue Ridge Mountains and StoneHill with a splendid lack of decorum. Days passed in a colorful blur, and most of the time she was able to ignore occasional twinges of anxiety. At night she fell into bed exhausted, her life full of newfound responsibilities and a sense of camaraderie she'd never before experienced. Devlin had given her the care of two horses—a dappled gray Percheron with intelligent eyes and a sweet disposition, and a mischievous Suffolk punch filly scarcely a year old. Under the careful eye of every stableman, including Devlin and Jeremiah, each day Thea gained confidence in her growing skills.

Bessie, however, also insisted on teaching her how to make some of her most famous recipes. "Because, miss, the day will come when you won't have me. You can hire a housekeeper, but a cook as good as me's hard to come by."

Her grandfather quit making plans to return to Staten Island, instead arranging for Mrs. Chudd to move permanently into their house until Charles decided whether or not to keep or sell. StoneHill, Thea mused fancifully, had become their Shangri-la, or perhaps El Dorado. At least, the pot of gold at the end of the rainbow.

Then another letter arrived, from her old friend who had married years earlier and moved to New Jersey. For months, Pamela had dutifully informed Thea whenever she heard a thread of gossip about Edgar Fane. In today's letter, however, she included some unsettling news, about:

> …a private detective, hired by Mr. Fane to search for some woman who disappeared after she broke his heart in Saratoga Springs. I will try to discover her name, if you like. But I do wish you would quit blaming Mr. Fane for your circumstances, Theodora. Nobody thinks less of you due to your reduced situation.

Along with admonishments, almost every letter from Pamela also included an entreaty for Thea to come home where she belonged. Pamela believed she and her grandfather to be rusticating in some southern backwater nobody had ever heard of, until they recovered from the "troubles of last year." Thea had not confided otherwise. Risky enough, to be writing her at all. They had both attended Union Academy College for Women; of all her friends, Pamela was the only one Thea trusted to secretly send information concerning Edgar Fane, and to keep her correspondence with Thea—as well as StoneHill's address—a secret.

So many secrets.

Perhaps her friend was right. It was time to give up on her hopeless quest for justice and focus instead on a future with the man she loved. Edgar Fane was beyond reach, and she needed to leave retribution where it belonged— with God. Revenge, she had learned at too great a cost, ultimately harmed the person seeking it. That long-ago afternoon at the Saratoga Springs police station, trapped within her own web of lies, she had listened to Edgar Fane—and seen herself. Enlightenment produced a shame almost as debilitating as her brief sojourn in a cell.

Devlin had freed her from that jail, loved her and given her his heart. But only Thea could make the decision that would free her soul.

She and Devlin had shared much in the past weeks about the Lord's Presence in their lives. "He reminds me of how you used to talk to God, when I was a girl," she'd told Charles just this morning. "As if God cares about him, and even communicates with him. Devlin's *praying,* Grandfather."

"And how does a praying man for a husband strike you, Taffy T?"

"For some reason, that strikes me just fine. I think I've discovered a—a similar hunger. This past year, it's been dreadfully wearing, believing God is no more than an indifferent Creator, indifferent to human suffering. But…" But she'd been angry at God; she'd spurned Him to pursue her own course. She had abandoned Him.

Charles pinched the end of his nose, then gave her a sheepish smile. "There will always be 'buts.' Most of them can be turned into faith, instead of flaws." And patting her knee, he rose. "But for Edgar Fane's interference in our lives, you never would have met Devlin."

"That's what Devlin says."

"Snared yourself a wise man." Chuckling, he left to go see how many autumn apples had fallen from the trees in StoneHill's orchard.

Now, as Thea stared down at the letter in her hands, she allowed a decision tugging at her for days to transform into certainty. She needed to release the past, along with her secret plans to pursue Edgar Fane. Nothing was worth the love of a man whose smile held the power of the sun whenever he looked at Thea. The man who had forgiven her own deceptions and seen beyond her flaws. To Devlin, she was beautiful. Worthy. Loved.

The way Jesus loved her.

*All right, Lord.* For months He'd been nagging her with wisps of remembered scripture, about His ways and His timing and His justice. *All right. I give up. Forgive my hard heart…restore the joy of salvation. Do as You will…* "But here's my final 'but,' Lord. Please, help me choose the right path?"

In a burst of energy she ripped Pamela's letter into confetti-sized pieces, and went to collect a couple of apples to feed her two horses.


Edgar strolled into Caruthers, a seedy gambling casino two blocks off Atlantic City's famous Boardwalk. Faded velvet draperies and crystal chandeliers were choked in a haze of cigar smoke. Ill-dressed patrons hunched around tables and roulette wheels, while aging ladies of pleasure pretended enjoyment in their duties.

Suppressing a shudder of distaste, Edgar walked over to a table near the center of the crowded room, where five men sat in a semicircle, playing blackjack against the house dealer. Only one player glanced up at Edgar's approach. The dealer shot a look toward the two bulky bodyguards who stood five paces behind Edgar, and kept his mouth shut.

"Good evening," Edgar said in his best Oxford-educated voice. "Is one of you Richard Langston?"

"Who wants to know?" a florid individual with squinty eyes demanded.

"Are you Mr. Langston?"

The man leaned back in his chair and jutted out his chin. "Any snoot who waltzes over and interrupts my concentration, he better be willing to give me *his* moniker before I answer a question."

"Now, Billy. No need to get testy." Rising, the only man who had acknowledged Edgar's presence adjusted his necktie and straightened his frayed cuffs. "I'm Richard Langston. What can I do for you, Mr.…?"

"I'll explain everything." Edgar swept the room with an assessing look. "Is there somewhere we can enjoy a private discussion, Mr. Langston?"

"Mr. Langston owes the house two thousand dollars," the dealer said. "And house rules require him to stay until he wins the money back, or pays in cash before leaving the table."

"House'll have to wait its turn," the squint-eyed man said. "You ain't leaving my sight, Langston, unless you fork over the thousand you owe me."

"How 'bout my five hundred? Cripes, man, did you pay this bloke to help you wiggle out from paying up? You been begging me for two weeks now ta give ya more time."

"Gentlemen," Edgar interrupted the jackals. Behind him, the bodyguards stirred uneasily but, obeying explicit instructions, did not approach. Next, Edgar made a production of withdrawing a small leather-bound notepad and gold pen from his coat pocket. "Other than two thousand for the house, how much does Mr. Langston owe each of you?" He pointed his pen at the most belligerent of the group. "Starting with you. A thousand, wasn't it?"

While Richard Langston's complexion deepened to the hue of boiled tomatoes, Edgar wrote down responses and tallied his quarry's total losses: over seven thousand dollars. "Not a good season this year?" He clapped Langston's shoulder. "I can change that. Allow me." He drew out his calfskin bill book and to the riveted attention of the watchers, counted out bills onto the worn felt that covered the table. When he finished, he planted one palm firmly over the money. "Now, Mr. Langston, if these gentleman will write receipts to verify your gambling debts to them are paid in full, that should free you up to join me for a private discussion."

"What extortionist interest will you require, in turn for this generosity?" Langston looked him in the eye, but he was sweating.

Good. The man still clung to some remnants of intelligence. Shabby gentility combined with a weak mind and bad habits offered little challenge. "You're a gambling man, Mr. Langston. You decide."

To give him credit, Langston chewed through the proposition. Finally, after a lingering study of the other players and Edgar's watchful bodyguards, he turned to Edgar with a shrug. "As a gambling man, the odds strike me as more favorable toward an unknown benefactor than my known acquaintances." He paused, and a reckless grin spread over his face. "How about double or nothing? One round, just me and you?"

"No." Edgar scooped up the seven thousand dollars. "Now or not at all, Langston. Think carefully. I'm neither a fool, nor a gambler. Before I stepped foot in this establishment I learned enough to provide for my own protection." He delivered the coup de grâce. "I also learned I'm the only person willing to arrange for yours. At least one of the men at this table, along with that pudgy gentleman lounging at the bar—to whom you owe another two thousand from a poker game a week ago, correct?—and finally, the management of this place, all plan to deprive you of whatever monies you possess at the end of the evening. If your pockets are empty, most likely you'll pay with your life."

"I...see. It's possible you're in cahoots with them all, and this is an elaborate hoax. On the other hand, you might be telling the truth. I like the odds of the latter." Langston nodded once. "I accept your offer. Now...mind telling me who the devil you are?"

Without comment Edgar handed over his calling card. Richard Langston's smooth pale face drained of color; he blinked twice, then like a hound brought to heel without another word followed Edgar and the two bodyguards across the momentarily silent room, and out into the brisk salty air.

# Chapter Twenty-Eight

"Thought it better to deliver the news in person," Fred Lawlor finished. With a grunt of exertion he helped Devlin load the final sack of grain into the back of the farm wagon. "Sorry."

Devlin rotated his head to work the kinks out of his neck muscles. "We knew all along StoneHill was only a temporary refuge. Now that Fane's putting all the pieces together it makes sense, him using Thea's father to lure Thea out of hiding. It's also probable he hopes to catch me, as well. But his motivation's never been that of a spurned lover seeking retribution. I told you about Thea's suspicions about Mrs. Gorman's death? This would indicate her suspicions hold merit. For some reason, the blackguard had her murdered. Might even have done the deed himself."

A chill he couldn't ignore iced down his spine. "It's imperative to discover how Fane unearthed Richard Langston. He's trying to get rid of all witnesses who can implicate him in the Cynthia Gorman murder. Since he can't know what Thea's told me, I'm on that list as well. This is no longer about catching a counterfeiter...."

Lawlor glanced around to ensure nobody else was in earshot. "That's our assessment about Miss Langston, yes.

We're not convinced of the threat to you personally. Appropriate actions are being evaluated in Washington. Devlin, you have to lay aside any personal feelings for this woman. Her protection, and securing proof that Fane is guilty of murder, is beyond our mandate, my friend."

"Obviously you don't understand something, Lawlor. This woman is going to be my wife. Nothing—*nothing*—is going to stop me from doing everything in my power to protect her. Have I made my position clear?"

"Completely." The other man lifted his hands in a placative gesture and backed away. "Take it easy, Devlin. I'm sorry. Until today we had no idea the two of you…you never mentioned…I—" He cursed under his breath, then offered a weak smile. "The one time I saw her, I should have guessed. Smart as a whip, isn't she? Pulled the wool right over our eyes, calling you by a fake name. Well, this will make for an interesting report tonight."

"No," Dev refuted, the word flat and final. "Until Edgar Fane is no longer a threat to Miss Langston, keep her name completely out of your daily reports. I've been working on my report for Chief Hazen, and will supply all mandated details. I'll also shoulder the consequences of flouting policy. Calm your conscience, all right?"

"Dev, I—"

"Subject's not open for discussion. I want to solve this case, now more than ever. But my first priority is my fiancée's safety." As long as he lived Devlin would never forget Thea's face when he led her out of the Saratoga jail. "All it would take is one careless word, and you know it. Give me your word, Fred, or Thea and I will disappear. Completely."

Lawlor's mouth thinned, but he quit arguing. "Much as it galls me to admit it, I see your point. You have my promise. If something changes, I'll do what I can to alert you. That's the best I can offer, Devlin."

"All right." Fred Lawlor was not a quick thinker, nor swift on his feet. But in the two years Dev had known him, Fred had kept his word. A careful, if pedantic Secret Service operative, he'd served honorably for fifteen years, and Dev also valued his insight. "Tell me the rest of why you came, then. I have to get back to StoneHill."

"Some of it's good news. A burglar arrested two days ago swears six ways to Sunday he was sent to Steven Clarke's residence in Philadelphia, not to rob the place, but to fetch counterfeit bills hidden in the Edgar Fane painting given to Clarke by Fane, just before they both left Saratoga. Fool of a burglar got too greedy and kept some of the bills for himself, along with half the Clarke's family silver. Bills recovered all bear the Hotel Hustler's mark. Operatives and police departments from Washington to Chicago are piecing evidence together to tie in the Hustler's work with paintings Edgar Fane donated to unsuspecting recipients. But…" He hesitated.

Ah, yes. Now for the bad news. "But we still need an operative to go in undercover," Dev finished for him. "The word of one no-name thief would never be sufficient to prosecute the son of Thaddeus Fane." He'd known ever since he heard about Thea's father what this personal visit from Lawlor was leading up to. "We've got to find some of those bills in Edgar's possession. It's possible Richard Langston's the next delivery boy."

"Won't be as workable as Saratoga. Jekyll Island is an exclusive haven for America's millionaires, not a world-famous tourist destination." Scowling, Lawlor kicked the wagon wheel. "Plenty of other southern resorts where Fane could pass the winter. But no, he has to take himself and

Richard Langston down to a blasted private island off the coast of Georgia."

"He needed someplace where Langston couldn't easily bolt," Devlin said thoughtfully, scanning the horizon.

Swollen clouds inched over the mountains to the west, blocking the sun. A gust of wind, smelling of rain, set the dead leaves heaped at the base of the two sycamores flanking the hardware store into a cyclonic frenzy. It was early November; back at StoneHill, he'd left a cheerful Thea swathed in one of Bessie's aprons, with Bessie barking instructions on how to make the best apple pie in the state of Virginia.

"I'll still be able to take care of my horses," Thea promised Devlin, waving flour-dusted fingers at him. "I might even squeeze in an hour to help Nab oil hooves. I plan to be an indispensable part of your life, Mr. Stone."

"You're indispensable, just by being you, Miss Langston."

Thea's face lit up like it did on those few occasions when he'd stolen a kiss. Over the past month his fiancée had flowered into full bloom, flitting between house, stables and Stuarts Crossing like a hummingbird. No more haunted shadows, no more vertigo spells, no more secretive, fleeting glances at Devlin when she thought he didn't notice. The insecure young woman who felt unworthy of love whisked through the days, radiant with confidence, soaking up life at StoneHill like a sponge. She and Bessie were planning a spring wedding, when dogwood blossoms covered the farm in drifts of white flowers. Edgar Fane, Thea had promised him three weeks earlier, had been exiled permanently from her life. "God gave me my very own miracle—the love of a wonderful man. What God brought together, I refuse to allow Edgar Fane to tear asunder."

Whirling abruptly away from Lawlor, Devlin slammed the wagon's tailgate shut and hooked the latches, his thoughts black as a crow's wing. He glanced over his shoulder. "The reason you delivered the news in person is because someone wants me to be that man on the inside."

Lawlor had the grace to look uncomfortable. "We know it's a fair risk. Obviously you can't go in under your real name this time. But he doesn't have a photograph, only vague, hearsay descriptions of Mr. Stone. You still have an advantage over all the other operatives, because you don't have to pretend to be a well-heeled gent."

"So did you bring along specific suggestions from Washington?"

"No. I was told to gauge your reaction, and hear what you had to offer. We're still doing research on Jekyll Island itself."

Devlin chose to interpret that as a compliment. "Give me twenty-four hours, Fred. I have a few ideas, but I need to think through them."

Resigned, his fellow operative shrugged back into his Norfolk jacket, donned his bowler and, using the wagon as a screen, handed over a thin sheaf of papers before climbing into his buggy. "That's everything we've collated since our last meeting, including the little we know about Richard Langston. It doesn't make for pretty reading, Devlin, especially since the man's Miss Langston's father."

On the twenty-minute drive back to StoneHill, Devlin chewed over his own strategy, and prayed his newfound trust in God would not be misplaced.

That evening, while Thea helped Bessie in the kitchen, and Jeremiah, muttering imprecations, retired to the study to do paperwork, Devlin asked Charles to join him in the parlor. "There's something I need to tell you," he said. "But you need to know up front that under no circumstances can you share this with Theodora."

"I've never been in the habit of keeping secrets from my granddaughter, Devlin."

"You will, once you understand that the repercussions from enlightenment might cost her her life."

# Chapter Twenty-Nine

A week later, Thea joined Devlin in the family parlor for a rare moment alone with him. Despite Saratoga, or perhaps because of it, at StoneHill they practiced as much propriety as they both could muster. Cozy trysts in the parlor after everyone else had retired were avoided. Well, mostly. A giggle escaped as Thea sneaked down the hallway. A round harvest moon glazed the windowpanes in a pearlescent sheen, and she blew the man-in-the-moon a kiss, her heart equally bright and swollen with love.

Devlin rose from the settee. "Sit here, across from me," he said. He gestured to the overstuffed chair her grandfather preferred, near the old-fashioned parlor stove, almost three yards away from the settee. "This is going to be hard enough…"

Laughing, Thea obeyed, wrapping herself up in her Scottish plaid shawl. But after he started talking, the bubbly urge to laugh fizzled and she squeezed her hands tightly together in the shawl's long fringes while she listened to her beloved regretfully inform her of a trip he had to make to Georgia. He would leave in two days.

"There's a breeder, near Savannah, with whom I've been corresponding for several years. He's given me first right of refusal on a yearling colt, a Holsteiner. If you and I were already married I could take you with me. Since we decided to wait until next spring to wed—"

"A decision I think I regret…"

"—and since I need to make this trip immediately, I'll make it as fast as possible. Thea, love…I don't want to go.…" Finally his words lagged, the light eyes half-hidden behind the screen of his lashes.

"A 'have to' instead of a 'want to'?" Thea finished, hoping to lighten the mood. "As you know, I've learned a lot these past months, distinguishing between the two." The tips of his mouth barely lifted. Thea fought a brief internal skirmish, and switched tactics. "I'll miss you terribly, of course. But I know how much the Holsteiner breed means to you. I have to agree they're as…as elegant an example of horseflesh as I've ever seen. It's just, well, could you explain the urgency of traveling to Georgia right now? Bessie tells me this time of year the weather down here can turn nasty between the tick and tock of the clock." And Thanksgiving was less than two weeks away.

"Trains these days can handle bad weather." He heaved a sigh, flexing his shoulders as though they were weighed down with a sack of stones. "The breeder needs the money now, but I won't pay for any horse sight unseen, especially a Holsteiner. Thirty years ago, while America fought a nasty civil war, Europe struggled with turmoil of their own. The Holsteiner's reputation suffered from some poor breeding practices, and a resulting lack of quality. In this country there's very few stock I'd want to add to Stone-Hill, but this breeder in Georgia owns some of them. I don't want to lose the opportunity." Leaning forward, he searched her face, his gaze still cloudy. "You know I love horses. But do you have any idea how much I love you? I'd give my life for you, Thea."

"As I would you," she replied, suddenly understanding. Desertion and betrayal left lifelong scars. Proprieties be hanged, she rose to join him on the settee. The heavy velvet drapes had been pulled, exchanging moonlight for coziness. Intimacy, however, eluded them; the hissing parlor stove tossed wavering shadows about the room; on the side table the milk glass lamp cast a feverish glow over the furniture. A life-size portrait of Devlin's father stared down at her, his expression grave rather than kind. *Don't worry,* she promised Eli Stone, *it might take years, but one day he'll learn to trust me enough to travel in peace.* "I'll miss you," she told Devlin, "every hour of every day. But I will be here when you return."

"It's not that."

He looked so miserable she rushed the words. "And I promise not to weep, or slide into feeling unloved, or afraid. My faith in God has never been stronger, even when I was a child. I know you've postponed several other trips over the past month because you were concerned about—"

"I'll have words with Jeremiah."

"He knew I was fighting guilt about stifling your freedom, and offered good counsel." She nudged the tough, muscular shoulder with her own, love and admiration prickling her skin. "Jeremiah said you'd go when you were convinced I'd be safe, and not before, so there was no use pestering you, or fretting. So I didn't, and now you're ready. We're both ready." Softly she stroked his forearm. "I'll be waiting right here, for you to come home. Don't worry about me, Devlin. Go buy us a colt."

Devlin dropped his head in his hands. "God, help me," she thought he said in a throttled undertone.

Frowning, Thea ventured hesitantly, "Devlin? Do you want me to ask Grandfather to chaperone and the three of us will all go? We'd have a delightful excursion, traveling to Georgia together."

"Not this time, sweetheart. I can't." Abruptly he turned and with a hoarse groan wrapped his arms around her, pressing kisses against her hair, her forehead. "Thea...I love you. No matter how long it takes, I will come back to you. Believe in me, Thea."

Believe in him? "I do, I do. Devlin...you're going to see a man about a horse. If the weather holds and the trains run on time, you'll be home in a week, won't you?" Despite her resolve, uncertainty stirred. Thea stared down at her lap, trying to ignore an emotion she hadn't experienced since she'd given Edgar Fane's fate into the Lord's hands.

"I'll try," Devlin said after an uncomfortably long interval. "Don't hold me to a promise I might not be able to keep. We've both had too many of those in our lives." His fingers tightened. "Too many broken promises," he repeated, almost reverently caressing her cheekbones, the line of her jaw. His gaze, dark, intense, bored into Thea's. "But I can promise that no man will ever love you as much as I do. God as my witness, Thea, nobody but God Himself loves you more."

The single kiss Devlin pressed upon her lips tasted of desperation as well as love, but Thea closed her mind to all the questions and held on to him with equal fervor.

Three days later she was in the barn with Jeremiah, helping Nab soothe an unhappy Suffolk punch gelding while Jeremiah examined the animal's mucous-crusted nostrils. Outside the wind whistled and roared, blowing up a Canadian cold snap, Nab warned everyone, "...'cuz my joints is aching something fierce. Whoa, boy, easy on now." He glanced at Thea. "You watch his hindquarters now, Miss Thea. He don't got a notion of how strong he is and how little you are. He just knows he's miserable."

"I don't like the look of this," Jeremiah said. "I'm pretty sure it's nothing but catarrh, but I'm not willing to risk a case of pneumonia, or strangles. Devlin will nail my hide to a tree in the back forty for sure if I don't call in the veterinarian, but I'll feel seven sorts of a fool if it turns out to be a simple cold."

"Do you want me to place a call on the telephone for you?" Thea asked. "Dr. O'Toole's information is in that ledger you keep in the harness room, isn't it?"

"Be a kindness if you did. Would you mind bringing back some leg bandages, as well? Might as well get the fellow as comfortable as possible while we wait."

Glad to have a task, Thea slipped away after giving Muggers's muscled withers a final pat. Moments later, however, she returned with bandages but the alarming report that the ledger was nowhere in the harness room. The oversize leather binder contained not only names and telephone exchanges, but also all the information on every single horse at StoneHill, from bloodlines to health histories. Due to its importance, the ledger was never removed from the harness room, where—until this moment—it resided on a small table situated below the wall telephone Devlin had installed six years earlier.

Jeremiah straightened, wiped his hands on his old dungarees and glared across at Nab. "I remember now. Confound the boy. Devlin himself took it up to the house before he left, to copy out all the bloodlines of our Holsteiners. In all the hubbub to get to the depot in time, looks like he forgot to bring the ledger back."

"I'll run up to the house and retrieve it," Thea volunteered. "I can make the call from the house telephone, then I'll bring the ledger back where it belongs."

"First thing when Devlin returns I'll string *his* hide to a tree," Jeremiah growled. "If you can't place your hand on it immediately, honey, try his desk. It's a mess, but I believe he stuffs telephone numbers in one of the cubbyholes. Come on, Nab, we may as well give this fella's legs a rubdown before we wrap 'em up."

Smiling, Thea stuffed her arms back into her coat and dashed outside into the wind. Once Devlin returned home, she'd have to poke a bit of fun at him over his extraordinary lapse. The evening before he left he certainly had been distracted, rushing around to prepare for a train trip that would probably, he grumbled, last twenty hours or more.

"I hope that Holsteiner colt is worth it," Thea said to him just before he'd ducked into the carriage, and a strange flicker came and went in his eyes.

"Sometimes it's hard to tell what's worth the trouble, until it's too late."

For the next quarter of an hour, while she and Bessie searched Devlin's bedroom and the study without success, Thea chewed over his portentous aside. "I'll take the library," Bessie offered finally. "Your grandfather's dozed off reading a book on Middle Eastern history, of all things, but I'll rouse him if we need another pair of eyes. You're Devlin's bride-to-be, so you go paw through his desk. Won't even let me straighten the papers on it when I clean, so mind you leave them as mussed up as you find them." She paused with her hand on the brass doorknob. "Year before last, when Devlin was gone, Jeremiah lost a horse to pneumonia. I don't want my man enduring that again. You find that veterinarian's number, y'hear?"

She bustled off toward the library, and Thea returned to the study, eyeing the massive walnut desk with trepidation. Full of drawers, cubbyholes and locked files, strewn with books and papers, an adding machine and several other contraptions, the thing hulked like a bad-tempered grizzly disturbed in its hibernation. And the ledger was nowhere in sight.

"After we're married," Thea announced to her absent fiancé, "we're going to tame this beast."

When gingerly sifting through the mess on the felt-covered desktop produced nothing, Thea knelt on the floor to tug on one of the drawer pulls on the two pedestals—and discovered the entire drawer swung open to disclose yet *more* cubbyholes and a stack of smaller drawers, along with slots for files. The ledger would have fit neatly in one of the file holders, except…it wasn't there. Nor was it inside the opposite pedestal, which also pivoted open. Aggravated, Thea blew hair out of her eyes and glared at the upper half of the desk. Behind the stacks of magazines and papers and letters were more drawers and cubbyholes. The two center drawers looked wide enough, and perhaps deep enough, to hold the ledger. She pulled the bottom one open, in her frustration yanking a bit too hard. The entire drawer flew out, scattering the pile of letters, one of which slid inside the empty space behind the drawer.

When Thea reached to retrieve the envelope, her fingers brushed against what felt like a circular indentation in the wood. Mildly curious, she pressed against it, and with an almost inaudible snick, a hidden panel popped open. "Oh, how clever," Thea murmured, wondering if Devlin even knew of the secret drawer's existence. This desk, he'd shared, was one of the few things his mother had left behind at StoneHill, because his father had loved the intricate patterns of inlaid wood on the top and side panels. Completely diverted, Thea shoved aside the envelopes so she could pull the hidden box behind the panel completely out. Perhaps Devlin's mother had left behind something all those years ago—a note would be romantic, but even a haberdasher's bill with his mother's signature would give Devlin a piece of history he'd lost.

What Thea discovered was a sheaf of folded papers tied together with string, the bundle practically filling the bottom of the drawer. A thrill of excitement fluttered beneath her breastbone and her fingers eagerly untied the string. The papers fell open, and instead of a long-dead woman's script she recognized Devlin's distinctive handwriting. Unlike his hopelessly cluttered desk, his penmanship was neat, precise and eminently legible. Thea liked to tease him that he would have made an excellent schoolmaster on the strength of his letters alone.

Her gaze fell upon the words halfway down the first page—and Thea's world exploded in a haze of shock.

# Chapter Thirty

"No. No…no…no!" The words blurred on the page, then sharpened into brutal clarity.

Richard Langston, estranged father to Miss Theodora Langston, has accompanied Edgar Fane to the Jekyll Island Club, located off the Georgia coast. Following instructions, I depart Paeonian Springs, Virginia, on the Washington & Old Dominion Railroad Friday, November 17, connecting with an Atlantic Coast Line Florida Special in Alexandria, for the purpose of going undercover at the Jekyll Island Club. As arranged with Club President Lanier, I will work under the moniker Daniel Smith as a seasonal stables employee. I hereby acknowledge receipt of two reports delivered to me personally by Operative Lawlor on Tuesday, November 14, which provided vital information pertaining to the Hotel Hustler case.

The rest of the words blurred. Thea shook her head, fought to breathe but there was no air, her lungs severed from a brain that continued to deny the evidence of her eyes. The bundle of papers slipped from her hands to fall with a soft rustle onto the desk. With the somnolence of a sleepwalker she stared down at them, at the condemnatory heading—*Daily Report of Agent. United States Secret Service.*

"God, You can't do this to me. It's a mistake. It can't be true." In a burst of frantic motion she pawed through the pages of the report, her heartbeat a concussive hammer against her rib cage.

Then she found what she was looking for—the signature.

Roaring filled her head and the neat inscription magnified, then receded down a dark tunnel. Thea stared at the name until the faintness passed, and hurt ignited in a conflagration of heat and red-tipped blackness. Devlin Stone, wealthy gentleman, horseman, breeder…the man to whom she had pledged her life, her love, *the man she had trusted with her whole heart*…Devlin Stone was an agent for the United States Secret Service. He could even have been one of the men who had her grandfather arrested a year ago.

"Thea? We found the ledger under a book in the library. Bessie sent me along to—" Charles's voice checked, and Thea heard him cross the room. "What's wrong?" He touched her shoulder as he peered down at the desk. "Heavens, what a mess. Well, I'll help you straighten things out a little. Devlin will never know." He reached to straighten the sheaf of reports, and went still. "Oh. Oh, my dear…"

All five of her senses felt as if they had been scraped over a washboard, leaving her raw, hypersensitive to every nuance. When she was able to speak, the words sounded strangely guttural. "You knew already. Devlin told you."

"Yes," he admitted. "He told me. Three nights before he left for Georgia. I gather there is some risk, what he's doing. He wanted me to know, because, well…" He hemmed and hawed, finally adding gently, "Thea, my dear, try to imagine how difficult this—"

"Does Jeremiah know? Bessie?"

In the lemony-yellow glow of a banker's lamp the lines on Charles's face deepened. "Yes," he admitted, his expression resigned. "Everyone knows. They also know how you feel, about the Service, and Edgar Fane. Taffy T…"

"Don't call me that again. The gullible little girl finally grew up." Like waves against rocky cliffs, the outrage of betrayal crashed over her. "You lied to me—*everyone* lied to me! How could you? How could Devlin?" She snatched up the first page of the report and thrust it beneath Charles's nose. "Did you know your son is part of this investigation? Your only living son, my *father?* The man who dumped his infant daughter and dragged the family name through the dirt of countless gambling halls is now in league with the very man who ruined you!"

Charles abruptly sank down into the office chair and covered his eyes with his hand. "I lost my son before you were ever born. As for his involvement with Edgar Fane, Devlin doesn't know what Richard is doing with, or for, him," he said, the words leaden. "Regrettably, if gambling money's included, I know Richard will do anything Edgar Fane demands. More troubling is Edgar's motivation for tracking him down at all. Devlin was disturbed enough to confide in me. He fears for your safety, and we both feared your reaction to the revelation that he's an operative for the Secret Service."

With every word, the hurt metamorphosed into anger. No, not anger—rage. A live monster with serrated teeth, beyond the scope of her experience. Not even her hatred of Edgar Fane or the news about her father matched the out-of-control emotions tearing through her, ripping open her heart, crushing preconceptions along with her bones. Devlin…Devlin. Eyes burning, she stared at her grandfather. "You feared my reaction?" Her tongue had difficulty forming the words. "So you both chose the coward's way out, hoping I'd—what? Never find out? Never discover that the two men I love most would rather lie to me than risk trusting me with the truth? While speaking our marriage vows to honor each other, would Devlin be breaking them with a secret life he refused to reveal?"

"Thea, the man's been torturing himself for weeks, waiting for a time and a way to explain, one which wouldn't precipitate this very sort of response. Try to understand from his perspective. You'd endured a horrific experience and spent your first weeks here wandering about like a shadow of yourself. And you've spent an entire year hating the Secret Service almost as much as you do Edgar Fane. You concocted a dangerous, implausible scheme, one which only by the grace of God didn't—"

"Don't you dare bring God into this!" A small metal postage-stamp box sat on top of a pile of bill receipts. Thea snatched it up, leveled a final scorching gaze upon her grandfather, then hurled the stamp box against the pine-paneled wall on the opposite side of the room. "That's what I think of yours and Devlin's avowals of faith in a loving God." Breathing hard, she stood, smothering in hurt darker than black tar until a strangled sob worked its way free. "After all these months together Devlin still didn't trust me enough to share the truth about his profession? Yes, I would have been upset, but why couldn't both of you have tried to understand how difficult the revelation would be for *me?* He says he loves me, he believed God brought us together until I believed, too. Ha! Jesus promised His truth would set us free, but Devlin never felt *free* to share it, did he? And you…you…" Blindly she shook her head.

The rage withered. The hurt expanded. "No. It's me, isn't it?" She pressed a fist over her heart. "It's me. I'll always be the daughter of a gambler and a saloon singer. No matter how hard I try, I'm never enough to be worthy of *anyone's* love."

Charles heaved himself to his feet. "My dear, please. Don't. You know we both love you. We just wanted to do what we thought was best. For the first time in over a year you were happy. I promise I was going to tell you—Devlin planned to tell you himself, if he returns—" He stopped dead.

"What do you mean, *if* he returns?" Thea braced her palm on the desk. A film of perspiration broke out all over her skin, and an ominous wave of dizziness glazed her vision. "Grandfather? What else haven't you told me?"

He took her hand; never had he looked so old, not even on the night he'd been incarcerated. "Child, Devlin did not apprise me of what he plans to do. But I believe he's gone to this Jekyll Island alone, undercover, not only because he's honor bound to obey orders. Apparently the Service has been trying to learn the identity of this Hotel Hustler for years. Devlin is convinced now it's Edgar Fane, and proof is finally within their grasp. But Devlin also convinced his superiors that Fane needs to be more closely investigated for the murder of that woman in Saratoga. Now do you begin to understand? You are likely the last person to have seen Mrs. Gorman alive other than her killer. For the authorities to have a case against Edgar, your testimony is vital. Yet for the past three months, my dear, Devlin has fought tooth and nail to keep your presence at StoneHill a secret, insisting the Service secure evidence on the counterfeiting charges alone because the risk to you was too great. After hearing about Richard, I have wondered if Edgar Fane is trying to lure you out of

hiding, using your father as the bait. A despicable tactic…"
He faltered, the tendons in his throat quivering.

Thea pulled away, wrapping her arms around herself. "I
don't care about my father." Under any other circumstances
she would have been ashamed of the self-deception. "Fane's
tactic won't work. Devlin should have told me. He should
have allowed me the opportunity to make the decision."
*If he died, she'd never forgive him, or herself.*

Charles inclined his head. "I agree with you. No matter
what you think, Thea, I'm on your side, and told Devlin
so at the time. But I will not condemn a godly man for
following a noble course of action. He's gone to this Jekyll
Island because he's honor bound to do his job. But I also
believe even more strongly his primary motive is to protect
you from a decidedly *un*godly man with enough money
and power to hunt you down until he finds you. Thea? Are
you hearing me?"

"Yes. I hear you saying it's acceptable for Devlin to
protect me at the expense of his own life."

"I can appreciate how you might look at it that way."
The lines crisscrossing his high forehead deepened to fur-
rows. "Devlin loves you, and he's doing whatever is necessary to keep you safe. Alive. He's also a professional with
a job to complete. Which means he's a man on a rack."

"He still lied to me about his true identity." Charles gave
her a sharp glance but Thea stolidly averted her face. "I
need to call Dr. O'Toole. Jeremiah's waiting."

"Bessie's taken the ledger to the barn. Theodora, Devlin's shared the best part of himself with you. His tactics
might have proven faulty, but his motives are pure. I'll be
honored to have him for my grandson-in-law. You don't
want to believe anything but the worst right now, but after
you've had a bit of time to recover from this conundrum I
expect you to behave like the astute woman I reared you

to be." He exhaled a wearied sigh. "These reports were never intended for your eyes, or mine. I don't know where you found them, but—"

"A secret drawer in his desk. It was by accident." Bitterness clogged her throat like gall. "Or perhaps it wasn't an 'accident' at all. Perhaps God wanted me to find them. Have a taste of Jesus' 'truth.'" She knew now what truth her grandfather believed, and likely the bitter taste would linger for a long time. "Of course, Jesus already knew better than to trust any man. Did you know that's in the Bible, Grandfather? How's that for truth?" With benumbed fingers she folded the reports up and tied them back together with the string, stuffed them inside the box and shoved everything back in its hiding place. "There. All gone, like they never existed."

She couldn't feel her feet, and shuffled backward one step, then two. "Sort of like me. Right now, I feel…invisible, as though my hopes and dreams, my heart, never existed. I finally believed what you wanted me to believe— that God should be Edgar Fane's judge, not me. I believed Devlin, that God had brought us together, had filled our hearts with love for each other, and Him. I was at peace. Until today. Tell me, Grandfather, what kind of God dangles peace in your face, then yanks it away? You want me to behave like a rational, intelligent human being, allow the man I love to hug his secrets, and perhaps die because of them. So what kind of God makes you give your heart to a man, then takes him away, perhaps forever? And what kind of man asks you to be his wife when he doesn't trust you enough to tell you who he really is?"

"Perhaps you need to reassess your understanding of the nature of God, Theodora? And the freedom human beings enjoy to make their own choices? You needn't look at me like that. I'm through lecturing, I promise—except for one final bit of counsel. Yes, I know you've not asked for it. One of the perks of old age is the prerogative to annoy loved ones with unsolicited advice. You're hurt right now, feeling betrayed. But be careful how you throw rocks at Devlin. The very nature of his profession demanded silence when you first met, the same way you demanded mine and Mrs. Chudd's when you played *your* dangerous game of deception."

A stronger blast of vertigo struck, making her stagger, but Thea lifted her chin and faced her grandfather down. "When I realized I was in love with Devlin, I confessed everything. For the past four months, I've been trying to relearn how to live a faith *you* seemed to have cast aside. Now I see why. It's impossible, isn't it, to believe God cares when everyone in your life betrays you?"

"Thea…I hadn't wanted to tell you this, but I believe you should know. You're not the only person Edgar Fane has been searching for all these months. He's also hunting for the Devlin Stone who secured a Miss Pickford's release from the Saratoga Springs jail. Devlin's undercover, but he's there alone, risking exposure for—"

"He shouldn't have gone alone! Does the Secret Service think so little of their operatives they sacrifice them like chess pieces? Excuse me, Grandfather. I'm not very good company right now. Perhaps by suppertime I'll be able to transform myself into that astute, understanding woman, and you'll be able to tolerate my company."

She walked out of the study without looking back; when she reached her bedroom she locked the door, then dragged down a pair of suitcases and began to pack.

# Chapter Thirty-One

*Jekyll Island, Georgia*
*Late November, 1897*

Devlin finished raking the dirt floor of the new stables, then trod down the aisle between the forty-six completed stalls, absently patting one or two equine heads that nickered a greeting as he passed. Most of these stalls, purchased in advance by owners for their private use, were unoccupied; few Club owners arrived on Jekyll Island before January. Boatloads of staff, however, commenced arriving as early as October to prepare the land as well as the buildings for the season. Yet access to the island was so closely scrutinized Chief Hazen had had to secure special permission from the Club's new president in order for Devlin to go undercover.

Over the past days, in between studying the plain but elegant Queen Anne-styled clubhouse, and shadowing Edgar Fane on a couple of his painting expeditions, Dev played the stableman, and helped construction workers install cypress shingle siding on the almost-finished stable complex. Many of the longtime crew eyed him cautiously, but some of the Irish construction laborers could talk the ears off a mule; he'd learned quite a lot about this southern hideaway to some of America's most prominent millionaires.

Jekyll Island was no Saratoga Springs choked with grand hotels, shops and amusements, visited by tens of thousands every year. Instead, the tiny island across the sound from Brunswick had been purchased by a French family in the late eighteenth century. They built themselves a home where they raised cotton until the War Between the States erupted. Twenty years later the island was bought and a private, very exclusive club was established whose list of first members read like New York's social register.

Yankees, Devlin mused sourly to himself, were the ones with all the money after the War.

One of several tiny islands dotting the Georgia coast, on the eastern side Jekyll boasted a sandy beach facing the Atlantic, while a serene intermingling of marsh, creek and river on the western side framed stunning sunsets. In between, Spanish moss–veiled forest, open fields and shimmering ponds offered a winter paradise to those who paid handsomely for the privilege. Strangely to Devlin, the place was considered a *family* retreat, not a men's club. Activities consisted of benign pastimes like bicycle jaunts and carriage rides and hunting parties; in the evenings, instead of raucous festivities, owners enjoyed elegant dinners, followed by billiards, games of whist—and talking.

A safe haven for political and economic machinations perhaps, but hardly a hotbed of vice—until Edgar Fane chose to spread his poison here. Lost in thought, just outside the stable entrance Devlin absently picked up a hammer one of the workers had left behind and laid it on top of a stack of pine boards. It was late afternoon, and thin wisps of cloud smeared the deepening coral of the western sky. If it weren't for Richard Langston's presence, and the timing of Fane's visit, Dev would be enjoying the sunset at StoneHill, preparing the horses for winter and basking in Thea's love.

*Lord? Keep her safe. Help me find the proof I need to bring this evil man to justice.*

A chipmunk darted across the path, eyeballed Devlin with a bright reproachful look, as though a heavenly Voice were chiding him. *All right, Lord. You judge Fane's heart. Just help me find the proof so we'll know one way or another what to do with him here on earth. Justice, Lord— not vengeance. Due process of law.*

Perhaps he wasn't so different from Thea after all. Dev might cloak his thirst for justice beneath the mantle of the law, but he still planned to stay on this island until he could handcuff Edgar Fane and formally charge him with crimes against the United States government.

And stuff a few of his bogus bills down his silver-tongued throat.

*Sorry again, Lord.*

What Devlin wanted most, however, was to go home, to StoneHill. To Thea. She deserved complete honesty; he needed forgiveness and reconciliation. The restlessness that had led his feet into service for his country had come full circle, evolving to a profound reverence for the blessings God had provided. Home, his horses, his family and friends. Most of all, the woman he wanted to spend the rest of his life with.

*Have to resolve this thing with Fane.* Only God knew for sure how fragile Thea's safety remained, with Edgar Fane still free.

*One more request, Lord? Help her understand why I had to come here....*

Fane normally arrived at Jekyll Island after New Year's

Day. His decision to depart Atlantic City in the family yacht two months early—and only four days after the discovery of Hotel Hustler counterfeit bills in Philadelphia—offered the Service a rare opportunity, well worth the risk, especially after one of the baggage handlers who'd trundled cartloads of trunks to the clubhouse confirmed Richard Langston's presence with Fane.

"Pleasant gent—tipped me a fiver. But he din't look like he was that glad to be here. I ain't never seen him afore, neither, so's mayhap he allus looks like a lost hound dog. But I did hear Mr. Fane call him—what was it now? Linford? Lane? No—Langston, that's it!" He beamed a toothless smile at Dev, content with the quarter tip he'd just received.

Stable hands wouldn't be able to afford a fiver.

On one of Devlin's first nightly reconnoiters inside the slumbering clubhouse, he'd also verified the guest's name in the register: Richard Langston. Unfortunately, no opportunity had yet presented itself for Devlin to search their rooms. A ferryload of nonmember guests had arrived to spend the Thanksgiving holiday, with a bevy of curious children constantly underfoot. Servants and staff, some of whom lived on the Island year-round, knew everything about everyone, and they were everywhere. There was also the problem of the assistant superintendent, a dedicated and observant man, who would definitely question a stable hand's presence anywhere in the clubhouse other than the servants' dining hall. If Devlin did not succeed in breaking into Fane's chambers and finding some Hotel Hustler bills within the next twenty-four hours, he would be forced to telegraph Washington, using the telegraph room...which would mean his life as Daniel Smith, stableman, would be over.

Nobody could predict the consequences if Devlin were

forced to reveal the Secret Service's suspicions concerning Edgar Fane. But after four days of futile undercover surveillance Devlin was desperate enough to risk a telegram, because the presence of Thea's father alarmed him on a visceral level impossible to ignore. He didn't dwell on issues of his own personal safety should Fane learn his real name.

"My good man, I need to hire a driver and buggy," a cultured voice spoke behind him. "But I can't seem to find anyone hereabouts."

Slowly Dev turned around—to face Edgar Fane himself. Behind him a colored servant carried an easel and a box of artist supplies. Dev hunched his shoulders and touched the brim of his old cloth cap. "Try the carriage room, down yonder," he said, exaggerating his drawl. He pointed, keeping his gaze respectfully averted. "It's a big 'un. This here's a brand-new stables. Forty-nine stalls when she's all finished, brand-new carriage room."

"Yes, I know that already. Imbecile." Fane swiveled on his boot heel and stalked off, muttering another imprecation about stupid cracker hicks and where on earth was all the help. The black man flashed Devlin a sympathetic white-toothed smile and a shrug before following after Edgar.

Very slowly Devlin's coiled muscles relaxed. Casually he stepped off the path, under the lengthening shadow of a palmetto, and flexed his cramping fingers while he watched. Moments later a shiny black buggy rolled out of the barn, one of the liveried drivers guiding the horse off down Shell Road until they disappeared into a stand of moss-draped oaks. Twenty minutes later Dev slipped inside the Clubhouse through the servants' dining room. Confidently he nodded to a cluster of chambermaids and some rough-looking men in dirt-smeared work clothes eating an early supper, then sauntered through the kitchen, snitching a piece of carrot from the chopping table and grinning at the flustered cook's helper.

He ducked inside the butler's pantry until the housekeeper marched past, her arms filled with unfolded napkins, then wandered down the quiet corridor, carefully peering inside the barbershop...reading room...card room, until he finally located his quarry—Richard Langston— disinterestedly shooting balls in the billiard room. He'd learned the first day not to think of Langston as Thea's father, or he'd go after the man like flies on horse dung.

Here at last was the opportunity he'd been waiting for through this interminable week: both men out of the rooms, and most of the guests with their younguns still outside enjoying the mild southern weather.

He would risk ten minutes.

Devlin darted up the U-shaped staircase to the chambers on the second floor, where Fane had rented two large rooms at the end. And discovered a chambermaid just unlocking the door to Fane's room, her cleaning supplies stacked on the floor at her feet.

# Chapter Thirty-Two

Thea arrived in Waycross, Georgia, with her spine straight as an iron rod and the rest of her body throbbing with exhaustion. A rattling, swaying local railroad that lurched to a stop in every rural village it passed finally deposited her in Brunswick a little past one o'clock Friday afternoon, six days after Devlin left StoneHill. The hurt had solidified into a spiny lump, permanently lodged just below her breastbone. But from the moment she asked the station agent in Paeonian Springs to have someone return the horse and buggy to StoneHill, a steely calm had encased her with impenetrable armor. She'd left a letter for her grandfather, another for Bessie and Jeremiah, and packed herself enough food to last for two days.

In Washington, while she waited for a southbound train, she posted her letter to Devlin—in care of the United States Secret Service.

Standing on the depot platform, a shudder of memory caught her off guard and almost punctured her frozen calm. She didn't know which she feared most—that Fane would learn Devlin's identity and kill him or, if her bold plan succeeded and Devlin captured Fane before Fane killed her, she might never be able to forgive Devlin.

She didn't let herself dwell on either possibility. Right now, she couldn't afford emotion.

Emotions were as untrustworthy as people, especially when love and hate intertwined. She had failed in Saratoga Springs because her hatred toward Edgar Fane had blinded her to her own ineptitude. But fear for Devlin had hurled her south nearly a thousand miles to carry out a plan born of equal parts love, anger, hurt and defiance. She wanted to succeed where Devlin and the entire Secret Service had failed, wanted to hand over proof and humiliate them as well as Edgar Fane. Then…then….

She didn't know what "then" entailed, so she ruthlessly throttled the surge of emotion and set all her resources on accomplishing her purpose.

At the Brunswick dock she found her way barred by a group of Italian girls freshly arrived from the northeast on a Mallory steamer. Surrounded by piles of trunks and carpetbags, everyone in the group seemed to be talking at once, their escalating voices drawing stares, though nobody approached the tight little cluster. One of the group, a slight young girl, half turned, and Thea caught a glimpse of a frightened, tear-bright gaze beneath her cloth hat. Thea stepped closer, her mind scrambling to recall the Italian she'd learned over the years from two of the typesetters at Porphyry Press.

*"Mi scusi, ma posso essere di servizio?"* she said to the young girl, asking if she could be of any help. The girl responded in a stream of incomprehensibly rapid words. Thea set her carpetbag down and lifted her hands in a calming gesture. "I don't understand. *Voi,* ah, speak English? *Qual è il problema?* What is the matter?"

A plump, middle-aged woman next to the young girl turned around, scrutinizing Thea with a blend of deference and desperation. "I speak English, *signora*. My name is Bertina, Bertina Giovanni. Please, a doctor is needed, but we do not know how to find, or pay. We have little money." Switching back to Italian, she spoke firmly and several women moved aside, allowing Thea to see a woman supine on the dock, her bandaged head in another woman's lap. Beneath the olive skin her complexion was chalk-white, her eyes closed.

"What happened?"

"On the ship, was yesterday, she fall, hit her head. There was a cut, but Carmella promise she is fine." She gestured to the hovering girl. "This is Maria, Carmella's sister. They are to be maids on the Island. They are new, this year. Now we are all afraid. We wait for the boat to take us across, and Carmella put her hand to her head, and then she fall down."

Slow tears leaked from Maria's eyes, and she silently pleaded with Thea, begging her to do something to help her sister. Thea finally clasped her hands and gave them a reassuring squeeze. "I will find a doctor. Um…*un medico*. Do not worry." After a quick scan of the dock, she addressed Bertina. "I'll be right back. Here—" hurriedly she unbuttoned her long coat and handed it over "—put this over Carmella, but don't move her. She might have a concussion."

"*Grazie, signora. Grazie.* You are a blessing sent from God. But…we have little money to—"

"I do," Thea interrupted. "Please do not worry. I'll be back, with a doctor, as soon as I can."

At the end of the dock she collared a barrel-chested man propped against an empty wagon. After a brief conversation the man tossed aside his cigar, handed Thea up onto the board seat and hollered at his two mules. Moments later, they pulled up in front of a neat frame house on the edge of town. "Ol' Doc Merton'll fix ya'll right up, ma'am."

Less than half an hour had passed by the time she returned to the dock in the physician's buggy; a lanky man of few words but shrewd eyes, Dr. Merton examined Carmella, now conscious but groggy and confused, and concurred with Thea's diagnosis: concussion. She needed complete bed rest for at least a week. After a verbal skirmish conducted half in Italian, half in English, Thea arranged to have Carmella transported to the spare bedroom in Dr. Merton's house, where Carmella would be well tended by the doctor's housekeeper and Dr. Merton's wife. Thea paid the doctor in advance, adding an extra twenty dollars to ensure the Mertons suffered no financial hardship for their care of a stranger.

After Dr. Merton departed with Carmella, the other servants gathered around Theodora, their expressions an amalgam of awe, gratitude and confusion. Maria wept quietly into a large red handkerchief.

"Why you do this, for strangers?" Bertina asked, apparently the designated spokesman for the group. "For—servants. You are a lady."

"You needed help. I couldn't pass by, when I knew I might be of assistance," Thea stammered, suddenly awkward. These days, she didn't feel much like a "lady."

Heavy black eyebrows drew together over Bertina's forehead. "Yet…you travel alone?"

"I travel alone," Thea admitted. "I too am bound for Jekyll Island. It is very important to me. I—I cannot explain. *Mi perdoni.* Forgive me, I will leave you now, for I must arrange for transportation myself. I hope Carmella recovers soon."

"You are expected?"

Bertina's soft question halted Thea's retreat. "Yes, and

no." Needles of shame stitched an ugly path across her conscience. Haltingly, because she no longer possessed the stomach to lie to anyone, ever again, she said, "There are… two men. One of them I believe is a very bad person. The other is—" the word stuck in her throat but she managed to force it out "—my fiancé. I don't know how to say…*mi innamorato?*" Color burned her cheeks. "He is in danger because he is a noble idiot. But it is my fault. I must go to him, to help."

Before Bertina could reply, Maria threw herself against the woman, sobbing and pleading, her words too thick for Thea to follow. For a moment Bertina allowed her to cry, then she set her away with a firm command to quiet herself. With a Gallic shrug she explained to Thea, "Maria is afraid Carmella will lose her position if she does not arrive today. She does not know these people. They have not met her or Carmella, so…she has no trust. I tell her I will explain to the boat captain, why we have one less number, that Carmella will still have her position when she is recover."

Abruptly she stopped speaking, her lips pursing as she looked first at Maria, then Thea. "Your *innamorato,* he is a member of the Club?"

"No, he's not a member," Thea confessed wretchedly. Her heart, which she had struggled to encase in ice, was awash in all the emotions she had tried to sever. Maria's wrenching tears, Carmella's bandaged head, her helplessness—suddenly all of Thea's hurt and rage against life seemed a paltry thing. The selfish tantrum-riddled reaction of a child. She focused her gaze on a small steamer chugging steadily toward the dock. "I will not bother you with my problems. You have enough of your own."

"*Signora,* I do not know how to say this. But you have shown kindness. I must do likewise. So I must say to you…is not allowed for visitors to come to Jekyll Island without invitation. Only members, their guests. Servants. The rules, they are to be followed." For another moment of prickling discomfort she studied Thea, then muttered something Italian beneath her breath. "Signora…I believe I have a way to help you, like you help Carmella. How long you stay on Island?"

"Not long. If I'm lucky, less than two days." *Luck has nothing to do with it,* she could almost hear Devlin's voice whispering in her ear. Like a snake, the quick bite of memory struck too fast, and she crammed a fist to her mouth to prevent an anguished cry.

"Signora, *scusi.* Please wait. I will talk to these girls." Wait? She may as well wait until she crusted into a barnacle if she couldn't find a way to reach Jekyll Island. Her thoughts swarmed without direction, horseflies buzzing in her head.…

At StoneHill, the horses would be out in the pastures, their winter coats a patchwork quilt of dappled grays and bays…and in the paddock, Percy with his soot-spotted rump would watch the lane, black ears pricked, waiting for his beloved master to return. The animal walked now without a limp. He had completely recovered.

If she lost Devlin, Thea would never recover.

Tears scalded her aching throat. She was so intent upon controlling them that she scarcely noticed that all seven women had suddenly formed a circle around her again.

"Signora," Bertina said, "we have talked. We have agreed. To help you is the right thing to do. But we must be careful." Pausing, she watched Thea, gesturing the others to silence while Thea in dawning awareness examined each somber face.

"The boat captain expects eight of you, doesn't he?" she

repeated slowly. "Not seven. He doesn't know Carmella. He doesn't know what happened."

Bertina nodded. "I have kept her papers, for safety." She glanced over her shoulder. The boat would arrive in less than five minutes. "You must be one of us, *signora*. This people, they no let you come if you not one of us. Here," she unpinned her own black cloth hat and held it out. "You cannot wear yours. Is too much like a lady."

"I don't want to cause trouble," Thea began, even as her pulse leaped with excitement—and resolve. She fumbled with her own stylish toque with its bird-of-paradise feather and ruthlessly stuffed it inside her suitcase. "I have no words...."

The other women commenced babbling in a stream of Italian and broken English, their gazes warm with sympathy. A lovely girl with thick dark hair and rosebud lips handed Thea a brightly patterned shawl, framing her sentences in slow, careful Italian so Thea could understand. "Do not be sad. You save Carmella. You follow your man to here to save him, no? This is why you come, all alone? We will help you."

"But you must not speak until we are safely to the servants' quarters," Bertina added drily. Then she grabbed Thea's shoulders and pressed a kiss on each burning cheek. "God is good," she pronounced. "God is good."

# Chapter Thirty-Three

The Jekyll Island Club compound faced Jekyll Creek, on the island's western side. As the Howland steamed toward the wharf, Thea clutched the damp iron railing and tried not to panic. Five months earlier, she had spent weeks at one of the most famous grand resorts in the world, surrounded by entire blocks of hotels, choked with thousands of guests. Yet this serene, deserted-looking island with its collection of buildings intimidated rather than welcomed. Jekyll Island was private, for millionaires and their families, not a social watering hole for the masses. The owners had deliberately retained as much of its natural state as possible, so forests surrounded by pristine sandy beaches abounded with wildlife and birds and beautiful scenery. *"È como il Paradiso,"* one of the servants promised her as they chugged across the water. So Jekyll Island looked like Paradise?

Well, if Thea failed to find proof of Fane's perfidy this time, her fate would probably land her at the real pearly gates. *Lord? I know my sins number higher than grains of sand on the beach these past few days. Is it too late to ask You to forgive me?* Certainly her motives for haring off to this place were ignoble as well as heroic. She wanted to scream her hurt at Devlin, pummel his chest with her fists—but then she wanted to wrap him in her arms and feel the beat of his heart against her ear. *Please, God. I don't want him to give his life for me, not like this.*

Shivering a little in the ocean breeze, she studied the Clubhouse, which vaguely resembled a castle with lots of square windows and a round tower on one corner. The four-story building next to the club, Bertina told her, contained eight private apartments for members. Some owners had built large houses, most within walking distance of the Clubhouse, but they usually brought their own staff. There were also servants' quarters, gardens and stables. Paths of sand and crushed oyster shells, and roads wide enough for carriages wound their ways throughout the buildings and around the entire island.

"But be careful of the alligators when you go for a stroll," Bertina warned her. "Also to remember everyone knows everyone," she reminded her again as the steamer pulled up to the long wharf. "Unless they new, like Carmella and Maria, who are for to work in the clubhouse. You must be careful with the housekeeper, Miss Schuppan— she is, how you say? Particular. Yes." She nodded firmly. "*Signora*...you will be careful?"

The next morning, clad in plain black worsted skirts, over-starched white blouses and striped aprons, Theodora, Maria and two others from what Thea privately thought of as "her troupe," presented themselves to the housekeeper. A surprisingly young woman, Miss Schuppan inspected them with the thoroughness of a drill sergeant. After warning them her word was law, that slovenliness in either appearance or work would result in dismissal and that she expected the clubhouse to shine like the sun by the end of the month, Miss Schuppan turned them over to an assistant. Thea was assigned the task of sweeping hallways and public meeting rooms on the first floor.

At present only eight of the sixty guest rooms were occupied. The assistant, Mrs. Dexter, ticked them off her work-reddened fingers; when she spoke Edgar Fane's name, then his guest Mr. Langston, Thea jerked. Mrs. Dexter paused, a questioning look on her face.

"*Scusi, signora,*" Thea managed with what she hoped was a Bertina-like shrug.

After a narrow-eyed look, Mrs. Dexter continued speaking. "For those of you working on the second floor, where Mr. Fane is lodged, you may clean the rooms as usual but under no circumstances are you to bother the large steamer trunk in the corner. Mr. Fane has been most specific, and as you know, we pride ourselves on catering to every need of our members. So do not even dust the trunk, or mention to Mr. Fane that there is sufficient room to store it in the basement or attic." She paused. "Miss Schuppan was forced to dismiss a chambermaid yesterday, for making that suggestion to him. He was—most displeased. Do I make myself clear? Very good, then. Now let's be about our duties."

By midafternoon Thea had finished sweeping and with a pleased smile hovering around her thin lips, Mrs. Dexter told her to help with the dusting until four-thirty, when she could have a fifteen-minute break as a reward for her diligence. Armed with feather duster, a stack of cloths, a bottle of linseed-oil-and-vinegar furniture polish and Mrs. Dexter's advice: "and make sure you rub the polish, not smear it over the furniture," Thea walked into the card room, where a gentleman sat alone at one of the tables. He glanced up at her entrance, his dark brown eyes disinterested. Then the cards in his hands fell with a clumsy slither all over the table as the man leaped to his feet.

"Hetty?" he whispered hoarsely. He passed a shaking hand over his eyes, and slowly took a step toward Thea, who had frozen where she stood.

Tall and spare, dark hair streaked with gray at the temples, neatly combed and held in place by a touch of pomade, Richard Langston approached, color draining from his face with every step. A vein throbbed in his temple. He stopped less than a yard away, close enough for the scent of bergamot and cloves to flood Thea's nose. "Not Hetty," he said finally. "But…you're the spitting image of her…Theodora."

With preternatural calm she set aside the dusting materials, her gaze never wavering from his. "Father." She tested the word, found the syllables as foreign as the Italian she'd been practicing. "I'm afraid I don't consider that a compliment."

He inclined his head. "She lacked maternal instinct. But to me, once she was the most beautiful woman in the world." He half lifted a hand.

"Don't." A hot trickle of bile slid down her throat. Her automatic backward step was instinctive, and the heat spread. A daughter shouldn't feel this way about her father. "You left her. You left us all. You never tried to stay, not once."

"Is that what your grandfather told you? Well, part of it's true." Moving away, her father clasped his hands behind his back, his face now an expressionless mask. "I did leave—after your mother kicked me out along with the baby who had spoiled her figure. I didn't know what to do. I was only twenty, and knew nothing about babies. You can't appreciate it, I know, but I did you a favor, leaving you with family who would care for you."

"You're absolutely right. I can't appreciate being abandoned by both parents. At least Grandfather didn't dump me in an orphanage when the rest of that caring family perished in the Hudson. I was only three, but I remember them. Do you?"

A muscle twitched the corner of his mouth. "Hetty's dead, you know. Smallpox. After that ferry accident I did go back to her, Theodora. I was willing to try, but it was too late. I sent you cards for a while, but decided you were better off forgetting me. Seems like a lot of my life has been too little, too late."

"I don't care." The childish fantasy that one day her mother would appear and ask Thea's forgiveness shattered, one sliver at a time. The lovely Biblical parable would never happen; if forgiveness was to be granted, she would have to extend it to the man who had fathered, then rejected her. Grandfather had warned her many times she may as well carry a gravestone as a grudge. Both marked the spot where death held the upper hand.

Hate and hope could not coexist. "I used to wonder what kind of a person I would have been, if my parents had loved me. Then I stopped wondering, and thought of all the words I would throw in your faces if we ever met. Now...I don't want to care at all," she said thickly.

A flicker of pain glimmered in his eyes, quickly extinguished. "Then you shouldn't have come here, Theodora. Why did you?"

"Perhaps because until I saw you, I didn't want to believe what I'd learned—that you'd become another Edgar Fane sycophant. Another lackey of the man who ruined our family. A man who continues to commit the same crimes against countless other innocent victims." When Richard merely continued to watch her with mournful basset hound eyes, Thea's outrage sparked. "Is the money he provides worth that much to you? In all your life have you ever considered anyone but yourself?"

"For the most part, no," Richard replied without a blink or a twitch. It was the face of a gambler—a poker face, Thea realized, and could have wept. "Mr. Fane hasn't chosen to enlighten me on the details of his life of crime," he continued evenly. "But I'm not here willingly, Theodora. If you won't believe anything else, will you at least believe that?"

For the second time his gaze searched behind Thea, through the open doorways on either side of a huge fireplace. "Which is why you need to leave, at once. Must I spell it out? I'm the bait," he confirmed, looking back at her. "This is a trap. For you, Theodora."

Bitterness coated his words, the same bitterness toward all of life that Thea had hurled at Grandfather in their last conversation. She flinched away from the comparison as though physically struck.

Richard didn't seem to notice. "Whatever you've done to him, this man is planning a nasty bit of revenge against you. You never should have crossed him. So please, Theodora. Leave now, before he returns from his bird hunting expedition."

"I'll leave—after I find proof to take to the Secret Service. You know precisely what I'm after, don't you…Mr. Langston? I'm pretty sure it's in his room, inside a locked trunk."

# Chapter Thirty-Four

The poker face cracked at last. "*Mr. Langston,*" he repeated under his breath, shame and desperation blurring the chiseled features. For a taut moment he stood silently. "I suppose I deserve your repudiation, perhaps your hatred," he finally said. "If I thought it would do any good, I'd tell you I'm sorry." Watching her, he put a hand inside his silk waistcoat and withdrew two keys, one a skeleton key, the other a smaller brass key. "When Edgar and his assistant left this morning, he told me they'd return at sunset. I'm to finish hiding the last of the counterfeit bills inside the frames. They're hollow—he has them specially designed. Man's developed quite a little consortium for his secret life."

Thea nodded, her mind almost as numb as her heart. "He's the man the Secret Service calls the Hotel Hustler, isn't he? He gives his paintings away to other guests, then uses one of his minions to steal them and retrieve the money. I don't know what happens after that." She hadn't had the stomach to retrieve Devlin's report before she left StoneHill.

"I can tell you," Richard said, a muscle tensing in his jaw. "By giving his paintings to guests, the bogus bills are circulated all over the country, far away from Fane. After the bills are recovered and distributed the frames are sold. From what I've seen his minions are so well paid they'd never snitch on him. Besides, he's Edgar Fane. So...poof. No evidence. The fellow's slicker than macassar oil."

And this was the man from whom she naively hoped to secure evidence on her own. What a stupid feather-head she'd been, not reading all the way through Devlin's reports. Thea grimly thrust aside the self-excoriation, the doubt.

"They've been trying to discover proof to arrest him. Well, I don't care if he is the son of one of the richest men in the country. I refuse to give up. There has to be a way and I'm going to figure it out." Now more than ever, because not only her life, but Devlin's, depended on it. Perhaps Richard could—

"How do you know all this, Theodora? Are you—don't tell me the Secret Service is using *you,* a young woman? I never thought a government-sanctioned organization could stoop so low. Vigilantes, that's what they are. A pack of baying hounds."

"You have no idea what those men do," Thea retorted hotly. For heaven's sake, no wonder Devlin had been afraid to confess his identity. So this is what spiritual scourging felt like—having all your pretenses whipped across your soul until it bled out. Well, she would try to atone for some of both hers and Richard's misconceptions.

"I've spent the last year reviling the Secret Service. But I was wrong. So are you. This organization you sneer at was formed to keep our country safe from fiends like Edgar Fane. These men choose to give up all hope of a normal life to...to perform a service for our country. Oh, excuse me. You wouldn't understand that, would you?" Uglier accusations pushed their way up. A single word—*forgive*—gave her the self-control to shove them aside.

"Those men put your grandfather in jail."

"Only because Edgar Fane paid him with counterfeit bills," Thea shot right back. "Fane's the villain here, not the Secret Service. So their operatives are human. Sometimes they make mistakes. And they have to live every day not only with the burden of their mistakes but with unjust accusations flung by people like you, and me, in order to bring cockroaches like Edgar Fane to justice. I've realized my error in judgment. Why can't you? You never should have agreed to help him, never!"

"If I refuse, he'll kill me, then find another way to get to you, Theodora."

"Don't you think I know that?" she hissed, belatedly realizing her voice had risen to a near shout. "But he won't have a chance if he's arrested. Now you will be, as well, for aiding and abetting a monster disguised as a man."

"I don't think it matters to me any longer," Richard said tonelessly. "Theodora…I don't have to tell you this, but I will. He's been using Porphyry Press. If you leave now, you'll be able to tell the Secret Service the location for the engraving plates, the ink and counterfeiting fiber paper from England." His mouth twisted. "He told me on the trip down, a smile on his face the whole time like he was merely sharing a joke. Well, the joke will be on him—if you leave now."

"You could have found a way to send out this information. There's a telegraph in the office. I don't see a guard with a gun, watching your every move. Club boats go and come all the time."

"I am watched, if I leave the clubhouse. I told you, you don't understand. He knows too much—I owe him."

Beads of perspiration gathered on his brow. "I don't have a choice, Theodora."

"You always have a choice to do the right thing. But you never have made that one, have you?"

In a swift move he snagged her wrist. "Here." He dropped the two keys into the palm of her hand, then closed her fingers over them. His were damp and cold, yet steady as a rock. "The last of the Hustler bills are inside a cigar box in the trunk. I'll be along in twenty minutes, to stuff them in the frame before Fane returns. Either tonight or tomorrow he'll select one of the owners or guests to be the latest recipient of an Edgar Fane work of art. Then..." He stopped, exhaled a wearied sigh. "Every day I dragged the process out, hoping you'd show up. Wishing you wouldn't. This is your only opportunity. Take what you need and get out of here. Blast it, Theodora, don't look at me like that! He owns me now, I told you. But regardless of the sins I've committed, I don't want to see my daughter murdered."

*My daughter.* A single punch of dizziness shoved against the side of Thea's face. The two keys bit into her palm, and she couldn't seem to draw enough air into her lungs. She could deny him until the day she drew her last breath, but here was an example of irrefutable truth: she was the daughter of Richard Langston.

"Theodora? What's the matter with you? I told you, you don't have much time—hey!" His arm shot out and steadied her when she lurched sideways.

"Give me a second," she managed, closing her eyes, trying in vain to blot the memory of Edgar Fane, standing over her with gloating eyes while he described the sight of Cynthia Gorman's corpse. Trying as well to comprehend that the man in front of her had after thirty years acknowledged her existence. The vortex inside her darkened, increased in speed.

Not now, not now. After a year of thwarted plans she had been granted the means, and the opportunity to collect evidence against Edgar Fane. She needed to be Esther of the Bible, placed in a palace to save her people from an evil man; Samson, the mighty but flawed judge, who after his adulterous affair with Delilah had given his life to do the right thing.

All right, she was more like Samson than Esther. She hadn't honored God like she should, though after watching Devlin's transformation these past months she'd yearned to follow his example. *I want to honor You, now. I do. Search me and know my heart, Lord. Help me…I can't function with this vertigo. Only You can take this affliction from me.*

*Only You*…and she didn't deserve anything but the condemnation she'd shoveled over everyone and everything, including herself.

Richard's chilly hold on her arm tightened. "What's the matter with you?" he repeated. "Look, I gave you the keys and the information. I'm no good with fainting women. Don't do this missish swooning on me now."

Even before her father finished speaking, the vertigo vanished. Blinking in astonishment, Thea opened her eyes, slowly glanced to the left, then the right. No symptoms. *No symptoms.*

God had answered her prayer—instantly. She didn't deserve His mercy, didn't deserve the grace or the miracle or His favor, yet He'd granted her plea anyway, from a love no human mind could fathom. The atheists and naturalists and scientists simply didn't understand the fundamental tenet of the Christian faith—Jesus' loving sacrifice of Himself on the cross. For everyone, including Theodora Langston…liar, hater, abandoned child, wounded woman.

Beside her, Richard swore, pacing the floor and darting her baffled looks. But the internal glow of transformation continued to flow unabated through Thea. She saw for the first time the flawed man too weak to accept responsibility for a baby—but strong enough now to offer her the way to escape.

"I didn't mean to scare you," she said, and briefly laid her hand over his wrist. "I have dizzy spells occasionally, particularly concerning Edgar Fane." Ten minutes ago she would have excoriated her father for his part in the lifelong secret affliction. "But I'm fine now. I'm fine…Father. I'm not really a delicate flower, you know."

"Good." They studied each other and a freshet of peace flowed between them. Then her father cleared his throat, strode over to one of the doorways and peered out into the hall. "Now go along, do what you've come to do. "

"I will. He's going to be arrested, very soon, then we'll both be free of him." *Thanks to You, Lord. All thanks to You.* Well…there was another father she needed to thank. After dropping the keys into her apron pocket, Thea gathered up the cleaning supplies and slipped beside Richard out into the hall. "Thank you for helping me," she murmured. "Perhaps later, we can talk?"

The poker expression returned. "I doubt we'll have an opportunity."

She paused. "We can make one." The blackened corner dirtying her soul for her entire life was gone like the vertigo, whisked away in an unexpected act of divine housekeeping. "I'm not going to let him win, Father. And you're going to stay alive."

The corners of his eyes crinkled; his shoulders straightened. Thea smiled at him, then set off for the stairs at the end of the hall.

## Chapter Thirty-Five

His lips pressed into a thin slash, Devlin sent telegrams to Washington and Fred Lawlor, who had traveled down separately to monitor things across the Sound in Brunswick. Defeat was a dull ax, chopping away at Dev's neck. His only "success" thus far was his continued anonymity; when neither Mr. Grob, the Club superintendent, nor Miss Schuppan caught him inside the club office, he considered it mercy from God rather than proof of his own cleverness.

Task accomplished, he stepped back into the wide corridor, automatically noting a waiter entering the dining room, and at the other end of the hall a gentleman guest with his back to Devlin. The gentleman appeared to be speaking to an aproned cleaning woman whose face was blocked by his shoulders. None of them glanced Devlin's way.

He was still a shadow, unremarked upon and unknown.

A discomfiting squiggle crawled along the back of Devlin's neck. Pausing, he risked another glimpse down the corridor, where the cleaning woman was now walking away. Something about her posture—or was it the tilt of her head and the glimpse of brown hair?—reminded him of Thea. *Not again,* he thought morosely. Over the past week his pulse had spiked several times for the same reason. Annoyed with the propensity to imbue every woman he passed with Theodora's traits, Devlin headed for the doors leading to the piazza. He had risked his professional reputation and his future to ensure that his fiancée remained safely ensconced at StoneHill, almost a thousand miles away. Missing her was automatic, like breathing, both of which he ignored. He could wallow in loneliness later, because until he received a reply to either telegram Devlin Stone needed to hide behind the persona of an unremarkable stable hand named Daniel Smith.

It was a little past four in the afternoon; he exited the clubhouse onto the piazza and stood for a moment in the shadows, wrestling with the disquietude. No operative achieved sought-after results one hundred percent of the time; Devlin could accept his inability to secure proof that Edgar Fane was the Hotel Hustler. What he could not accept was his failure to protect the woman he loved. With Fane alive and free, Thea could never be safe, never stop wondering. The vertigo attacks, in abeyance for the past few months, might return.

When Devlin confessed his profession as an operative she might never forgive him.

She might repudiate him altogether.

Inevitably, Edgar Fane would discover her whereabouts.

*I made the choice to trust You, Lord. But…do I have to lose the woman I love to prove my faith?*

Luminous streaks of gold-and-orange-tipped red painted the western sky, signaling the end of another day. From the direction of the marshes, he heard the plaintive honking of geese and, down Old Plantation Road, the distant voices of members, returning from their day's outing. As the sound of hooves and carriage wheels drew closer, Dev decided to head on over to the stables. Might yet hear something about Fane he could at least pass along to headquarters for the next operative assigned to the case.

A pair of buckboard carriages rolled into view, jammed with several women as well as men, most of them carrying shotguns. In the first carriage, tongues lolling, a pair of hunting dogs peered between the driver's legs. And behind the driver lounged Edgar Fane, looking smug and relaxed in his Norfolk jacket, yellow sweater and knee breeches. His personal assistant Simpson sat beside him. The carriages passed by, heading for the covered porch around the corner.

Instinct took over. Hands stuffed in his pockets, whistling a tune and shuffling his feet in the sandy soil, Dev leisurely followed. When he reached the hunting party, people were still mingling, talking about the day. Mr. Grob had joined the group, a deferential smile showing beneath his handlebar mustache. He congratulated the man who bagged an eight-point buck and a woman who had nabbed half a dozen quail, commiserated with those who had returned empty-handed, including it seemed Edgar Fane.

"I'm no good with guns," Edgar said with good-natured aplomb. "No doubt *un*masculine of me, but I prefer to potter with a paintbrush."

"I'm so dreadfully sorry to hear you're leaving us," one of the women gushed. "Next week, was it? And so soon after your arrival. You will return, I hope?"

"Alas, 'downward the voices of Duty call, to toil and be mixed with the main,'" Edgar responded, with a flourish kissing the back of her hand. "Incomparable words from Sidney Lanier's poem, written for the marshes of this incomparable island sanctuary." He glanced at his expressionless secretary. "Simpson, that last painting I completed day before yesterday? I think you should present it to Mrs. Butler tonight after dinner."

"Yes, Mr. Fane," Simpson replied stolidly while Mrs. Butler squealed with delight.

Using the buckboard carriages for a screen, Dev maneuvered closer. After nodding to the colored driver standing beside the horse, he knelt to pretend to retie the laces of his work boots.

"…and sorry Mr. Langston couldn't join us today.…"

"…worse than I, at the sport of hunting…prefers taking risks with a deck of cards…likely still in the card room.…"

So the man Dev had glimpsed at the end of the hall had been Richard Langston, Thea's father. Apparently he was trusted enough, or cowed enough, to be left to his own devices while Edgar Fane enjoyed the island amenities. Dev filed both tidbits of information away.

The unwelcome news of Fane's apparently imminent departure would have to be investigated with—

"'Scuse me, suh? You be the new stableman what's got a dab hand with horses, right?"

Devlin's head whipped around to the driver, whose eyes flared in alarm. Dev offered a placatory smile. *Stay in character,* he reminded himself as he straightened. "I am," he said. "You're…Wiggins, isn't it?"

The driver nodded, pulling off his hat to run a hand over his head of kinky gray hair. "Would you mind looking at Brownie's right leg? He was favoring it just now. Might be nothin' but seeing as how you was walking by, thought I'd ask."

Dev throttled the frustration and approached the lightly sweating gelding harnessed on the right side of the team. After a rapid but thorough examination of all four legs, he showed Wiggins two fragments of oyster shell. "Likely these were the culprits—one was lodged in the central cleft of the foot on the right foreleg, but there was also a smaller piece in the left hind sole. The shoes are still properly nailed, so I don't think he'll suffer from lameness, but I'd let him rest for a day or two, just to be safe. Good man for noticing." With a final pat on Brownie's neck, he surveyed the dwindling crowd still clustered around Edgar Fane.

"Would you mind coming along to the stable with me?" Wiggins asked. "I can drive a carriage fine, but my knees give out on me when I have to stoop down." Anxiously he searched Devlin's set features. "You won't tell, will you? Me and the missus, we get to stay here year-round now, and I'd hate to be let go."

"Your secret's safe with me." Torn, Devlin hesitated, but Fane was already extricating himself from the group to "freshen up before dinner."

Suppressing a sigh, Dev told Wiggins he'd be glad to take care of Brownie.

Some ten minutes later, while gently cleaning the horse's feet with a hoof pick, the squiggle of unease he'd felt earlier returned to irritate his brain. He remembered the cleaning woman with more clarity, remembered her turning away from the man to walk toward the staircase. *It was the walk,* he abruptly realized. That walk…the first day he'd followed Thea down the steps of the Grand Union Hotel in Saratoga Springs, memorizing her unique blend of femininity and firm assurance… Would a servant, a cleaning woman hired to mop floors and dust furniture, walk like a woman of purpose, of power?

And why would Richard Langston converse with a servant at all? *What if Theodora weaseled the truth from her grandfather—and was playing another part?* If instead of a wealthy socialite with a titled fiancé, like Devlin she'd somehow slipped onto Jekyll Island in the guise of a servant?

Devlin had come to know his beloved and her propensity for impulsiveness very well indeed. For a fraught second he rested his forehead against Brownie's shoulder and absorbed what instinct already knew. He might have been within shouting distance of the woman whose courage far outweighed common sense. Never mind the wishes and elaborate schemes of the man desperate to keep her far away from Jekyll Island.

*God, Thea's here, isn't she?* And for some reason God hadn't alerted Devlin until now.

Urgency rolled through him, thundering its intensity; tail swishing, Brownie's skin quivered beneath Dev's hands. He automatically calmed the animal before obeying the insistent hum of warning.

Five minutes later he headed back to the clubhouse.


Thea heard the voices in the hallway. Fear exploded inside her stomach, but she managed to close and lock the trunk, stuff the last of the counterfeit bills in a hidden pocket of her skirt, then gather up her cleaning supplies. Several more bills were hidden beneath the rags at the bottom of the bucket. By the time Edgar appeared in the doorway, a scowl on his face and a shotgun balanced in the crook of his elbow, she was on the other side of the room, feather-dusting a lamp.

"What the devil are you doing here? The rooms were supposed to have been cleaned this morning."

"*Scusi, signore,*" Thea bobbed a clumsy curtsey and with her face averted, aimed her feet for the opened door. "*Io somo finito. Lascio.* I finish. Leave now."

Fingers slippery with fear, greasy nausea filling her

throat, she had almost managed to gain the hallway when she sensed him looming behind her.

"One moment, girl."

Servants would never disobey such a command; if Thea ran, his suspicions would be aroused enough to chase after her. Yet if she obeyed his order, when he saw her face he would most certainly recognize Miss Pickford. *Into the lion's den,* Thea thought. Squaring her shoulders, she turned around.

*"You!"* Triumph flared in eyes gone hard and bright as polished black marbles. "So. My little plot worked. I thought it would, though you cut it close, my dear. Later, you'll have to share where you've been hiding all these months. For now, have you enjoyed the reunion with your long-lost father?"

Thea raised her chin. "What difference does it make? You never should have used him as bait. You might think you've outmaneuvered us all, but this time, Edgar Fane, you'll be the one in a jail cell. Not me, or my grandfather. Or my…my father." The bundle of rags wouldn't faze him, but if she threw the bucket, screamed to draw attention…

"Ah, then you have spoken to him. Sorry to have missed the exchange." He whipped out an arm, yanked the bucket out of her hand and tossed it through the doorway behind him. When the clatter ceased he resumed talking as calmly as though he'd plucked a dead leaf from his sleeve.

"Definitely didn't inherit your father's poker face, did you? Good thing I left my shotgun in the room. Of course, your weapon of choice is words. You verbally cut a man to the size of a mouse—one of your less-attractive traits, my dear Theodora." He made a tsking sound and shook his head. "Poor Richard. Did you eviscerate him like you did me at Saratoga? I might feel sorry for him, except he handed you the keys to my kingdom. Too bad. I was going to let *him* go."

More voices echoed up the stairwell; seconds later a couple with three children crowded into view, a confusion of noise and movement with the children racing between Thea and Edgar, calling to one another while a flushed nanny scurried after them. The couple stopped to speak to Edgar, forcing his attention.

Thea dropped the rest of the cleaning supplies, gathered her skirts in fistfuls of fabric, and ran for her life down the staircase.

## Chapter Thirty-Six

"Excuse me," Edgar explained urgently to the mystified Randolphs as Theodora whisked out of sight. "I must speak to Mr. Grob. I'm afraid I caught that cleaning woman trying to steal several personal articles from my room. She must be apprehended immediately, before she can hide what she stole."

He dashed down the stairs; fury and triumph throbbed to the beat of his racing footsteps. Based upon Theodora's expression of guilt and horror, Langston had double-crossed him. Likely his irritant of a daughter had stolen some of the bills, but her pathetic plan to outwit him was doomed to failure. Some of his work was probably at the bottom of that bucket. Some, but possibly not all. The wench had fled onto the piazza, and was scurrying down the path that led to the servant quarters.

She couldn't run far enough or fast enough to escape her inevitable fate, but blast it all, she'd just forced him to drastically hasten his plans.

Edgar found Simpson and Langston in the card room, talking in a corner while a threesome dealt cards at one of the tables on the other side of the room. "Simpson, one of the wagons from the hunting expedition was still under the porte cochere a moment ago. Go out there at once. Don't let the driver leave for the stable. I need that buggy, *now*."

He turned to Langston. "Wipe the smugness off your face. You gave her the keys, of course."

The older man stroked his sideburn for a second, then shrugged.

Only the presence of witnesses compelled Edgar to rein in his temper. "Deal yourself aces and eights, Langston, because you're a dead man."

"Everyone dies, Mr. Fane. Even you."

Edgar stepped close, keeping his back to the three card players. "I have men waiting on my yacht, with orders. It will be a pleasure having them carried out."

Langston's only reaction was a raised eyebrow. "You might be richer than Croesus, Fane. Like I said, every man has a day of reckoning. Perhaps mine's today. But yours, my friend, is just around the corner."

Edgar mouthed a vicious curse, swiveled on his boot and stormed out of the clubhouse. As soon as he caught Theodora and had her stashed safely aboard his yacht, everything else would fall back into place. He was prepared. He'd been prepared for her inevitable arrival, just as he'd been prepared for Richard Langston's belated streak of paternal instinct.

He had not expected Thea to sneak across to the island in the guise of the maid, however. Resourceful, he'd grant her that.

But like Cynthia, she'd made a big mistake, the last one of *her* life.

Outside, Simpson was arguing with the driver, who insisted the horses were too tired for another outing. In the distance, Edgar could just make out Theodora's dark skirted figure with the white splash of her shirtwaist, fleeing not in the direction of the servants' quarters but toward one of the roads that led into thick woodland. He had to capture her before she found a hiding place.

"I'm taking this vehicle." Unceremoniously he shoved the liveried driver aside. "Simpson," he bit out to the slack-jawed assistant, "see to that painting, and have Langston escorted to the yacht. He is not to be left unattended, do you hear?"

After grabbing the reins, he snatched the whip out of the holder and applied it to the two horses with the unleashed violence he longed to perpetrate against Richard Langston and his daughter. Half rearing in surprise, the animals leaped into motion and almost jerked Edgar over the dashboard. Cursing, he shook the reins, and finally the horses lumbered into a canter, careening headlong down the path where Theodora fled, the proverbial rabbit fleeing the hounds.

Dusk had fallen, the vivid colors of sunset a fading memory on the western horizon. Heedless of the crunching sound of the oyster shells, Devlin ran toward the clubhouse. At the bend in the road, just past the old duBignon house, a flash of movement distracted him. It was a person, a woman, running toward one of the roads that led into the island's interior—not a destination one would choose with night fast approaching. Denial and ice-edged terror streaked through Devlin, because he knew in his gut the woman was Thea. Knew she was that cleaning woman and Fane—

Panicked hooves thudded hard on the road behind him, coming from the direction of the clubhouse. Dev dropped to a crouch behind a shrub and watched while scarcely a dozen paces away, Edgar Fane drove past in an open buckboard carriage. White-eyed, their flanks wet with terror, the two horses who had been out on the hunting excursion all day had been pushed into a full gallop by Edgar's maniacal recklessness. His lips were stretched in a rictus of fury, and as he flew by Dev glimpsed murder blazing from his eyes.

Devlin would never reach Thea in time. *Dear God in heaven.* "Thea!" He roared her name as he sprinted after the buggy, an agonized cry of impotence swallowed up in trees that loomed like vultures over the road. "Thea, I'm coming! Watch out! *Thea…*"

A hundred yards down the road he watched her falter, glance over her shoulder, watched her throw herself to the side to avoid being trampled. Watched Edgar bring the horses to a snorting halt…watched him leap from the buckboard and manhandle Thea, kicking and punching, back up onto the seat beside him.

Sand and dirt and crushed shell from the churning wheels flew up close enough to spit in Devlin's face as the horses sped away beneath moss-draped live oaks and palmettos. The buggy disappeared from sight less than five seconds after Devlin arrived at the spot Thea had fallen. A deadly calmness settled over him. Calmness, clarity and determination. Running like a stag, he raced back to the stables in a diagonal dash through the undergrowth, burst into the courtyard and down the aisle to the stall where Lancer, a former Thoroughbred racehorse, was idly munching hay. "I need you, fella." His movements calm but swift, Devlin led the horse back down the aisle, stopping only long enough to grab a bridle. Then he mounted Lancer bareback and, once they left stable, kneed him into a canter.

Less than two minutes had elapsed since Edgar abducted Thea.

The horse's big muscled body surged into an effortless

gallop at Dev's soft command. Balanced like a centaur, he funneled thirty years of rapport with equines into the task of winning the most important race of this horse's life—and prayed God would protect Theodora, for just a few more moments.

# Chapter Thirty-Seven

Thea battered Edgar with fists and elbows, squirming every way she could to break either the iron bar of his arm around her shoulders, or the hand holding the reins, shouting at him all the while in a vain attempt to rattle his composure. The carriage swayed wildly, knocking both of them about on the seat, and at one point they swung almost completely off the path, the side wheels bouncing into a rut that rattled Thea's teeth. She didn't care, didn't cease yelling and struggling despite the certain knowledge that she was about to die.

She fought because she had heard Devlin, calling her name. *I love you,* she told him silently. She wanted to yell the words out, to answer the faint voice she'd heard just before Edgar tried to run her down. *I love you with all my heart. God? Please let him know I'm sorry...* She managed to wrest an arm free, and landed a solid punch to Edgar's jaw.

He mouthed a foul curse. The arm crushing her against his side shifted, squeezing her rib cage until she was light-headed from lack of oxygen and the dreadful certainty her ribs were about to crack and puncture a lung. Her efforts to escape grew wilder but lost force; abruptly the buckboard slewed to a halt. Edgar's hand closed around her throat and his face in the powder-gray gloaming loomed over her, an evil bird of prey poised for the kill.

"This ought to make you more manageable." She sensed movement, then something shiny appeared in her whirling vision. "Do you see this? Do you?" He spat the words and Thea managed a jerky nod. "A hunting knife is a useful thing, I'm told," he said. "This one fits in a man's pocket. It was a gift—from Cynthia. I've always appreciated irony. Let me think…where's the best place to—*be still!*" The command rasped out viciously. "Shut up and don't move another inch, or I promise I'll feed you to the alligators a piece at the time."

Amazing what passed through one's mind at the point of death. Thea stared up into the glittering dark eyes and silently thanked God that she could at least face them without the vertigo. That she felt no fear, only a ripping grief for Devlin, and a gritty determination to spit in Edgar Fane's eye.

"Devlin will hunt you down," she choked out, gasping when his fingers cruelly bore down against her windpipe. "He'll…find the evidence. Hotel Hustler…"

Pain suddenly exploded in her side, a spear of white-hot fire that stole the last of her breath.

"That ought to do it," Fane said, thrusting her away. "As for your pathetic Mr. Stone, he'll never find you. He's nothing but a gullible Southern gentleman who still believes in chivalry. When he learns the woman he rescued from jail is the daughter of a bawdy house singer and a gambler, he'll consider himself fortunate to be rid of you."

"The Secret Service…" The shock of pain had weakened her. She slumped, managed one last challenge. "They'll find you."

"Bah. Fools, the lot of them. They can't find their way

across a street. Neither the Secret Service nor any other authority will be able to prove a thing. They never have. They never will. I'm Edgar Fane. It's quite delicious, you know, having all the power and wealth one desires."

Thea collapsed like a rag doll against the seat, her hands instinctively fluttering to the source of the pain in her left side. The white cotton shirtwaist blouse was wet, sticky with what dawned upon her in shock was blood. "You… stabbed me."

"You shouldn't have hit me. Here." He tugged out his handkerchief, pressed it with ungentle force against her side. "If you apply sufficient pressure, you should survive long enough to make it to my yacht." The carriage lurched back into motion. "If it's any consolation, after you and your father are disposed of, I've decided cold-blooded murder's not really my style. Frankly, I don't care much for blood, so if you don't mind, try not to bleed all over the buggy. As for the Hotel Hustler, I'd already decided it's time for him to retire, sail to the Fiji Islands. I plan to paint satisfying but mediocre art. The thrill's been gone for a long time. Tell me, did you hide some of my best work anywhere else other than the bucket? Perhaps somewhere upon your lovely person? Well, not so lovely now. But you were, Theodora. You were."

Pain and shock had weakened her resistance, but Thea smashed the heels of both hands over the handkerchief and pressed while she gritted her teeth, forcing her sluggish brain to ignore the dusting of regret in his voice and *think*. "Too many people know, this time. You're…no longer impervious."

"Remains to be seen, doesn't it? You'll never know, having tragically fallen overboard once we set out to sea." Suddenly his head lifted. Twisting, he looked behind them, then muttered a curse. Lifting the buggy whip, he slashed the horses' hides until their light canter erupted back into a frenzied gallop.

The buggy rocketed down the road. Winding curves with gigantic trees close enough for the Spanish moss to brush their heads flew by in a blur as twilight deepened toward night. Dizzy, depleted, Thea clamped her elbow against her side and wondered if the next bounce would propel her over the armrest. Then she heard it—a voice, calling out in the tropical wilderness of Jekyll Island. Devlin's voice.

Somehow Thea managed to turn, though an agony of pain sliced through her side. Her heart gave a leap of gladness. "Devlin." She tried to shout the name, but the word dribbled out in more of a whimper. Fane flicked her a single savage glance bristling with challenge. A taunting smile twisted his lips before he leaned forward to focus all his attention on the horses flying at the edge of control.

The sound of thundering hooves crescendoed off to her right, until the rolling rhythm filled her ears. Hope blossomed inside Thea's laboring heart and she managed to turn her head toward the sound. A horse's head appeared, mane flying, ears pricked forward, bright dark eyes focused on the two harnessed animals racing a few strides ahead. Then Devlin came into view, riding bareback, one long arm stretched out toward Thea. Across the low armrest of the buckboard their gazes met.

"Take my hand, love," Devlin told her in a calm, commanding voice.

"Not a chance!" Fane shouted, and abruptly the buckboard swerved away, almost crashing into the underbrush before settling back into a shuddering path along the center of the road. "Catch me if you think you can!" he yelled over his shoulder.

Less than a hundred yards ahead, the road curved sharply to the left.

Thea stiffened her spine, never taking her gaze from the magnificent sight of Devlin riding a beautiful chestnut Thoroughbred as though he were part of the horse. Love and determination and—peace—washed over her. *I can do all things through Christ...soar on wings of eagles...walk on the heights with hind's feet...* Time stretched into a bright supple ribbon, wrapping Thea in an unearthly blend of strength and weightlessness. Grasping the wire arm rail, she pulled herself forward in the seat, watching the horse lengthen his stride until he and Devlin galloped less than a yard away alongside the carriage. Devlin had tied the reins together over the horse's neck and he was leaning, both arms now stretched toward her. Thea sucked in a deep breath, lifted her arms toward his, and as the ricocheting buckboard tossed her off balance and she toppled forward, Devlin's hands closed around her waist and lifted her out of the buckboard.

# Chapter Thirty-Eight

Dev...Devlin. He had rescued her after all. Joy filled Thea's heart until pain from the knife puncture shrieked through her body. The joy and pain wrapped around her in blinding whorls of gold and scarlet. Sobbing, she drifted toward a fog of semiconsciousness while Devlin settled her sideways in front of him, his hard muscled arms on either side holding her in a safe protective cage.

"I've got you, love," his voice murmured in her ear. "You're safe, Thea."

He spoke to the horse, and a moment later the animal slowed to an easy walk, nostrils blowing hard but as quiescent as a purring kitten. Down the road, Fane and the buckboard carriage flew around the corner and out of sight. "Whoa, boy," Devlin said, bringing the horse to a standstill. He slipped to the ground, then reached to haul Thea down.

"You crazy little fool! You almost died!" His voice broke and he abruptly wrapped her in a smothering embrace, his arms shaking. "Thea...Thea...Thank You, God. You're alive. Lord, thank You..."

"Amen," Thea breathed waveringly before her legs collapsed beneath her. "Devlin...sorry. Had to come. Found out your secret." His face turned gray as the Spanish moss and she tried to lift her hand to soothe him. "Don't care. Love you…"

"Thea, I wanted to tell you, but I didn't know how. I—hey! What's this?" He grabbed her hand and stared. "This is blood. Did that monster hurt you?"

"'fraid so." She could feel herself sliding back down a slippery slope into darkness. "Knife. Left side. Then he gave me a handkerchief. He doesn't like blood.…"

Before she finished the sentence Devlin had her stretched out on the path, his jacket under her head while he ripped open her shirtwaist with scant ceremony. "I see it. All right, sweetheart, you're all right. It's actually not too bad, only a couple of inches deep. Still bleeding a bit but it's starting to clot. You'll need stitches but—you'll live."

A single shuddering breath escaped before he shrugged out of his shirt, then tugged a flannel undershirt over his head. In a few swift tugs he ripped off the three-quarter sleeves and tied them together. After folding the shirt into a wad he carefully covered the wound, then used the tied-together sleeves to wrap around Thea's side to hold the makeshift bandage in place. Edgar's blood-soaked handkerchief was hurled into the undergrowth.

Then he was covering Thea's face with desperate kisses. "Don't ever do this to me again. I love you. I never should have kept my profession a secret. I never want to keep sec—"

A loud scream ripped the air, then was silenced with the abruptness of a snuffed candle. A pall of stunned, absolute silence quivered in the twilight.

Devlin sprang to his feet, standing literally over Thea in a protective stance that moved her to tears. Yet his reaction awakened in her a longing wide and deep as the ocean to cover *his* face with kisses. When he knelt beside her once more, she fumbled for his hand, holding it against her wet cheek. "Go find out what happened," she told him. "I'll be fine."

Devlin shook his head. "I'm not leaving you alone in the darkness. If I hold you, can you stay on the horse?"

"Absolutely. I'll even ride astride. The pain's much better."

"Liar." He covered her mouth in one brief, hard kiss, then stroked his index finger down her cheek. "I love you for your bravery. But no more secrets or lies between us, all right?"

"All right. But I do feel much better. You're here."

Gently, he lifted her into his arms, settled her on the horse. After mounting with a breathtaking display of masculine strength, they set off down the road at a smooth, controlled canter. When they reached the bend in the road Devlin pulled the horse to a walk, and used the shadows of a thick grove of live oak to conceal their presence as much as possible.

A dozen yards into the bend, they saw the two livery horses standing near the side of the road, heads drooped, sides heaving, globs of white foam coating their flanks. The empty buckboard carriage was tipped sideways over the branches of a fallen tree which protruded halfway across the road.

Edgar Fane was nowhere in sight.

"Can you stay on the horse by yourself?" Devlin began urgently, just as the sound of a low groan reached their ears, followed by a garbled string of illegible words, then silence.

Thea passed her tongue around lips gone numb and sand dry. "Be careful. Please. He still has the knife."

"I'll be careful. Thea…"

"Don't worry about me, Devlin. I've discovered I've a knack for horses. Lancer and me, we'll be fine."

The stormy blue-gray eyes lit up for a moment, then he melted into the shadows, using the screen of the buckboard to shield him from sight. Thea sat still, basking in the afterglow of that expression. She might be sitting astride a lathered horse, her side might be on fire and shivers still racking her body, but nothing could dim the wonder of this moment. Devlin was here, alive. She was very much alive despite Edgar Fane's evil intentions.

Amazing, how love could transform a knife wound to a pinprick.

Devlin returned quickly. "It's not a trap. Thea..." He paused, then added simply, "Fane was thrown from the buggy. He broke his neck. Right now, he only has a few moments to live. He asked for you."

"He—what?" She couldn't absorb the words, couldn't grasp their significance.

"Hold on to Lancer's mane, love. I'll take you to him. It'll be faster if I don't try to carry you myself."

Fane lay without moving in a patch of dry weeds, his head twisted at an unnatural angle, inches away from the trunk of the fallen tree. The last beam of burnt-orange light streamed over his body in macabre illumination. Silently Devlin lifted Thea into his arms and carried her over; she knelt beside Edgar.

His eyes were open, watching Devlin. He spoke with difficulty. "Not just...Southern farmer. Secret Service?"

Dev nodded. "But I'm also a Southern farmer."

"Would have made a good jockey. Looks like...you win...this race, after all, Stone." The opaque gaze drifted over Thea. "Will she live?"

"Yes," Thea answered. "God willing, for a very long time. Long enough to learn how to forgive you, I hope."

"Ah." A rattling breath struggled to escape from his throat. "Always did like…straightforward women." A strange baffled look drifted across his face. "Can't feel anything. Can't move…tell Simpson…sorry, about Cynthia. I was wro—" The final confession sighed out unfinished as Edgar Fane breathed his last.

# *Chapter Thirty-Nine*

Clean, milk-white skies and mild winter sunshine greeted Thea the next morning. Stitched up and sore, her body squawked in protest the entire walk to the clubhouse from the infirmary, where the compound doctor had insisted she spend the night. Thea didn't mind the discomfort; she and Devlin were both alive, and safe. *Thank You, Lord.* The grateful prayer winged upward with surprising naturalness.

When she opened the door to the office, the first voice she heard was her father's. "One villain dead, the other captured. You've certainly earned a gold star for your 'Secret Service,' Operative Stone."

"That's one way of looking at it." Devlin's back was to Thea and she couldn't see his expression, but he responded to the light sarcasm in a deceptively lazy Southern drawl.

Another Secret Service operative, the "reporter" Mr. Lawlor, lounged against a desk. No difficulty reading the contempt in his expression, she thought sadly. But then, her father deserved it. Neither the Club superintendent nor Miss Schuppan were anywhere in sight. Feeling like a trespasser herself, Thea awkwardly cleared her throat. "Good morning," she said.

Devlin swiftly turned and started toward her. "Thea! We didn't expect you much before noon."

He said something else but she didn't hear because she had just seen the handcuffs around her father's wrists. For an instant time telescoped backward, and she felt the cold heavy manacles around her own wrists. Remembered the hopelessness inside that barren cell. *Every member of her family...* Blindly she focused on Devlin.

He reached her side in two long steps, filling her vision, calming her senses. "You're still pale. Did you sleep? Did the doctor give permission for you to leave?" The intensity of his loving perusal mitigated the churning in Thea's stomach. His anxiety made her want to wrap him in a hug.

And yet, her father's hands were shackled together. "I slept. The doctor grumbled but gave in. I'm stiff. Sore. Grateful to be alive...Devlin? Why is Richard...why is my father handcuffed?"

"Mr. Langston," Mr. Lawlor said, answering for Devlin, "is under arrest for aiding and abetting a notorious counterfeiter guilty of abduction and committing bodily harm, who may or may not also be guilty of the crime of murder." For some reason he scowled at Devlin, then walked over to stand with folded arms in front of the door.

"Don't fret, Theodora," Richard said. "It was inevitable from the moment I followed Edgar out the door of an Atlantic City casino. The arm of the law is long and unrelenting. Unfortunately, so was Edgar Fane. At least I'm still alive." A corner of his mouth curved. "As are you."

And Edgar Fane lay covered in a shroud on his yacht. The men who would have killed Richard and tossed Thea overboard had been taken to the jail in Brunswick.

Fane's crimes were at an end…but their consequences still remained. For a painful moment she studied the man who for almost a quarter of a century had pretended she didn't exist.

And yet… "Devlin, my father also aided and abetted *me,* knowingly put himself at risk so I could secure the evidence—for you. For the Secret Service. Doesn't that count for something? Must he be treated like a criminal?"

Deep lines furrowed Devlin's forehead, and shadows smudged the blue-gray eyes. But he allowed Thea to speak, not interrupting or defending himself. Suddenly she realized with a sharp internal click that she'd fallen back into the same toxic trap that had poisoned her spirit for much of her life. Her father had never escaped. With God's grace leveraging some spiritual muscle, Thea could.

"I'm sorry," she said. She darted a glance at the impassive Mr. Lawlor, then stretched up and right there in front of the Lord and everyone else pressed a repentant kiss to Devlin's cheek. Beneath her lips the muscles in the hard cheekbone jerked once, then stilled. "I'm sorry." She breathed the apology again, into his ear, and stepped back. "You're right. You're upholding the law, and I know it's also the right thing to do. It was just…"

"You don't have to apologize. I understand." Softly he brushed her clenched knuckles. "Mr. Lawlor?" he said without looking away from Thea. "Can we have a moment, please?"

"Why am I not surprised? Come along, Langston. You and me'll—"

"Leave Mr. Langston here, Fred."

"Oh, all right." The other operative winked at Thea— *winked.* "You're the boss." He sauntered out, quietly shutting the door behind him.

"My dear man," Richard began, "if you're needing to

assert your power over my daughter by ogling her in front of me…"

He hushed up fast when Devlin whirled around and leveled a look that could fry an egg. "You lost your rights as a father a long time ago, Langston. And this woman is going to be my wife. You will treat her with respect. I don't want to regret what I'm about to do."

He turned back to Thea, his tone altering to the deep warm syrup drawl that flowed over Thea in a healing balm. "Your father abandoned you, robbing you of self-confidence. A year ago, another man robbed you of your inheritance, and your grandfather of his self-respect. Then the Secret Service, albeit unintentionally, robbed him of his reputation."

He paused, searching Thea's face, regret carved like old scars in his own. "Not even God can change the past. He can only help us heal from it. But I can try to make some sort of reparation, by giving you a choice. Theodora, nobody outside the Service—except for you—knows your father was forced to become one of Fane's accomplices. Fane's dead. Simpson has sworn in an affidavit that Richard Langston was threatened with death for refusal to comply with Fane's demands, and was used with ill will as a tethered goat to lure an innocent woman to her own demise. To everyone else on Jekyll Island, Mr. Langston was just another guest. Last night, I sent another telegram to the head of the Service. His reply came fifteen minutes ago. Mr. Lawlor and I have been granted the authority to determine Richard Langston's fate. We've decided to pass that determination along…to you."

Disbelief wrapped Thea in barbed wire suspense. Slowly she sank down into Mr. Grob's desk chair. "What are you saying, Devlin?" she managed through stiff lips.

With easy masculine grace Devlin knelt in front of her.

"I'm saying your father's fate rests entirely in your hands. I can't undo what operatives up in New York did to your grandfather last year. But Fred and I agreed we can balance the scales here, perhaps a little bit. Say the word, dear heart, and your father walks, free to choose the course of his own life."

Blindly, she reached out, and his hands closed around hers, warm and strong and sure. "What he did was still wrong. He could have approached the Secret Service before leaving Atlantic City. He could have appealed to someone here."

"He could have turned you over to Fane," Devlin murmured. "But he gave you the keys, which allowed you to collect the evidence we needed—knowing the gesture would probably cost him his life. So. Judgment or grace, Theodora? The choice is yours."

Thea looked over Devlin's sturdy shoulder to her father, who stood in profile gazing out the window, his face expressionless, his posture relaxed. The shackles holding his wrists together might have been a figment of Thea's imagination. *What am I supposed to do here, Lord? What?* When she stirred, Devlin helped her to her feet, tucked a tendril of dangling hair behind her ear, then stepped aside so she could approach the man who had given her life, yet who she knew in her heart still wanted nothing to do with her.

"If you're free, what will you do?"

"If he decides to take up counterfeiting as well as gambling for a profession," Devlin put in smoothly, "he'll be hunted down without mercy."

Richard shrugged. "I'm too old to pretend in the game of life any longer, Theodora. Fane did teach me something, though. In the future, I won't gamble with money I don't have, and haven't legitimately won. As for the rest,

Operative Stone, your warning is duly noted." The chains rattled as he made a restless move with his hands. "Charles did a good job with you, Theodora. You might look like your mother, but you're nothing like her at all." He laughed a light, bitter laugh. "An upstanding professional government agent with a heart wins over a professional gambler without one, every time. Though in my opinion, any man willing to toss away his career for a woman is gambling more than he ought."

# Chapter Forty

"Toss away his career?" Thea retorted furiously. "Is that a taunt, or a threat? Never mind, it doesn't matter. Since that's your attitude, you can go straight to jail. And I won't regret one bit being the one who sent you there. I will not allow Devlin to ruin his career because of a poor decision on my part and poor judgment on yours."

Devlin joined her and touched her shoulder. "Thea, it's not a threat. We've had a long talk with your father. There's something I haven't had a chance to tell you."

Richard shook his head ruefully, admiration sparking behind the shuttered expression. "Let her be," he said. "Fierce in her defense of you, isn't she, Operative Stone? I could envy you that, but what's the point? Deal the cards, Theodora. Freedom or jail, whatever hand I draw, it's up to me to play. No obligations on your part either way."

"I know," Thea admitted. "I learned that lesson from you a long time ago. But lately I've learned a few others, as well." Moisture gummed her throat as she struggled, the words halting and hoarse, to set both of them free. "Thank you, for what you did, yesterday. For caring enough to try to save my life. I…don't want you to go to jail, not for this. Let him go, Devlin." She glanced up, and his smile erased any lingering doubt. "I want you to let him go. I believe in my heart it's the right choice."

"I agree," he said, and tugged a key out of his vest pocket to remove Richard's handcuffs. Then he held out his right hand. "You'll always be welcome at StoneHill Farm. But the only games we play there are chess and dominoes."

Richard stared at the outstretched arm, then with another shrug shook hands. "I've seen my share of grifters and green goods. Maybe we can work something out." His shoulders squared as he lifted his chin and looked straight at Thea. "I haven't been a good father, but I want you to know—I've never cheated. Not once." After a final glance he strode across the room toward the door.

Two betraying tears rolled silently down Thea's cheeks. "Father?"

He stiffened but turned, hand on the doorknob. "Yes, Theodora?"

"Every now and then…send Grandfather and me a postcard?"

The poker face crumbled suddenly, and for one fleeting second she glimpsed the shadow of a weak, vulnerable young man trapped between responsibility, and a compulsion that refused to relent. "I'll try," he promised. "I'll try…daughter."

With a firm click, the door shut behind him.

Thea closed her eyes. So this was what it felt like, to see someone through the eyes of Jesus. When Devlin carefully drew her into his arms, she laid her head against his chest. "Thank you," she said after several long moments, soaking up the love, the kindness, the exquisite compassion of this man God had brought into her life. "I love you with all my heart, Devlin. But…your career? What will happen? I know you have to write a report. You have to be honest.

You have to, or I'll never forgive myself. No, wait. You'll do the right thing, no matter what I do or don't do." She listened to the steady rhythm of his heartbeat, and was content. "I'm learning...."

Devlin chuckled, then led her over to a table, picked up a sheet of paper and handed it to her. "Before I came down to Jekyll Island, I visited the man who persuaded me to join the Service, Micah MacKenzie. We had a long talk. Then I went into Washington and talked with the Chief. I've resigned, Theodora. As of this morning, it's official. Operative Lawlor has taken over to tie up the loose ends, your father being the final thread. You and I can go home."

A long, cleansing breath ruffled Thea's hair. "Home," he repeated. "For three years God allowed me to wander in the desert of deceitful, greedy souls and dirty cities full of crime. I like to think that, in my wanderings, I at least honored Him by serving my country. But StoneHill is my promised land, and I don't ever want to leave it again." Searching her face, he lifted his hands to tenderly cup her cheeks. "I want to marry you, and raise horses and babies with you. On our way back to Virginia, I want to stop by that breeder and hopefully buy a Holsteiner colt."

His eyes closed, then opened, dark now with desperation. "But what I need more than anything, Thea, is to know you forgive me for hurting you. For not telling you months ago I was part of an organization you hated. If you can forgive your father enough to give him his freedom...?"

"Devlin..." Wincing a little, she carefully wrapped her arms around his waist and hugged him close again, inhaling the wonderful scent of soap, starch and the most dear man in the world. "Of course I forgive you. What woman could resist a dashing hero who rides to her rescue?" Then she balled her fist and punched him hard enough in the ribs to surprise a whoof of discomfort from Devlin and an internal screech from the wound in her side. "But don't you ever do anything that dangerous again, do you hear? I came down here to find proof and save you from Edgar Fane myself. If he'd discovered you, he would have killed you."

"Looks like we saved each other, and God administered divine justice to Edgar Fane." He rested his head against her hair, his palms warm against her back. In all her life, Thea had never felt so protected. So at peace.

"Devlin?"

"Hmm?"

"If I told you that I believe God's looking down on us right now and smiling, would you think I was an emotional mush head?"

"No, sweetheart. Because I sense Him, too. As warm and real as the fire burning in the fireplace."

"Fires in fireplaces burn out...."

"Ours won't." Devlin pressed a gentle kiss to her eyelids, forehead, then each cheek. "Because we'll work to keep it alive, every day, for the rest of our lives."

Theodora gave herself over to the embrace of her beloved, and with a yielding internal recklessness, finally abandoned everything else to God.

\* \* \* \* \*

Dear Reader,

In *A Most Unusual Match*, I had as much fun with the research as I did creating all sorts of problems for Thea and Devlin. There is something magical about old photographs that pulls me right out of the twenty-first century. (Check out saramitchellbooks.com!) In fact, my patient editor had to gently remind me not to let the setting dominate the characters! At one time, my office floor and most of the surfaces of the furniture were covered with books and maps of 1890s Saratoga Springs, New York, and Jekyll Island, Georgia. StoneHill Farm was easier, since I live in Virginia and it was no trouble at all to take long wandering drives, then erase this century to create a magnificent horse farm built in the 1800s. Believe it or not, in this state a lot of houses even older than the fictional StoneHill still survive.

As I write this letter spring is freshly arrived, with daffodils and hyacinth blooming, and buds sprouting on all the trees. Since this book is scheduled for publication in January, I can't help but smile, wondering how many of you will be curled up by a cozy fire while a snow/sleet/rain winter storm rages outside...unless of course you live in Florida.

But no matter the season of your life, my prayer remains that this book offers a few hours of pleasure, inspiration—and in some small way kindles a desire to deepen or develop your relationship with God. Please feel free to share your thoughts—I love to hear from readers, the twenty-first-century way via saramitchellbooks.com, or the old-fashioned, nineteenth-century way in a letter c/o Steeple Hill Books.

As for all the readers wanting to know what happened

to Jonathan Tanner, Micah MacKenzie's assistant in *The Widow's Secret,* well, somehow he and I lost touch. After leaving the Secret Service, Jon spent several years in limbo, unable to figure out what to do with his life. Sometimes, you know, people have great difficulty figuring out who they are, and how God could possibly love their confused, messed-up selves. But because I refuse to countenance anything but happy endings in my stories, I believe Jonathan did eventually discover he could trust himself to God's faithfulness. Did he ever find a woman to love? Of course! I write love stories, don't I?

With joy...

*Sara Mitchell*

# QUESTIONS FOR DISCUSSION

1. Theodora Langston is outraged by what happened to her grandfather. Do you think her decision to pursue justice on her own, assuming a false life to prove the case, was appropriate—or reckless?

2. Was Thea justified in her hatred of the Secret Service? Have you ever been wrongly accused of something? What was your reaction?

3. Both Devlin and Thea are pretending to be someone they're not. Have you ever found yourself in a relationship where you're doing the same thing? What happened?

4. Part of *A Most Unusual Match* takes place in Saratoga Springs, which by 1897 was well-known for its casinos and horse-racing culture as much as its international fame as a hotel resort. What did you think of Thea's response to Edgar Fane and his dinner guests, when she was queried on her views? Did you agree? Disagree?

5. Thea manifests a particular symptom of anxiety with her episodes of debilitating vertigo. Have you or someone you know ever wrestled with an anxiety disorder? What did you do to overcome it?

6. Edgar Fane is initially presented as a fairly decent fellow. But evil can be seductive, even attractive. Did you find yourself wondering how such a popular and

attractive man as Edgar could possibly have a darker side? Were you surprised by his actions later in the book?

7. Both Thea and Devlin are "surface believers"— people who acknowledge God and have a passing understanding of Jesus, but who live their lives following their own wills and wishes. What was the turning point for each of them, when they realized that life without God was not how they wanted to live any longer?

8. Do you think if Christians try to live a life in accordance with God's will, that they will always enjoy peace and freedom from temptation?

9. Thea asks Devlin, "Is there a truth that stays the same, and no matter how a person twists and turns things about, the truth remains?" What would your answer to this question be?

10. When Thea learns that Devlin has lied to her about his Secret Service identity, do you think her reaction was appropriate? Why or why not? Has someone you loved and trusted ever lied to you? What was *your* reaction?

11. Devlin cannot hold back his declaration of love for Thea, yet he refuses to ask her to marry him because he is still a Secret Service operative and afraid of her reaction. Was his fear justified? If you were Devlin, would you have told her before leaving for Jekyll Island?

12. The scene between Thea and the Italian maids on the dock is symbolic of one of Jesus' most famous parables. Which one?

13. Discuss the differences between Thea's relationship with her grandfather, and her father. Do you think Richard Langston will try to restore a relationship with his family?

14. Devlin loves horses and has a family home with a thriving vocation. Yet he abandons both for several years because he feels something missing inside his soul. What is this missing piece? When does he realize it?

15. Good people who make poor decisions with noble motives get into all sorts of trouble! But those troubles offer wonderful opportunities to illustrate how God can work His amazing grace. Describe scenes in *A Most Unusual Match* where, despite their lies, doubts, anger and fears, God still speaks to Thea and Devlin.

# HISTORICAL

## TITLES AVAILABLE NEXT MONTH

### Available February 8, 2011

**RESCUING THE HEIRESS**
Valerie Hansen

**THE OUTLAW'S RETURN**
Victoria Bylin

**ROCKY MOUNTAIN REDEMPTION**
Pamela Nissen

**THE BLACKMAILED BRIDE**
Mandy Goff

# REQUEST YOUR FREE BOOKS!

## 2 FREE INSPIRATIONAL NOVELS
## PLUS 2
## FREE
## MYSTERY GIFTS

*Love Inspired*

# HISTORICAL
### INSPIRATIONAL HISTORICAL ROMANCE

**YES!** Please send me 2 FREE Love Inspired® Historical novels and my 2 FREE mystery gifts (gifts are worth about $10). After receiving them, if I don't wish to receive any more books, I can return the shipping statement marked "cancel". If I don't cancel, I will receive 4 brand-new novels every other month and be billed just $4.24 per book in the U.S. or $4.74 per book in Canada. That's a saving of over 20% off the cover price. It's quite a bargain! Shipping and handling is just 50¢ per book.* I understand that accepting the 2 free books and gifts places me under no obligation to buy anything. I can always return a shipment and cancel at any time. Even if I never buy another book, the two free books and gifts are mine to keep forever.

102/302 IDN E7QD

| Name | (PLEASE PRINT) | |
|---|---|---|

| Address | | Apt. # |
|---|---|---|

| City | State/Prov. | Zip/Postal Code |
|---|---|---|

Signature (if under 18, a parent or guardian must sign)

### Mail to Steeple Hill Reader Service:
**IN U.S.A.:** P.O. Box 1867, Buffalo, NY 14240-1867
**IN CANADA:** P.O. Box 609, Fort Erie, Ontario L2A 5X3
Not valid for current subscribers to Love Inspired Historical books.

**Want to try two free books from another series?**
**Call 1-800-873-8635 or visit www.morefreebooks.com.**

* Terms and prices subject to change without notice. Prices do not include applicable taxes. Sales tax applicable in N.Y. Canadian residents will be charged applicable provincial taxes and GST. Offer not valid in Quebec. This offer is limited to one order per household. All orders subject to approval. Credit or debit balances in a customer's account(s) may be offset by any other outstanding balance owed by or to the customer. Please allow 4 to 6 weeks for delivery. Offer available while quantities last.

**Your Privacy:** Steeple Hill Books is committed to protecting your privacy. Our Privacy Policy is available online at www.SteepleHill.com or upon request from the Reader Service. From time to time we make our lists of customers available to reputable third parties who may have a product or service of interest to you. If you would prefer we not share your name and address, please check here. ☐

**Help us get it right**—We strive for accurate, respectful and relevant communications. To clarify or modify your communication preferences, visit us at www.ReaderService.com/consumerschoice.

LIH10R

*Enjoy a sneak peek at Valerie Hansen's adventurous
historical-romance novel RESCUING THE HEIRESS,
available February, only from Love Inspired Historical*

"I think your profession is most honorable."

One more quick glance showed him that Tess was smiling, and it was all he could do to keep from breaking into a face-splitting grin at her praise. There was something impish yet charming about the banker's daughter. Always had been, if he were totally honest with himself.

Someday, Michael vowed silently, he would find a suitable woman with a spirit like Tess's and give her a proper courting. He had no chance with Tess herself, of course. That went without saying. Still, she couldn't be the only appealing lass in San Francisco. Besides, most men waited to wed until they could properly look after a wife and family.

If he'd been a rich man's son instead of the offspring of a lowly sailor, however, perhaps he'd have shown a personal interest in Miss Clark or one of her socialite friends already.

Would he really have? he asked himself. He doubted it. There was a part of Michael that was repelled by the affectations of the wealthy, by the way they lorded it over the likes of him and his widowed mother. He knew Tess couldn't help that she'd been born into a life of luxury, yet he still found her background off-putting.

*Which is just as well,* he reminded himself. It was bad enough that they were likely to be seen out and about on this particular evening. If the maid Annie Dugan hadn't been along as a chaperone, he knew their time together could, if misinterpreted, lead to his ruination. His career with the fire department depended upon a sterling reputation as well as a

Spartan lifestyle and strong work ethic.

Michael had labored too long and hard to let anything spoil his pending promotion to captain. He set his jaw and grasped the reins of the carriage more tightly. Not even the prettiest, smartest, most persuasive girl in San Francisco was going to get away with doing that.

He sighed, realizing that Miss Tess Clark fit that description to a T.

*You won't be able to put down the rest of*
*Tess and Michael's romantic love story,*
*available in February 2011,*
*only from Love Inspired Historical.*

Mom-to-be
Kelsey Anderson is
finally following her dream
when she moves into her
late grandmother's lake
house and makes plans
to open a quilting shop in
town. But when former
army doctor Luke Turner
moves in next door, he
stirs feelings in her that
soon make her rethink
all her plans....

# Child of Grace
by
# Irene Hannon

*Available February*
*wherever books are sold.*